Home Means Nevada

The Adventures of W. W. Ronin
Book Five

By Gregg Edwards Townsley
Two Bears Books, Saint Helens, Oregon

Western fiction by this author:
East Jesus, Nevada
Lady of the Lake
The Pinkerton Years
True Believer

Also by this author:
Kauai Getaway: Tommy Valentine, PI

Home Means Nevada

Copyright 2015 by Gregg Edwards Townsley

Cover design by Olivia Passieux
Cover photo by Josh Townsley

Published by Two Bears Books
245 N. Vernonia Road
Saint Helens, Oregon 97051 U.S.A.
www.twobearsbooks.com

ISBN-13: 9780692486665 (Two Bears Books)
ISBN-10: 0692486666

To my brother Scott, who has made a home
for himself on the East Coast, and
to my father-in-law Del, who has made a home
for himself on the West Coast.
Good and very different men. I love them both, dearly.

TABLE OF CONTENTS

"In men whom men condemn as ill
I find so much of goodness still.
In men whom men pronounce divine
I find so much of sin and blot
I do not dare to draw a line
Between the two, where God has not."

Joaquin Miller, aka
Cincinnatus Heine Miller, 1837-1913
"The Poet of the Sierras"

"We have this treasure in earthen vessels ..."

2 Corinthians 4:7

Home Means Nevada
December 1881

Chapter 1

FIRST EDITION

W. W. Ronin left the train on Telegraph Street, as he had many times before, dragging an over-stuffed valise behind him, and an over-stuffed friend as well. This time was no different, save for a copy of the *Los Angeles Daily Times* folded underneath his arm. "A first edition," said the man who handed it to him. The headline, "A Vial of Vitriol," had been shamelessly borrowed from a *Philadelphia Times* story a few months before.

"My hometown."

"Los Angeles?" the man asked. It was near midnight. Everyone was tired, particularly those who had journeyed far.

"Philadelphia, more or less."

Ronin had seen the story in a Sacramento paper before leaving for Elko a few weeks before. "Horrible thing to happen," he continued, referring to the unexplained burning of children and adults in a former Philadelphia roller rink. The assailants had dumped "a full gallon of acid" on their victims, throwing bottles and glass from an overhead balcony. They'd escaped through a skylight.

"Seven dresses were ruined," the man said, "silk dresses. A number of hats and bonnets were stained as well. What kind of people would do such a thing?" the man mumbled to no one in particular.

Ronin looked at his friend, Ormsby County Deputy Marcus T. Slade, who hadn't stirred despite the conductor's announcement that they'd arrived in Nevada's capital city. Their nearly month-long trip—to Elko and Wells, "and a thousand points in between," he'd complained before leaving a Wells saloon two days before — had left both of them exhausted. Storey County Sheriff Thomas Kelly and Augustus Ash, the U.S. marshal, had exited the train at the top of the hill in Virginia City.

"Time to get up, Dusty," Ronin said to his friend while looking around for his hat. The man's insensitivity to the pain and suffering of those who had been disfigured in the Philadelphia attack didn't surprise him at all. Nothing surprised him anymore. An ex-priest and later ex-Pinkerton detective, now a bounty hunter, he'd seen the worse things. Their Elko adventure, the pursuit of a violent Utah man and a Virginia City psychic, had left him wondering if anything good could be found in human beings at all.

"I know," said Dustsucker, a name only Slade's best friends could call him.

"You can bunk in with me tonight if you like. The Ormsby House might be a good deal more comfortable until you get cleaned up. I'd hate for the widow Rogers to see you this way."

"She's seen worse," the big man said, lifting his bag onto his shoulders with one hand while patting a vest full of pockets with the other. "Any idea where my badge is?" he asked, stopping under a lamp on the train platform to search.

"You gave it to the kid."

"Shoot, I meant to get that back." Three-hundred pounds heavy, the Ormsby County deputy put his bag down on the platform and took a deep breath. He was waiting for his horse.

"You really ought to name that nag, you know."

"Jesus, Ronin. Will you let up?"

"I'm just saying, if you're going to ride her, you might as well give her a name. What if she wandered off? What would you say ... 'Here, horse, horse, horse? Here, horse?'" He whistled three times, low and then high, as if calling a dog. "See how silly that sounds?" he said before pulling Jackson from the train and grabbing what's-her-name for his friend.

"Whatever."

The two friends walked a couple of hundred feet before deciding to ride the remaining half mile to the stables. They tied their bags to their saddles. "What do you want to do tomorrow?" Dustsucker asked, fastening a loose strap so that it wouldn't get caught in his spurs when he lifted his leg.

"I don't know what *you're* going to do, Dusty. But *I'm* going to check in with my friend."

"Your *friend?*" Dustsucker said. "Why don't you just say it? Your *beloved?* Or maybe your *intended?* The lady you hope to marry. She has a name, you know ..."

"I know."

"Well, I'm just saying," Dusty mocked. "She'd probably like to hear you say her name every so often."

"You're right." The ex-priest smiled. "And she's probably all of that. I'm going to make an honest woman out of her yet."

"It's about time." Slade put his boot into the stirrup and threw his right leg up and over. "You'll be doing a good thing if you do," he wheezed. "Tomorrow's Christmas, you know."

"Oh, man," the detective said, "I totally forgot."

"It's a Sunday."

"Geez, that's even worse."

"How's that?"

"The stores will be closed."

"Not all of them. We'll find something."

Chapter 2
BEFORE MORNING

It was after midnight when they got to the livery. A clear sky signaled that Sunday would be cold and crisp. A subtle dusting of snow had blown down from the Sierra. The white stuff sparkled, like a hand-colored print by Currier and Ives.

The lithograph "Winter Morning in the Country" was published in 1873 by New York printers Nathaniel Currier and James Ives. Ronin first saw it in Wichita, while still a priest at the St. John's Episcopal Church. He had found it fascinating. Who could say who the original artist was, they had used so many over the years. The quiet picture of an apparently happy man and woman, riding in a single horse-drawn sleigh carrying milk cans along a snow-covered lane, and the working barn and farmhouse nestled up against the wintry, gray mountains of God-knows-where had gotten him to wondering if it was time to move on. The picture fanned a disquieting fire. It was a flame he had hidden from his congregation.

Perhaps he wasn't fit for the Episcopal Church. Maybe it was ministry in general, he wondered as he gazed at the quiet colors — gray and white, pale blue, mountain green and alpenglow pink and red. His experience as a priest had felt empty at times. The more difficult days made him wonder if there wasn't a call more meaningful than the frontier ministry he had worked so hard to establish. Weary of it all, he left the ministry. A brand new Colt revolver was his only prize.

In time, he realized he'd left a lot behind. But the farther west he went, and the further apart he grew from the rigid set of rules he'd embraced as a part of the priesthood, he came to understand the ecclesiastical expectations to be typical of an older America, a Yankee, urban and industrial America. In the West, men were what they made of themselves. A young man's identity wasn't defined by his name or occupation. And women? He didn't fully understand women—save to say there seemed to be in Western women an equally fierce independence of the traditional constraints. And that was okay. A man might want a lady who reminded him of his mother, who could bake a biscuit or sew a shirt or make a pie. But a man didn't want to marry his mother. Something more striking was needed, and in the West — Nevada anyway — there was no shortage of exceptional females.

Emma Nauman, for instance, the directress of the American Gospel Mission south of Carson City. He'd known others. The woman he'd fallen in love with years ago, for instance. He'd met her as a Pinkerton detective, trailing her and an emerging entourage of previously unknown husbands and lovers across three states. He'd been terminated from the agency as a result. It had been embarrassing for sure. But the experience — in all of its moral failure and foolishness — had been utterly intoxicating. He'd never learned her real name — "Madame Bovary," she'd said, *Emma* Bovary it turned out, simply a character in a well-known French novel who lived beyond her means and marriage so as to escape the emptiness of everyday life. The women that followed, the second Emma included, had all suffered in the painfully long shadow the first Emma had cast. As a result, he left not only the Pinkertons but his faith as well. His life as an unattached bounty hunter was the end result. He was a wandering minstrel of justice — he found wanted men in a way that few could, and delivered them their just rewards in a way that few would.

The smell of sage blew across the Carson Range as they dismounted behind the Ormsby House a block north of the St. Charles Hotel, across from the government buildings. He handed Jackson's reins to a tired stable man anxious to earn a two-bit tip. "He's already eaten," he said before gesturing with his thumb toward his friend behind him. "Our horses have. My friend and I haven't. We're headed into the bar if you need some information."

"Mister Ronin, you need no introduction here, sir," the man said. "You're home. Your room is ready, as it always is. And I'll take real fine care of Jackson and old what's her name."

"Thank you, then." Dustsucker pulled a blanket from behind his saddle before handing over his reins. "Dusty, you don't need that. There are plenty of blankets in the hotel."

"That may be, Ronin. But I'll be a good deal more comfortable if I bring in one of my own, if you don't mind."

"I don't mind."

They lifted their rifles from their scabbards, an 1866 Yellow Boy and the more popular 1873, guns that were winning the West, someone had said. They untied their saddlebags. "Then why are we standing here?" Dusty said, grinning.

"You tell me."

"No reason that I can see," Dustsucker said. He looked at his friend. It had been a tiring couple of weeks, and before that an exhausting couple of months dealing with situations in Carson City, Virginia City, and finally three hundred miles east of there in Elko and Wells. The wear and tear on the ex-priest — his best friend and perhaps the finest non-lawman he'd ever met — was obvious.

"Listen William," he said wondering, "I know it's late. But there's beef and beers waiting for us, and to be utterly frank, there's a story waiting for us, too. I need to tell it to you before morning."

Chapter 3
BEAR CLAW

"William Washington Ronin, how the hell are you?" the big man blurted out while blocking the door to the Ormsby House's Supper Club.

The late Major William Ormsby, who had founded the hotel, wasn't much of an Indian fighter. He'd died in the First Paiute or Pyramid Lake War in May of 1860 a few months after the hotel was built. But he was a real live Nevada pioneer and had erected a first class hotel and eatery at the corner of 2nd and Carson Street. The hotel was Ronin's favorite, and the Supper Club — a brilliantly lit restaurant carved out of the hotel's main welcoming space — afforded Ronin a fun yet formal place to conduct business and entertain guests. A specially lit derringer display was featured on one of the Supper Club's walnut paneled walls.

"Good evening." It was almost midnight as Ronin approached the hotel. He stopped a few feet away from the door because the man — a large, bushy-bearded bear-sized man with a Pinkerton star on his chest — didn't move. Instead, he'd wedged his 6 foot, 6 inch frame into an intractable position, fondling his pistols, which were tucked backwards into his waistband and carried cross-draw, Hickok-style, as if their pearl-handled stocks were the ends of a well-waxed handlebar mustache named Remington. Ronin waited patiently.

"Thought we'd had this conversation before, friend," Slade said, pushing past his friend. "And the shield, I told you to take it off." The badge, a gritty gray and silver star that read Pinkerton National Detective Agency, was apparently pretend or out of service. Ronin had checked when Slade had pistol whipped the man a year before for the same issue. He was standing in the way of hotel guests.

"He's a lethargic slug," Goodwin had explained when asked at the time. "He's well beneath the usual standard of employment for hotel staff," Goodwin argued in his usual caustic manner. But Victor Goodwin was nowhere to be seen. The daytime manager of the hotel, restaurant and saloon, he'd been at odds with the doorman for years for unsaid reasons but would have handled the situation if he had been present. Which he wasn't, the towering doorman said as a way of suggesting that their conversation would remain uninterrupted until they could work out a solution.

"Look, Mister … I'm afraid I never got your name."

"It's unimportant."

"Well, Mister Unimportant," Ronin said, grinning past his upset friend. "We're about to head upstairs for the night but thought first we'd have a beer or two in the Supper Club. Mind moving to the side, son?"

"I've got this, William."

"That's good Mister Slade," the doorman interjected. "I've got no beef with Ronin here."

"He's got no beef with me, Dusty." Ronin looked at him calmly. "Son, move out of the way." He palmed a couple of silver dollars in his right pants pocket, making sure the man saw that he wasn't reaching for his gun, and gave him another chance. "Is there a problem, son?"

"No problem, Mister Ronin. It's just that Mister Slade and I have some history."

In a painfully inopportune moment a year prior, the upset Ormsby County deputy had picked up the doorman and rammed him into a hitching post, securing him there with handcuffs until he and his friends had finished breakfast. It had become a bone of contention between them. So too between Ronin and Emma, as the ex-priest saw nothing wrong with his friend's actions at the time. "Some people don't listen the way you and I do," he'd explained when Emma and her physician friend had arrived to eat.

"Some people can't get past the cruelty," she'd said later when encouraging him to stay in town rather than continue his independent ways as a man tracker and detective.

"It's what I do, Emma," he'd explained. "You have a right to live safely," he had said, "the kids, too. I offer reality to the riffraff no one else wants to deal with. At your service," he'd said, tipping his hat. Emma didn't find the exchange at all funny. Nor would she see the humor in this conversation.

"That you do, son," Ronin said. The man was a good five or six inches taller than him and out-weighed him by more than a hundred pounds. "But we're both rather tired. And I'll not vouch for my friend's actions if you get him any more riled up. Fair enough?" he said, with a look that would cause most men to crumble.

"Fair enough," the big man replied, moving to one side. Ronin relaxed.

"Oh, and Mister Unimportant?"

"It's Bob, sir. Bob Bear Claw."

"William Washington Ronin, Bob. At your service," he said, smiling. "Mister Bear Claw," he continued, "you seem like a nice man. And I've appreciated your being here at night to keep things safe. But my friend and I are hoping that you'll put behind you any little convenience you previously suffered at the hands of Deputy Slade."

"It wasn't little, sir."

"Well, that may be. And it wasn't very thoughtful. But he's a good man, too. And I'm sorry you both got off on the wrong foot. Can we start again?"

Bear Claw and Dustsucker stood there, their mouths open. W. W. Ronin had earned a rough and tumble reputation in these parts. Patience was not a part of it.

"Dusty? What do you say?"

"Um ... I guess it's time to make friends."

"That's what I was thinking," Ronin replied. "Mister Bear Claw, what do you say?"

"Friends it is," the man said, blinking his eyes and swallowing hard. The two men, both easily tipping the scale at 300 pounds — overweight if it wasn't for Bear Claw's breadth and height or Dustsucker's jolly good nature — grasped hands, looked each other in the eyes, smiled and shook hard. When finished, they stepped back from each other and waited, as if waiting further instructions.

"Mister Bear Claw ..."

"Yes, Mister Ronin?"

"... lose the badge. I've been a Pinkerton, and I don't much appreciate your pretending to be one."

"Yes sir. It was the only badge we could find."

Ronin smiled. "I'll talk to Mister Goodwin in the morning about getting you something more suitable to wear than that old shield, son — something shiny, maybe something that says, 'special police' or 'house detective.' How's that sound, Dusty?" Bear Claw was smiling. He'd become a fixture in Carson City. People enjoyed seeing him, even the little children.

"Don't imagine there'd be anything wrong with that," Dustsucker said, bending down to pick up his saddle bags and blanket. "In fact, it might be real nice."

"Well then, we'll be back in a few minutes to grab our bags, Bob. My friend has a story to tell me. Please keep an eye on things."

"I will that," he said. "I don't miss anything, Mister Ronin, I don't miss anything at all."

Chapter 4

ORRIN HICKMAN

Orrin Hickman pulled a crumpled piece of newsprint out of a rhododendron bush by the front door of his house in Genoa. He'd done his best to keep his property up after the Prophet Brigham Young had called the Saints to return to Utah. He'd even tried selling it as the Mormon seer had suggested. But it seemed such a shame to let go of so nice a homestead for pennies on the dollar. And by the time he'd gotten around to letting people know his ranch was up for sale it was worth even less than those of his neighbors.

In time, the much-feared government invasion of Utah had come to naught. Instead, an uneasy peace had been forged, despite rigorous federal maneuvers of infantry and artillery units and his Mormon brothers taking up strategic positions in many of Utah's mountains and valleys. When the final shot was fired — and there weren't many shots fired at all — the fifteen-month "Mormon War" became known as President James Buchanan's "Blunder." A New York newspaper man reported on the Utah War, "Thus was peace made...Killed, none. Wounded, none. Fooled, everybody."

Hickman had half-expected everyone to return, as the western expansion of the church and its mission to restore the true church was so much more important than whether Mormon brothers and sisters had gone home to Utah, as requested by the president of the church. The western states still needed missionary settlers. The Mormon Corridor — the church's goal to establish a chain of settlements and forts from Salt Lake City to the Pacific Ocean — had been a good idea, a real revelation he thought, although with the passing of time he wondered if the prophet remembered what God had caused him to say.

When Hickman had first settled in the Carson Valley — having traveled with a group of fifteen Mormons and a company of non-Mormons westward through Wells then called the Humboldt Springs to the lip of the Sierra — seven of them decided to remain on the east side of the mountains to establish a supply station where passing emigrants could buy salt, beef and flour. They'd made a lot of money over the years, until the Mormon prophet called some of them home, all of them to be honest, though a few remained, Hickman among them.

He'd painted the front doors he'd shipped from a Palmyra, New York, woodworker, who assured him the hickory had been harvested in the very village that the church's founder, Joseph Smith, had grown up in, though he knew the man's claims to be untrue. Smith had been born in Sharon, Vermont, he wanted to tell the man, though by the time Joseph was twelve and was grappling with the mysteries of God he was living in Palmyra. It wasn't much of a difference, he figured, as God first spoke to him there, not in Vermont. Any time before that was merely butter for the bread, he thought when he first brushed the crimson-colored paint onto the doors, mounted the hinges to the sturdy oak frame and called his Carson Valley house a real home.

"A holy home," his bishop had said, insisting the color was the very shade of Christ's blood, though he didn't know how a man could know that, even a consecrated Mormon bishop. "You know the Hebrews smeared the blood of a sacred lamb on their doors to protect their first born from the angel of death," the bishop had said before sitting down at his dining room table, where his wife had prepared a beautiful meal of wild quail, winter potatoes and broccoli. Hickman had brought the broccoli over from California the week before, after counseling a Placerville family about the latter-day restoration of God's good news in Jesus Christ.

"It's not the same as being Presbyterian," he'd told the husband and wife, who had gathered their children in the great room of their mountain home above Hangtown to hear him preach. "It's different," he said. "It's real. It's really real," he told them, confident that he'd stumbled onto the key of what it meant to build a Great Basin kingdom, a place where God and God's people would reside in perfect harmony and peace.

"The color of Christ's blood" was a particularly morbid thought, the words his bishop said, given that it was the first time the church leader had been to his home. Most of his neighbors simply remarked when visiting there, "You have a beautiful house." Or "I like the color of your doors." But in time, when he began to deeply study the Mormon scriptures, he realized the subtle blessing his bishop had brought to his home that night almost twenty-five years before, before the bishop and others had left at the beck and call of the Prophet Brigham Young to defend the Mormon Zion from a possible federal invasion. "Turn your barns into bullets, your cows into cudgels, your homes into a holy zeal for what is right and true," the bishop had said before leaving.

He'd held on to the blessing, thinking that the others might return some day. And if they did, they'd pray together, those who had left and those who had stayed behind. They'd understand the color of the doors, he figured, red like the blood of the Savior, who had not only spared the Utah territory but the areas west of there as well. Someday, all of the West would be theirs as part of a united kingdom, doing God's will and led by God's people, the Latter Day Saints, who had worked so hard to establish communities and forts between the Church's Utah center and the promising gold fields of California.

The red doors had reminded him of Christ's love and sacrifice and protected him, more or less, though his family had long moved back to Utah, his wife having married someone else instead of remaining. His children had written and "were still hopeful," they said, "in returning someday." The beveled crimson-colored hickory doors from Palmyra, New York had kept him safe from the scorn of his Gentile neighbors, too — those who made fun of those who left and equal fun of those who had remained — despite having greatly benefited from the sacrificial gifts of the Mormons, who had sold everything so as to arm themselves against an invasion that had never really come, save for a few battles here and there where men, women too, didn't even fire their guns but had fallen nonetheless.

The red doors swung heavy and wide, and were as big as his heart, though it didn't seem fair, his being there alone beneath the mountains, where pioneer John Reese had built a trading post, laying claims as far north as Jack's Valley and as far south as the hot springs. Colonel Reese had come from New York as well. He'd have understood how he was feeling, and might have actually remembered the tree from which his doors had come. Reese had stayed behind for business, he remembered, thinking business would be good with the others gone. But ultimately, even Reese couldn't hold on. He left for Utah in 1859, two years after everyone else, as if there was more important work to do there instead of here on the east side of the Sierra.

Hickman pulled the crumpled-up Carson City newspaper that had blown some sixteen miles south of Nevada's capital and gotten caught in his bushes, clapping up against the windows of his Carson Valley home. He sat down on the damp, oiled-stained steps leading to his crimson red front doors and thought for a moment. It was Christmas. And while the Church didn't make a big deal about the birth of the Christ child — it was Christ's death that mattered, everyone said, a blood atonement for those who would come to believe on his name and follow his gospel — it seemed right to muse a bit about the dream he'd brought with him to Genoa, formerly called Mormon Station because Reese and others had been among the faithful just as he had been, and still was. And if it hadn't been for those early Mormon settlers, he liked to say, there'd not ever have been a sacred city in the now great *State* of Nevada, the very first settlement in the state except for the Indians, who seemed nice enough but needed the gospel also.

It seemed right to muse about the dream Reese and others had had because so much of it was now cold and shattered and over and gone. Some had blessed him as they left him behind to do what he could to keep Christ at the forefront of the Mormon expansion. But now, though it was not any fault of his own, Nevada was a non-Mormon state, no longer a part of the Utah territory, which he hoped would someday be a state, too if the federal government would just look the other way on the Church's holy and sacred ordinances of plural marriage and such. Still, all that remained of that dream — the Mormon dream, though really it was a part of a much larger American dream, to build a kingdom on a continent on which God had shined his divine and everlasting light — was an ancient Mormon curse by one of the community's founders.

An ancient Mormon curse — the more he thought about it while sitting there on the well-oiled steps of his Mormon Station home, looking east past the Carson Valley toward mountains and cities he couldn't see except through the eyes of faith in a someday still-hoped-for Mormon state named Zion, the more he realized God had raised *him* up, like the prophets and apostles and long forgotten men of old, to do something about it.

Chapter 5

EMMA NAUMAN

"William!" she exclaimed, opening the door to her single-story home at the American Gospel Mission just south of Carson City.

An Indian school had been the Naumans' dream, Emma's more or less after her husband Henry disappeared. No one knew whether he had fled the state — and the charges that awaited him should he return — or if had tragically fallen prey to the darker criminal elements of the capital city. It turned out that he was intimately acquainted with them, though testimony of such no longer existed, some folks having died and others having simply moved away.

Emma had continued on without him like a good Christian soldier. And despite initially struggling over the school's finances and the expectations of its donors — pressures she hadn't needed to deal with prior to the kidnappings or her husband's disappearance — the mission to Washoe, Shoshone, Paiute and other children had actually begun to thrive, as did Emma in her husband's absence.

A West Virginia native raised on a simple farm in the shadow of Steubenville, Ohio — a mill town having first been formed as a fort to protect government surveyors looking west of the Ohio River — Emma was moving the mission along like a seasoned river boat captain. She worked carefully, methodically even enthusiastically, as if there was a hidden magic to the maneuvering involved.

"I've missed you so much," she said, skating across a porch of native-colored stone and masonry, a product of the school's families. She blew through the door in a simple white house coat, the morning light hardly announcing that it was Christmas Day.

"It's early, I know." He embraced her as if they had known each other their whole lives, lingering silently for a few moments, in the crisp December air a few degrees above freezing, a dusting of snow caressing the ground as they held on to each other. "I've missed you so much."

"And I have missed you!" Emma repeated, smiling. She raised her chin so that Ronin could kiss her, their lips hungry for an intimacy they hadn't yet allowed themselves to experience, and yet each knew it was just around the corner.

They'd be married soon, he'd told her by telegram from Elko, "if she'd have him," he said once he realized that he hadn't asked her — he'd only assumed.

"I can't wait," she'd replied, as if each word was a sentence and the thought an expression of everything she had ever hoped for.

It wasn't as if the decision had come easy for W. W. Ronin, who was used to living on the range or in the woods, having a traveling jacket or coat as his comforter, a smooth stone for a pillow. He'd known a few women in his thirty-some years. None had captured his imagination as fully as Emma Nauman. In time, he figured he'd found in Emma the woman he wanted to marry. She was a curious mix of everything he had ever desired — the wild adventure that had waited for him in the West, an eight-year journey he'd enjoyed since leaving the St. John's Church despite the disapproval of family and friends. She was also the softer but just as substantial "coming home" he'd always hoped for. Reminiscent of Abraham, the biblical patriarch who had left his birthplace to seek a land he had never seen, a home he had never known, Emma was the Promised Land. She was the jeweled city set on a hill that could not be hidden or any longer denied. The path before him — a holy house of sorts, spoken for, agreed to and now in full construction — was like a light, shining brighter and brighter until it would become their perfect day.

"There's so much to talk about," he said as he allowed her to step back so that he see the entire woman he loved — a beautiful brunette, thin-framed, delicate in appearance, her green eyes hiding just enough fire to make things interesting. Despite her calm demeanor, she was a door slammer to be sure — he imagined that he'd like that. Ronin placed his hands on the outside of her arms as she raised them above her head, and smoothed her housecoat downwards until his fingers rested on her hips. He leaned forward to kiss her right eyebrow. "And you have so much to tell me," he said, knowing that if his head was full, hers was even more so. "Tell me, dear one. What is foremost in your heart today? What do you need?" he asked.

"I can't imagine a moment more perfect than this," she replied, pulling him close to her and whispering "I love you" into his left ear. Doing so, she noticed that Jackson was still tethered to a post outside her home. Ronin had not put him away. "Are you staying?" she asked, a library shelf full of old thoughts and feelings beginning to shimmer within her head. *It's Christmas. Can it be that he's not staying?* she wondered, hoping that her anxiety didn't show and that her anger — that he could be away for so long and could be considering leaving again — was misplaced.

"I am, my love."

She'd known the ex-priest for only a couple of years, having met him in a doctor's office while she was being treated for dizziness, he for a broken leg. They'd become fast friends and almost lovers ever since then. She knew his every movement and mood like the biblical book of *Proverbs* or the *Psalms.* But his answer seemed only partially true, tentative like the morning clouds still pressed up against the Sierra, deciding whether they'd offer snow or allow a brilliant and crisp sunny Christmas day.

"But first …" he continued.

"Oh, Ronin…"

"I know ... but there's so much time ahead of us, and this, this thing that Dustsucker has raised ... he says it can't wait."

"This thing?" she said, curtly she thought though she hoped it didn't appear so. "Come inside, William. Leave your things there if you have somewhere to go. If you bring everything in, I'll want you to stay." She stopped in the doorway for a moment and then turned around. "Do you know where you want to be, William? Are you clear in your mind?"

"Here," he said.

"Here," she said, "our home, the two of us together."

"Exactly," he repeated, kissing her on the forehead.

And the two of them — the former preacher turned gunfighter because the world needed him that way, and an almost ready school teacher who knew that her heart and future belonged to a traveling man — walked hand in hand into the front room of the director's home at the American Gospel Mission, as if beginning their life as man and wife.

"Ronin, do you love me?" she asked.

"I do, Emma. You know that."

"Then that will have to be enough. Whatever it is that you've got to do, William, wherever it is that you have to go — we'll do and go there together."

Chapter 6
THE OLD DANITE

What Emma didn't know of course was the future and full extent of her promise. But then who does, when one says, "I'll be there Thursday," or while engaged in a series of nameless pursuits or pledges, "You can count on me"? Promises have a way of biting a man in the ass, if he's not careful. And a woman? Well, she can find herself in quite a quandary if she's assuming that following her man is going to be anything other than difficult or dangerous.

W. W. Ronin didn't take those kinds of commitments lightly, though he figured he would want to be the first to excuse Emma's unbridled optimism for their new relationship and the commitments that relationship could someday bring.

Capturing kidnappers in the Washoe Valley a year before, despite involving a dozen children from Emma's mission, was no place for a Christian woman. And while she had distinguished herself by keeping in touch with her man — thinking about him, praying for him, showing up for him at just the right moment and saying all the right things — Emma was a Protestant missionary at heart. She was not a killer, or a lawman, or even an exhibition shooter like Annie Oakley, who he'd seen splitting the edge of a playing card with a .22 once, and putting several more holes in it before it could touch the ground. Having Emma nearby when capturing or killing criminals was a hazard. Not that he believed in it the concept, but hell would surely come to the man who permitted her to be hurt in a dark or deadly situation.

When he tracked down the murderers of the two Washoe men at Lake Tahoe, Emma had kept her distance except to tug at his heart strings at the most inopportune times. The distraction had caused him to wonder if he really wanted a full-time, committed relationship with a woman. An evening here, an overnight there, offered a totally different set of circumstances than waking up next to the same person every day for the rest of one's life. And while some inner sense of morality argued for the latter — if there were children, for instance, and shouldn't spouses care for each other as they get sick or grew old — he felt ill-equipped to face the subtle nuances of a life-long relationship, especially if he was working. "It's life and death out there," he explained during one particularly frozen time in their "friendship and more," as Emma sometimes called it. But the comment fell on deaf ears. It was as if he was talking a different language.

The Bible was clearly written by *men*, he mused. There was no other reason that the first book of the Bible, *Genesis*, blamed women for men taking their eyes off of the important things. They were that damned dangerous and distracting.

Ronin pulled the rocking chair away from the wood in Emma's front room and placed it so that it faced the large leather sofa where Emma was seated. He sat silently for a moment, looking at her, appreciating her, feeling the love that he had for her, and then began. "Dustsucker told me that he was worried," he said, "and that the sheriff had no one else to ask."

She squirmed and pushed both of her hands underneath the cushion she was sitting on. A pillow slipped beneath her right elbow. She didn't move. "Tell me more," she managed, when what she really wanted was less — less adventure, less anxiety, less danger and less business and the less chances of seeing their whole life dance away before their eyes, as if listening to a rousing tune but knowing they wouldn't or couldn't participate. Too much time had been wasted between them. Too much distance had been created between where she wanted to go and where Ronin always seemed to end up. He was in the midst of a giant adventure. At times, she wanted less of it. "You know," she said, "just because it's right to do doesn't mean that you're the one that has to do it."

"I know."

"So why *you*? Why *now*? Why not someone *else*?" She waited, but patience wasn't a gift God had given her.

"Because the Mormons won't talk to the sheriff about the problem," he answered after a few moments. "They wish it would go away. 'It's not a Gentile thing,' they say, so it's none of our business."

"I don't understand, William."

"Orrin Hickman, Emma. He's angry again, and he's fixing to do something about all the damage that ever happened to any of them, whether they stayed when Brigham Young told them to return, or whether they left, it doesn't matter. Hickman's angry, and he wants the rest of us to pay."

"I thought Orrin was an old man by now."

"Everyone did."

"Well then," she said, pulling her hands out from beneath the cushion and pointing her index finger into the air between them, "what's an old Danite going to do about the even older business of who owns what and why and how much they paid? God, seriously?" It wasn't like Emma to curse.

"Honey, I'm not going to argue with you about it. I know you've got feelings for some of the Saints living in the valley, and I do too. But when a man begins to think of himself as an avenging angel for all of the economic suffering Mormons have been through in this state, someone's got to control the damage."

He took a deep breath and leaned forward in the rocking chair she had used each and every day he was gone — praying for him, supporting him in his journey and wondering how things were going. He took hold of her finger, folding it and the rest of her hand in between his own hands. She would be sitting in that chair again she figured, looking out the front windows of her home at the early morning mists that sat uncomfortably upon the Sierra. She'd be sitting there soon, whether she wanted to or not, whether they were married or not. It simply was what it was. There was no other way to think about it.

"To be frank, dear," he continued, "and I know you don't want to hear this, but the sheriff is hoping *that* person is going to be me."

It was a commitment he'd made, she figured. And he needed to keep to it.

Chapter 7

A MORMON OATH

They opened a few gifts — he a brown wool sweater to keep himself warm in the dry, cold, wintry air of northern Nevada, she a tiny gold locket that Dustsucker had picked up for him early that morning to give to her. "We'll get it engraved," Ronin said, feeling poorly he hadn't given any real effort to picking out the necklace. A suitable Christmas gift was the last thing on his mind.

The "Mormon Minutemen," as some journalists had called the Danites, had spread a kind of righteous rage across non-Mormon settlements in 1837 and 1838. It was a long time ago. But he'd recently read the former Danite Bill Hickman's book — no relationship to the Genoa rancher, and written by an avid non-Mormon a few years back — and wondered if any of the "Destructive Angel's" story of wide-spread murder and mayhem on the part of Latter Day Saint militias was actually true.

When Horace Greeley interviewed Brigham Young in July of 1859 — the first such interview of the Latter-day Saint prophet — the two of them talked for two hours according to the account printed in practically every American newspaper. The night before, Dustsucker had given him a copy of the article from the *Sacramento Bee.* "I know of no such person or organization," the Mormon leader replied when asked. "I hear of them only in the slanders of our enemies."

Still, the evidence seemed overwhelming. Mormon soldiers had, at some point in the Church's history, scouted the borders of non-Mormon settlements and chipped away at them, committing robberies and even killing some folks. "Thereby building up the kingdom of God," Dustsucker had said, smiling. The Gentiles — or non-Mormons, Ronin insisted — had done pretty much the same thing.

"Their name comes from a verse in Genesis, Ronin," Dustsucker said. "'Dan shall be a serpent by the way, and a snake in the path that bites the horse's heels …'"

"I know," he'd replied as they'd headed up to his room at the Ormsby House the night before. Ronin couldn't remember if the church's founder had actually disbanded the movement, as some of his Pinkerton friends had said, or if it had grown at the direction of the next Mormon prophet. Not that it mattered.

"William? Are you listening to me?" Emma asked, after a lengthy description of the mission children's holiday activities. "You don't appear to be."

"I'm sorry," he said, blinking his eyes a couple of times to clear his mind. A seminary professor named Culbert Rutenber had suggested the practice in a classroom of almost-ministers, after they'd confessed that they were sometimes bothered by inappropriate thoughts when speaking to the women in their congregations. Ronin had found the habit equally effective in getting his mind back on track when caught musing about other things.

"You were talking about some of your fonder memories from when you lived in Steubenville."

"*Near* Steubenville, Ronin. I never lived *in* Steubenville."

"Right," he said, looking about for a glass of water.

"So as I was saying, our family much enjoyed setting up a tree in the center of our living room. Henry and I did the same thing when we moved to the Carson Valley. Some of the children had never seen an indoor Christmas tree. You know that the Christmas tree first appeared in Ohio, right?"

"I did not," he said.

"It did. A man named August Imgard set up the first Christmas tree in Wooster, Ohio, in 1847 …"

"I thought the Christmas tree was a German custom," he interrupted.

"I'm talking about the first *American* tree, William. Aren't you listening?" She shook her head. "When Imgard arrived in America, he was so lonely for the German traditions he cut the top off of a nearby spruce tree, brought it indoors and hung small paper ornaments on it, and candles as well."

"I've never been much for putting candles on trees, Emma. It doesn't seem at all safe ..."

"I'm not talking about *candles*, Ronin. I'm talking about missing my family and my own traditions, and wanting to share some of them with the Washoe and Paiute people here at the mission."

"Right," he said, thinking that at some point he'd have to mention what he was thinking about — how dangerous the Danites had been to people in Missouri and elsewhere. And how some of them, maybe 400 or so of them, had surrendered with the Mormon movement's founders, Smith and Rigdon, among them, and that both of them were armed. Some of the Danites had continued on it appeared as Nauvoo policemen and body-guards, despite being formally disbanded. He had never heard of any of them being so far west as Genoa, Nevada's first settle-ment, a Mormon settlement. But there'd been a meeting recently he found out of similarly-minded men on the porch of the old Kent house, now the Gardnerville Hotel. An ancient oath had been mentioned, suggesting that the men support the church "in all things that they say or do, whether right or wrong." While he didn't know what that meant, it certainly didn't sound safe or easy.

"Ronin, I'm talking to you."

"I'm sorry, dear. I don't mean to ignore you. I've just got this other thing on my mind."

"Perhaps you could enlighten me, then." Emma's tone seemed pricklier than usual.

"Maybe when Dustsucker comes?" he offered, hoping to lay down for a bit and think. He turned to head into the bedroom.

"William Washington Ronin, it is Christmas Day — the day that our Lord and Savior Jesus Christ was born. It is not a day to sleep away. Nor is it a day to keep secrets. I don't believe the baby Jesus would appreciate such things."

"No, I imagine not," he murmured, though he had real doubts that the baby Jesus would have minded anything other than being denied his mother's milk or a clean wrap or diaper. *If the Holy One could tolerate shepherds attending a little boy's birth, he could certainly allow a tired man a short snooze.* "What would you like to do next?" he asked.

"Well, I want you to see the children's tree, of course. It's all we've been talking about."

Ronin began counting the subjects he thought they had covered since his entering the house a couple of hours ago. He stopped at nine and thought better about mentioning it. "I'd love to, dear." He took her hand and they walked hand-in-hand out the back door onto the rear porch, where a small assemblage of children was beginning to sing.

A half-dozen of the younger kids were squeezed into a small line next to the kitchen's woodbin. Another dozen or so older ones stood behind them. They'd obviously just learned the words to an old wine-maker's Christmas poem, written at the request of his parish priest a long time ago.

"O holy night, the stars are brightly shining. It is the night of the dear Savior's birth." Ronin smiled as the children kept to, more or less, the difficult rhythm and tune.

One of the practices he'd most appreciated as an Episcopal minister was teaching the younger children to sing. He had a reasonable voice — "not anything to write your grandmother about," his mother used to say, his father usually grimacing at the remark — but it was enough to lead the few children who gathered each Sunday at the little log church in Wichita. It was a pleasant memory, the breadth and beat of the music set against the painful bleating of the church's adults: "Why isn't so and so singing a solo this week?" And "How come you taught them *that* song?"

Something happened to the hearts and intentions of little children when they grew older, Ronin thought, though he could never figure it out. It was as if the happiness drained out of them, the kindness, too. Ultimately, the meanness of a few parishioners led the otherwise enthusiastic priest to leave parish work for something gentler and more interesting.

He began to mouth the words of the second verse. "Led by the light of faith serenely beaming, with glowing hearts by his cradle we stand. So led by light of a star sweetly gleaming ..." The gentle ups and downs of the music were pleasing. He pulled Emma closer to him. She had grabbed his new sweater as they'd walked out of the kitchen. He pulled it up around her neck and made sure it covered her shoulders.

Christmas is a good time of year, he mused, remembering intermittent moments of calm with his father in Tennessee while riding with Biffle's Cavalry. The memories were intermixed with the pain of seeing fellow soldiers and friends shot, their limbs growing gangrenous in hospitals where Confederate medical personnel knew too little to be of any help and had even less to use or apply if they did. The promise of peace and serenity — the mainstay of the Christmas holiday's meaning — seemed distant then, and now, with the threat of violence just south of them in the Carson Valley. If any of what Dustsucker had said the night before was real, the risk that people and property could be harmed was genuine. *What is it about religion that it harbors such crazies?*

He began humming as the children started the third verse. "Truly he taught us to love one another." He couldn't remember when he last sang a Christmas carol. This one had been one of his favorites. "O Holy Night" was written by an agnostic Frenchman during a particularly bumpy coach ride into a capital city to celebrate the renovation of the church's organ. Ronin looked over at a couple of boys who were enjoying the bounce of what was becoming a familiar tune and smiled. The mission children — Washoe, Shoshone, Paiute and others — were dear to him. "His law is love and his gospel is peace. Chains shall he break, for the slave is our brother, and in his name all oppression shall cease."

Maybe that would be the case, he thought as he listened to the children begin the familiar chorus. "Fall on your knees ..." He'd not be spending any time at all on his knees in the next few weeks. His backside would be glued to a horse. And his hands — as uncomfortable as he was with killing, he touched his Colt .45s — might be busy as well.

Life could get bumpy again if "that old Danite" Orrin Hickman was going to gather the support of similarly-minded neighbors and head their way. Mormon or not, faithful or not, Christian or not — Hickman was a dead man if he thought he could spread violence in the Carson Valley, particularly if it came anywhere near those that he loved and the woman he hoped to marry.

Chapter 8

A MORMON CURSE

Dustsucker pulled the napkin from around his neck and pushed away from the table. "It doesn't please me at all to take your man from you," he said. "You've waited so long for some clarity, not that it's any of my business."

"You've been witness to the back and forth," Emma replied, covering Ronin's hand with her own. "Neither one of us have had a good experience with these things. I don't know that Henry ever really cared about the things I care about. And William here has had his ups and downs as well."

"Let's not be talking about that, dear." Ronin pulled his hand away, took hold of her plate and stood up to begin clearing the table. "The past is past. That's what I always say."

Dustsucker and Emma looked at each other. Generally, they'd heard him say the opposite. "I'm not following," Emma said, folding her napkin and placing it where her plate had been. Dustsucker nodded.

"I mean, what's done is done." Ronin picked up his utensils and stacked the two plates together, pausing by his friend who didn't appear to be finished. "It seems to me," he continued, "that the only sure way a man can find peace is if he focuses on the present moment. That's been my experience."

"And the thought that someone's past is a good predictor of what he or she will do in the future?"

"Well, I guess I've said that, too. I'm just saying, this new thing of mine — hanging up the guns for a while, working on my relationships with people, taking care of the people I care about most — I've got to make a go of it. I'm not getting any younger or any less angry. There's got to be something more to life than evening the score and catching up to people who need catching up to."

He turned to put the plates on the counter behind him. The kitchen shelves had recently been refinished. A new cast iron sink had been installed where a blue table used to be. "This is nice," he said.

"Everything changes, Ronin," Emma said, smiling. "You didn't notice?"

He knocked his knuckles on the side of the heavy metal white colored sink. "Some things don't. I doubt this is ever going to move," he said, laughing. He pulled a towel from the countertop, draped it over his gun hand and looked around for some soap.

"So Marcus, what's happening with this thing in Genoa? William says that you and Sheriff Swift need him."

The big, bear-sized man pulled his chair back to the table and put his fork into a still-steaming piece of Christmas ham. He shoveled it into a mound of mashed potatoes before pushing it into his mouth. "I don't want to share too much, Emma," he said, chewing. "I mean, I don't want to get you worried and all. Ronin's typically kept this sort of stuff to himself."

"Go ahead," Ronin said, looking around for a pan to put the dishes into.

"Just put them into the sink, dear. There's no need to use a pan anymore. The sink holds the water."

"Of course." He pulled on the pump handle and watched as cold water began splashing into the basin. "Huh. Fill her up, she might have a perspective or two."

Dustsucker shrugged and pulled a hunk of coarse ground wheat bread from a loaf in the middle of the table. He began to mop at the warm, brown sugar and raisin gravy at the edges of his plate. "Emma, this is amazing. I don't ever eat as good as I do when I come here."

Emma smiled. "As well, Dusty... good is the adjective, well is the adverb."

"Right. Let me start at the beginning. Then I'll tell you why Shubael insists that we involve the reverend."

"The reverend thing is ancient history. I don't see how it has to do with anything nowadays," Ronin said from the sink, where he was stacking wet dishes.

"Well, let's see what Emma thinks." She leaned forward, her elbows on the table. She looked into his eyes, waiting. *A man could fall in love with a look like that,* Dusty thought. "Here's how I put it together, ma'am. And the sheriff agrees. It all started with a couple of sacks of flour. It always starts with food."

Emma laughed as Ronin pulled his chair out from underneath the table and sat down. "Not for everybody." The ex-priest was thin as a rail.

"Yeah, it does," Dusty replied. "I don't remember when the first Mormon got to the Carson Valley. It was long before I did. But in June of 1850, thirty-some years ago, seven Mormon men built a station out of pine logs at the base of the mountains in what we now call Genoa. There was plenty of water, pine trees for fuel and shelter, and lots of feed. You've been there, Emma."

"Absolutely. William and I have taken carriage rides out that way. We love Jack's Valley."

"Well, folks along the trail appreciated their settling there, as it helped them replenish their supplies before heading over the mountains."

"Prices were high. Prices are still high in Genoa."

"Give me a minute, ma'am. As you can imagine, it cost something to situate supplies there, it being so far from everywhere. But people did what they what they did and the commerce went both ways. Story is told, for instance, that folks on this side of the mountain sold snow to the people of Sacramento, though I can't imagine anyone paying for snow. But with the money they picked up on the other side of the mountain they restocked their shelves here so that they'd have coffee, bacon, meat and such to sell to people along the way. And the circle went on from there."

"Sounds like good business," Ronin said. "Grabbing something you can get for free and taking money for it in return." He laughed, until Emma glanced his way and raised an eyebrow.

"Look, nobody's ever faulted a Mormon for knowing how to make money," Dustsucker answered. "It's always been a cardinal teaching of the church that a religion that doesn't have the power to make people prosperous can't much be depended on for anything else."

"Joseph Smith."

"Exactly, Emma, though I have no opinion on the matter. I'm just saying they worked hard at it. And their efforts to establish a trading post and ultimately a settlement were much appreciated. In fact, Mormontown couldn't keep up with the demand."

"Hmm," Emma said, taking a sip from her coffee. "I had no idea."

"Well, in time, I'm told the original ownership of the fort passed to a man named Reese and another man named Beatty. They built the hotel and much of what you see there today. It was Reese that gave the two sacks of flour to some Washoe Indians to release any future claims to the land."

"Not the first time a white man cheated a brown man," Emma said.

"I don't know anything about that either, ma'am. But I do know that by 1852, there were some pretty strong anti-Mormon sentiments in the area. Some folks didn't want to be part of the Utah Territory, or the Mormon Church either. Others, I suspect — who knew the future was coming a good deal faster than anyone wanted it to — simply hoped for local control. Despite it all, the Mormons ..."

"Latter-day Saints," Emma corrected.

"Right, the Latter-day Saints caught a vision for the Carson Valley and began to think of it as part of a corridor of land they had acquired to extend the Utah Territory — their territory, their kingdom if you will — to the Pacific Ocean. So in 1855, the church sent Orson Hyde." The name hung there in the air, shimmering as if it were a special part of the Christmas story, or as if Hyde had been recently headlined in Carson City's *Morning Appeal*. Emma and Ronin looked at each other. Finally, Ronin spoke.

"Who cares about Orson Hyde?"

"You do," Dustsucker said. "You just don't know it yet. Hyde was an accomplished man in the Mormon Church."

Emma nodded.

"The Latter-day Saint Church, I mean. It was Brigham's hope that he'd help organize the territory. Given that there were some who wanted Nevada to be a power unto itself, and others who despite the surveys wanted the area to belong to California, Hyde did what he could to strengthen the church's hand in the matter."

"There were many Mormons, but not all of them were Saints."

"Exactly, Emma — Hyde put it the same way. He kept real busy working to keep his church faithful, growing his business interests, serving as a judge and focusing on his missionary work."

"To the Washoe tribes?"

"I mean toward everyone. You and me, for instance, though the missionary enterprise has slowed down in the last few years. The church calls us 'Gentiles ...'"

"... and tells us the problem with Hickman is none of our business ..."

"Exactly, Ronin." The former preacher hated the word. His dealings with Mormons over the years had been neither good nor bad. But the word "Gentile" had a sense of exclusion to it. It signified an outsider, worse still a heathen. Over the years, despite his training and traditions, he'd decided the most dangerous man in the world was a man who thought himself better than others.

"So?"

"So," Dustsucker smiled, "when the church's new prophet called everyone back to Utah, many Mormons abandoned their hard, heart-felt work in the valley. And I'm not just talking about ranches and real estate, but religion as well."

"So folks were pretty upset?" Ronin asked.

"That's an understatement, William, though I'm sure there were some who walked with the baby Jesus, as you like to say. Lots of people — not just in the Carson Valley but in the Eagle and Washoe Valleys as well, folks from all over the West — sold their ranches and businesses, picked up their guns and headed home to Zion. They didn't all arrive with smiles on their faces. And, as you already know, there were a few similarly upset folks who stayed behind."

"Orson Hyde?"

"No, Hyde did what the prophet asked him to do. But Reese stayed, for a couple of years anyway. And Hickman did, too."

"And why do I care about this?" Ronin tapped the corner of his coffee cup, hoping Emma would get up to freshen it. Emma didn't move.

"You care because Orson Hyde became a very angry man. Maybe not immediately, maybe it took a few years, but by the time he got back to Utah the money that was due him for his piece of the Mormon prize — his business in Washoe Valley, his house and land — was already being spent on something else. He, and certainly others, never did see what they were due."

"Dusty, this was a long time ago. And Nevada has a history of people being cheated of what belongs to them if it has a history of anything. But my coffee has grown cold. Emma has baked us a pie. And I'm hoping you'll get to the main point of why you think I need to be involved with all of this before it's time for all of us to go to bed."

"Well, that's why Shubael is so interested in your being a part of things. You can understand *all* this stuff."

"Sure. So your point is?"

"The sheriff says that Hyde had a saw mill in Washoe Valley that he sold before returning to Utah. But all he ever got for it was a span of weak-assed oxen and an old wagon. I'm sorry, ma'am."

Emma smiled.

"The rest, about $10,000 in all, was never paid. Five years later — and the sheriff just gave me this afternoon, before I came out to dinner — Hyde wrote an open letter to everyone who lived in the Carson and Washoe valleys ..."

"Dusty, get to the point."

Dustsucker put his fork down and took a piece of newsprint from his vest pocket. "Here it is," he said. He unfolded the paper and began to read.

"The Lord has signified to me, his unworthy servant, that as we have been under circumstances that compelled us to submit to your terms, that He will place you under circumstances that will compel you to submit to ours, or do worse." He looked up to make sure his friends were paying attention.

"That mill and those land claims were worth $10,000 when we left them. The use of that property, or its increased value since, is $10,000 more, making our present demand $20,000. Now if the above sum be sent to me in Great Salt Lake City in cash, you shall have a clean receipt therefore in the shape of honorable quitclaim deeds to all the property that Orson Hyde, William Price, and Richard Bentley owned in Washoe Valley. The mill, I understand, is now in the hands of R. D. Sides, and has been for a long time. But if you shall think best to repudiate our demand or any part of it, all right. We shall not take it up again in this world in any shape of any of you. But the said R.D. Sides and Jacob Rose shall be living and dying advertisements of God's displeasure, in their persons, in their families, and in their substances. And this demand of ours, remaining un-cancelled, shall be to the people of Carson and Washoe valleys as was the ark of God among the Philistines. You shall be visited of the Lord of Hosts with thunder and with earthquake and with floods, with pestilence and with famine until your names are not known amongst men,

for you have rejected the authority of God, trampled upon his laws and his ordinances, and given yourselves up to serve the god of this world — to rioting in debauchery, in abominations, drunkenness and corruption ..."

Ronin interrupted. "I've never heard a bigger barrel of sh..."

"William, you will not use that word in this house," Emma interjected.

"Of course not. I apologize. Dusty, but that's a load of crap ..."

"Or that word, either."

"That word, too?" he asked.

"Yes."

"Alright," Ronin grimaced, biting his upper lip. A man needed to be who a man was, he figured, though a man might take some getting used to. Most good things were worth waiting for. Emma had a lot of things going that he was willing to wait for as well. He took a deep breath and paused, hoping for the feelings to pass. "Let me express my thoughts another way."

Dusty nodded.

"If Shubael thinks he needs an educated reverend to decipher what these crazy-assed bastards were thinking *way* back then ..."

"Ronin ..."

"What was that, twenty years ago?"

"About that," Dustsucker answered.

"Well then, he's as nuts as they are, or were anyway. It's hocus-pocus, my friend — superstition, religious nonsense, bullshitery. There's no need for me, or any other thinking person to get involved. I'm way past being an expert on religious things," he said as Emma continued to wince. "And as for this Orrin Hickman character— this former Mormon militia man, this old wrinkled-up Danite living in the Carson Valley — well, I've changed my mind. I've got more important things to do. He's simply an tired, worn-out old man..."

"He's also an angry man," Dustsucker insisted.

"Old and angry, then — I don't care. He's not likely to bother anyone over something so ancient and silly as a thirty year-old Mormon curse."

"Ronin, calm down," Emma said.

"Don't tell me to calm down." He looked back at his friend. "I'm just saying I've got better things to do, Dusty."

"Ronin, I'd agree with you, really I would, if it wasn't for the people in Franktown."

Chapter 9

FRANKTOWN

Franktown had seen better days. When the mills were running, when there was still timber on the mountainside and the Comstock's gold and silver strikes were such that it was tough for a quartz-laden cart or donkey to get a place in line, the little town west of Washoe Lake and south of Bowers Mansion had maybe a couple hundred people living in it. There were some Canadians for instance, even some Chinese.

But when the area's economy crashed — farms, timber and quartz mills, even a railroad station at one point, a Mormon-owned mecca before the Latter-day Saints flew back to Utah to protect the church from invading federal troops — no amount of magic could bring the good days back again, not that people didn't try.

Take Alison Oram "Eilley" Bowers, for instance.

Ronin had met Eilley, sometimes called "the Washoe Seeress" because of her fortune-telling talents, earlier in the year. A widower, Missus Bowers had shared a perspective or two regarding an attractive set of twins he was investigating in Virginia City, prior to pursuing one of them to Elko and Wells. While Eilley was no longer the millionaire owner of the mansion — having been arguably the richest woman in Nevada a few years before — her attention to the lore of the valley and to the people who lived there made her a valuable asset when attempting to corral the Livestock twins, who were defrauding a group of Comstock businessmen.

Bowers Mansion at the time had been long empty, having fallen prey to the woman's escalating financial difficulties after her husband's death. Sandy Bowers owed pretty much everyone, it turned out. And those he didn't *owe* money to he *loaned* money to. The declining economy didn't help.

Thirty years prior, the valley was one long strip of industry. Between Virginia City and the Sierra Mountains, highways, homes and mills dotted the landscape like spring seedlings, hoping to become a full-grown forest of plants and prosperity. Eilley had been a part of that. A few years later, the valley's mansions and businesses lay empty. The dreams and machinery of a golden age of mining had moved north with the railroad to the new city of Reno. The quartz mills were torn down, and Franktown, progress' casualty along with three other Washoe Valley towns — Galena, Washoe City and Mill City — was a mere shadow of what it had hoped to become.

Eilley had found new fame and fortune using a crystal ball and other expedients to speak to lost loved ones or to locate lost pets and treasures. Local legend included the tale of a man who had accumulated $85,000 through various felonious pursuits and then hid the money in Franktown. No one had ever found the money, though not for want of trying.

When the flood came, those who hadn't moved away yet moved away. And everyone, north and south along the Carson Range remembered the old Mormon curse.

"It's a desert, Dusty. I mean, not literally," Ronin said, "but figuratively it is. The only person who lives out that way, the only person I've ever seen, is Happy Hands."

"You know that's not true," Dustsucker said.

"I'm just trying to make a point, my friend. How faithful folks could be so wrong-headed is beyond me," Ronin said, looking over at Emma, who was beginning to cut into an apple pie. "I'm just saying, this thing with Hickman will blow over. And there aren't enough people in Franktown to make it worth my time. It doesn't need my attention. It doesn't need yours either. What's the sheriff's interest?"

Emma lifted a piece from the pan and put it on a plate before setting it in front of her man. "French apple," she said softly, knowing the simple butter and sugar-iced pie to be a regional favorite of folks in Pennsylvania and Maryland. Ronin had grown up in Pennsylvania.

"You never mentioned liking it this way," she said, sliding a large piece of pie onto a man-sized plate. "And I don't know if you enjoy raisins. But the recipe says it's sweeter, and I loved the thought of orange and lemon juice setting off the cinnamon, sugar and nutmeg."

Ronin looked down at the plate set in front of him, a shiny silver utensil balanced on its edge, inviting him to believe that there was a God in heaven and that God had given him this woman to be his stomach's wife. "Oh my," he said, his friend looking on. "This looks *real* nice," he said, lifting the napkin to his mouth. "I don't remember when I last saw a piece of French apple pie like my mother made."

Emma smiled. Nothing pleased her more than to cook for her man. "It's been a good number of years, I imagine," she said. "How long has it been since you've been home?"

His mother and father were now gone. The house he had grown up in was gone as well, though he had lived with his father for a good number of years prior to the Civil War. Ronin counted up the time. He'd been on a professional journey for almost ten years — first a priest, then a Pinkerton detective and now — *what is it that I'm now doing?* All of a sudden, the only thing he could think of was the hollow inside of him, and the hope that he could fill that awkward emptiness with the thought of getting married. Angry Mormon militiamen would have to wait. If this was the future of his heart and soul, he would be content. If it meant his stomach would be filled with sugary delight, home-cooked meals and a personal intimacy he had only previously sampled but would now live with the rest of his life, well then the sooner the better.

"Emma," his voice trailed off as he picked up the dessert fork and began thinking of all that had brought him to this place — an almost frenetic need to see the great American West, a sometimes careless expectation for justice, in the sense that the law didn't always matter. If his personal ethics demanded an aberrant action to right a wrong, then so be it, even if it included an intense and athletic enjoyment of the pugilistic arts. He preferred his hands, his fists and his feet to the two Colt handguns that most days and nights hung at his sides.

So much seemed to be floating in the air right now. His emotions were a circus — on the high rise, next rolling in the dust like an acrobat, then tromping through the city's streets as if he was an elephant, the giraffe, the lion or tiger. *What am I to do? How is it a piece of pie can bring all of this to mind?*

"Can I have a taste of that?"

Some things did change. Others things remained the same. He didn't know what he was going to do. "I'm sorry, Dusty, what were you saying?"

"Can I have a piece of pie?" The Ormsby County deputy had picked up his fork and was twiddling it like *it* was baton and *he* was a marching girl out front of a carnival band signaling that the circus was in town. It all felt like a circus, this back and forth at Emma's house. *I'm a gunfighter. I'm a detective. That's what I do best. After the bearded lady comes the fat man and the midget.* He smiled.

"No, before that," he said. Emma looked away.

"I was saying that the people in Franktown are afraid. The few folks left there, piled high up on the mountain more or less, they're expecting to see a Mormon uprising."

"That's bat sh..." Emma looked over. Ronin caught her eye. "That's plumb crazy."

"Well, that may be. There aren't enough Mormons left in Nevada to cause any kind of trouble. But with Hickman talking about folks taking a "Danite Oath" again, Sheriff Smith is saying you'd be the perfect person to look into things, it being a religion and all."

"I am not that man, Marcus. Shubael Smith shouldn't have run again. The city was doing fine doing just fine with Lloyd Hill as sheriff."

"I don't know anything about that, Ronin. But I do know this — Shubael says no one is more right for this job than you." Dustsucker looked at the pie and licked his lips before gazing up at his friend. "What do you think?"

"About the pie?" Ronin smiled.

"No, about our request."

"I'll do this, my friend. I'll think about it. I mean, we'll think about it. Won't we, Emma?" But when he turned around, Emma had already left the room.

Chapter 10

ANGER WON'T, ACTION WILL

Orrin Hickman gathered his papers in his hand and tapped them on end so they'd lay straight in the upper right hand drawer of the sitting room's desk. "I'll not listen to another damn word," he said, looking around the room. At six-foot-five, he was taller than anyone present. Save for the hair — "a lion's mane" someone had said, a full head of hair he was happy to point out and white as snow "like a Saint's hair should be" — the Sunday afternoon gathering at his home looked a lot like church. Except that Hickman was the elder and he hadn't been to Mormon church in some time.

Quick tempered, independent thinking and long upset with the movement in general, the "LDS authorities," as he put it, in particular — Hickman was as much a part of the church as a broken wagon wheel was a part of a pioneer wagon laying in the 40-mile desert. Not only did the church have little use for him, he had no use for the church, particularly the new Mormon prophet. Brigham Young was bad enough. John Taylor was tall — taller than Joseph and Brigham anyway — but prophetic character didn't apparently come with extraordinary height. Joseph less so, Brigham more so and Taylor even more so, the Mormon church's leaders had been sleeping with the enemy. The political philandering had to stop.

"Every time I hear that man speak, I wonder why the angels ever bothered with us, goddamnit." Hickman hadn't heard the prophet say anything, not recently anyway — he'd received letters instead, hoping to encourage him to take a more restrained view of things. "Be at peace with all men," the last letter counseled. "Follow me as I follow Jesus Christ." He didn't care that the words came directly from the Bible. The ancient writers could be as much at fault saying them as the Prophet John Taylor was repeating them. People's salvations were at risk.

"Fact is, the Mormon footprint will be long gone in this valley if we follow the wisdom of Salt Lake City," he said, very much aware that he had used the Lord's name in vain. *An effective leader is a righteous leader,* he reminded himself.

John Taylor, for all his faults, had been with Joseph Smith in the Carthage jail when he was martyred. He carried the scars of having been shot that very night. He had contributed to *Doctrine and Covenants*, part of the Mormon scriptures being a record of ancient prophecies and promises. And his earlier testimony, "the Kingdom of God or nothing," from a sermon in the Tabernacle in Salt Lake City when he was just an apostle, had been most remarkable.

"'Are you not afraid of being killed?' you may ask me. No. Great conscience! Who cares about being killed? They cannot kill you. They may shoot a ball into you, and your body may fall; but you will live. Who cares about dying? We are associated with eternal principles: they are within us as a well springing up to eternal life. We have begun to live forever. Did not Jesus also say: And fear not them which kill the body, but are not able to kill the soul: but rather fear him which is able to destroy both soul and body in hell."

Hickman had sat there, ten rows up from center twenty-four years ago, and been mesmerized by the man's rhetoric and faith.

"What is the first thing necessary to the establishment of his kingdom?" Taylor asked. *"It is to raise up a prophet and have him declare the will of God; the next is to have people yield obedience to the word of the Lord through that prophet. If you cannot have these, you never can es-*

tablish the kingdom of God upon the earth. What is the kingdom of God? It is God's government upon the earth and in heaven."

John Taylor's words had been mesmerizing, and had as an apostle rekindled for him an earlier faith in the church and in the men who were leaders in God's church. But in more recent years, Taylor now a prophet seemed less the prophet and more a pastor in Latter-day Saint circles. Not that many didn't need that, given the continuing persecution of so many.

"We need to do what's right," he said, "not what's fashionable." He noticed a couple of men to his right who seemed less than satisfied with the evening lesson. "Is there something else I should be talking about, Brother Smith?" he asked. "I say that with respect, of course," though he wasn't really speaking with respect. Hyrum Smith was a newcomer, and a Negro at that. But the man occasionally inferred that there was some relationship with the church's founder. He shared his brother's name, for instance — "Hyrum," who had also been killed that night in the Illinois jail where the two founders of the faith, Joseph and Hyrum, had been martyred.

"There is not, sir," Hyrum said, though no one really believed him when he said that, as the tall Negro's fondest desire was to fit in and to be seen as faithful. Still, he had lobbied for a more judicial use of force, should defending their faith come to that. He'd been through the better of the southern states and endured treatment in some that were less than friendly, not that he often spoke about it and not that anyone was interested. A black man was lucky to get a seat in some church circles, and while the Mormon church had been better than some, he didn't like to push things. Life as a logger was tough enough. And only God knew when that would end, though he was certain it would end sooner than later, the Sierra foothills being virtually denuded of timber for the still ravenous mines in Virginia City and elsewhere.

"You looked as if you wanted to say something then," Hickman interrupted while hanging off one side of the crudely built lectern he had made himself from a downed cottonwood tree found alongside his Genoa ranch. "It looks a bit like a cross," his wife had said prior to leaving a half-dozen years back. Those were her last words. "It looks a bit like a cross." *Jesus.*

"I meant no disrespect, Orrin. I meant simply to raise the question if we should be a little more like Jesus and a little less like Jehovah." Hyrum Smith was an educated man, despite having been a slave, having never learned to read or to write. The word "Jehovah" was evidence of that, Hickman figured. An Old Testament name for God, "a personage of spirit," Joseph Smith had taught, Jesus being "a personage of tabernacle," not that he understood the difference. He was certain the black man didn't understand the prophet's words any better than him. He was black, after all. He couldn't hold the priesthood.

"Jesus and Jehovah are one," Hickman said, feeling pretty certain that the LDS Church would agree.

"I don't know anything about that, Orrin. I'm just saying …"

"And maybe you ought to be calling me Elder Orrin, Hyrum, I mean given that we're in a sacramental meeting of sorts."

"I'm sorry, I didn't realize that."

"Perhaps there's a lot all of us aren't seeing," Hickman said, redirecting the conversation to include the other eleven men gathered in his Genoa home. "Maybe we're not seeing the main point of our coming together like this."

"Well, that's my point, Orrin."

"Hyrum, I think I've heard enough," Hickman said, straightening his frame by pushing up with his hands. They were the size of melons, he'd been told. He was proud of that. He stood smiling, until it was clear that he towered over everyone in the room, including the tall Negro who had sought out their fellowship when he'd moved to the Sierra Mountains a couple of years ago. And they had let him into their fellowship, despite his being black. "What I'm saying is simply this." He took a few moments for his words to sink in. "Anger won't get us to where we're going, any more than oxcarts got us to the sacred state of Deseret. And when they took that away from us — making us call our Zion 'Utah' of all things, an Indian word at best, 'mountain top,' who gives a damn — well, they stripped us of our calling. They took away from us our birthright as the children of God." His words floated there in the expanse of his living room, cedar paneling on the walls, decorative tile and oak flooring flowing into a kitchen that invited people to meet, and stay, and to be one family. "And now the church wants us to 'be at peace with all men?'" he shouted. "Anger won't get us there, my friends. Only action will."

"And that action?" Hyrum Smith said, jumping to his feet. *The man will simply not back down.*

"Hyrum?"

"Yes sir."

"Sit down or be put down." Hickman's words had never been more clear.

"Yes, sir."

"Who's with me, my brothers? Which of you is willing to do what God wants in this place and time? Who among us will answer the upward call of our brother Jesus, the Christ, who gave his life so that we might have life?" It was then that the fistfight broke out, though no one could remember who started it.

Chapter 11

NEW SOFA

Ronin spent a long night on the new sofa in Emma's front room. Tufted leather, ornate wooden legs —"all the rage," Emma had said, after he'd returned from his business in Elko. She repeated the same at supper, prior to not speaking to him over the issue of his picking up some work with the Ormsby County sheriff's office. The "warm in winter, cool in summer" custom three-cushion sofa was an unexpected replacement for the floral davenport Emma had brought with her from the Ohio Valley a dozen or more years earlier.

He'd sat on the sofa since supper, after Emma mysteriously disappeared after having served him a nice dessert. The thought of his picking up his guns again, of putting his gloved hands and cavalry-shod feet to people who needed his attention — a "character adjustment," he liked to say when criminal intent was threatened — had driven Emma from the room crying.

"You're not responsible for her feelings," Dustsucker said, before standing to get a slice of the French apple pie she'd prepared. Seeing the pieces were cut small, he slipped a second slice onto his plate before returning to the front room.

"I know I'm not," Ronin replied, though the feelings he was somewhat to blame for Emma's emotional storm lingered. "She's got to realize that the chase is apparently important to me, I guess."

Dustsucker nodded, scooping a big piece of apple and icing into his mouth before moaning how nice it was that Emma had thought of them that way. "I'm no expert," he said while sitting back in the rocking chair next to the wood stove, "not being married and all …"

"Having never been with a woman …" Ronin added, smiling.

"Don't rub it in." The deputy, despite being a congenial sort of fella, had come to regard himself as not the marrying kind.

"I know it's not like you haven't tried, Dusty."

"No, that's true. Being a night watchman when the city was young, and then a full-grown deputy, it's not like I have a lot of energy left." The job was a source of pride in Slade's life, despite it being, for the most, part-time.

"That's understandable," Ronin responded, stirring a cup of hot water with his fork. The water aided his digestion, he figured. He hated coffee, thinking it tasted too much like dirt. And drinking coffee always left him a gastronomic mess. "And who can figure women, anyway?" he said, looking up to meet his friend's eyes.

Dustsucker looked at his friend. It was tough to see him so unhappy. "I'm sorry, William," he said.

"Yup." The two of them sat there a while, finishing what was left on their dessert plates before turning their attention to other subjects. "Have you seen Happy Hands?"

"Not since we've been back."

"I'm thinking we may want to include him in this," Ronin said. "I've missed his wisdom. And he has a special place for holy men, you know."

"He likes them so," Dustsucker said, laughing, "though the two of you seem to have worked things out." A Washoe medicine man, Happy Hands lived in an abandoned house just outside Franktown. "But I thought you wanted to think things through first?"

"Well, given that the 'us' has already gone to bed, it doesn't seem that there's going to be too much of a conversation on the matter, Dusty. And I've got to say," he whispered, "when you have the talent for something, and enjoy doing it, it sure doesn't seem right to leave it all behind."

Ronin stood up, leaving the room to put the dishes in the kitchen sink. Dustsucker followed. The detective pulled a key from his shirt pocket and unlocked a small padlock on one of the cabinets, pulling a belt and a couple of holsters from a lower shelf. Two strong-side, high ride buckets appeared. Dustsucker noticed an unusual dip or cut to the front of both holsters.

"What's that about?" he asked.

"The holsters?"

"Yeah."

"They allow a little bit more speed," Ronin said. "I can clear leather faster this way. You've seen me dump my gun over the back of the holster at times?"

"Right."

"Well, this gives me a tad bit more room. I blew the front out of one my holsters in Wells, you'll remember." He felt around the top shelf in the cabinet until he was able to grab two short-barrel Colt handguns, his .45s.

"That a new gun?"

"It is. I had one made to match the other," he said, smiling. "They're both four inches now, and while I can't hit shit with my left hand, I've been practicing." He touched the tip of his nose with his left hand. The problem, however, had to do with eyesight — which eye was more dominant. "If I don't look, and I just point, and things aren't too far away, I can hit. But not by much."

"I thought you liked the long gun best."

"You mean the Yellow Boy?"

"No, the 7½-inch Colt you've been carrying for as long as I've known you, cross-draw."

"Well, I do. But you know, Dusty, I've been thinking there will come an end to all this madness at some point. Sheriff's offices, police departments, the Pinkertons, whatever — sooner or later the West won't be the West anymore. The criminals will be in jail. The Indians will all have jobs. And women will be running for public office." They laughed as Ronin strapped on his gun belt and began spinning one of the Colts with his right hand. "The only thing that will be left of the West will be fast guns and twirling."

"Oh God, you're kidding me!" Dustsucker knew his friend's distain for fancy gun handling. Neither one of them were strangers to shooting imbeciles who, instead of using guns for their intended purpose, had taken too much time to look good. Ronin slipped the handgun back into its holster, pulling a strap over each hammer to secure things before removing the belt from his waist.

"I am," he said, chuckling. "I just wanted to give you something nice to remember the evening by."

Dustsucker walked toward the kitchen door, but looked back at his friend before leaving. "Ronin," he said, "you be kind to yourself, my friend. Life is hard enough without trying to be someone you're not."

Ronin spent the rest of the evening thinking about what his friend had said, before pulling a blue blanket from atop the chair Dustsucker had been sitting in, Emma's prayer chair, and lying down on the couch. "Emma?" he called out. But there was only silence. And before he knew it, sunlight was shining through the kitchen windows. It was a new day.

Chapter 12

BACK PORCH

Ronin stood on the back porch getting ready to split some wood. The boys at the mission had brought in a couple of cart loads of mixed pinyon and white pine a few days before Christmas. The sun was barely up when he heard the screen door shut and Emma came up behind him. She touched his back. He shot a gloved, right hand jab to one of the porch posts. His habit was to stand strong-side forward. The impact caused the porch roof to shudder.

"You upset?" she asked.

"No," he smiled. "I was just deciding whether to practice a bit or to chop some wood. I'm fine, thank you. How was your sleep?" She pulled her hand away and waited. While he'd learned to not be too direct with her given her reactions, she'd never gotten used to the pulling away. They both did it. It made her crazy.

"You miss boxing?" she asked.

"Savate, dear. Boxing is just with your hands."

"Of course," she said, looking at the wood pile and wondering how to continue the previous evening's discussion. "Want to get some wood going and I'll make breakfast?"

"Sure," he said, firing three vertical punches at the porch post. Never full power, he'd moved one of the posts last spring when practicing. It had left the shed roof a little askew. Rather, he preferred to hold something back, even with his gloves on. "Just give me a few moments with this and then I'll be in. There's still a bit of a fire in the front room if you like. Maybe you can do your devotions there before we fix breakfast?"

She nodded and padded into the front room. It was an odd relationship, him and her. They'd taken their time — he an ex-priest with no discernible religious practice, she a missionary at heart but hardly interested in other people's points of view. She'd been praying about changing that, hoping that Jesus would do something new and good within her. But try as she did to be a different person, a kinder and more accepting person, a gentler and more generous person, she felt like she hadn't changed at all.

She took the folded blue blanket from the top of the rocking chair by the stove and sat down. She was confused about what had happened the previous evening and embarrassed she had reacted so sternly. Nor did she understand Ronin's interest in shadow boxing by the wood pile. Opening her Bible to the *Psalms* she found herself unable to concentrate. "William?"

Pat — pat, pat. Woomp. Woomp, woomp, woomp.

"Dear?"

The lighter, more vertical punches were meant to "set-up" his opponent for what was to come. They measured his range. They kept his opponent at bay. The stiffer strong-side jab cut and confused his prey. He delivered his more powerful weapons after the fact. Ronin slapped a couple of heavy strikes with his palms to the cedar post in front of him, swinging in from the side with each of his hands, one after the other while pivoting on his front and back legs. The metal roof stuttered, making it hard to hear.

"I'll be in in a minute, Emma."

He pressed forward, as if the post was an opponent. *Never backward always forward,* he reminded himself — words his bishop used to say when he was in the Episcopal seminary and the boys, or men rather, would box for exercise. He soon found he had an interest in the martial sciences, and had come to appreciate the contribution they'd made to his life.

Whoomp. Whoomp.

He lifted his front leg until his knee sat up against his chest. Extending his leg slowly, he pushed the ball of his foot toward the post until it touched. *If I really kick this thing, the whole house will come down.*

"Are you finished, dear?" Emma called out from the front room. *Really?* He pulled his leg to his chest, his knee in position to deliver another kick. He extended it again. He then did the same with his left leg. *It'd be easier not to answer,* he thought. "Dear, can you hear me?" she said.

He shook his head, right to left, touching each of his shoulders with his ear to make sure his neck and trapezius muscles were limber. He then lifted his right leg up so that it sat sideways, like a dog getting ready to pee. He extended his foot forward until his shin touched the post, his left leg turning so that the supporting heel pointed forward. He pulled his leg back and did it again.

"Honey, can you hear me?"

Jesus. "I said I'd be in a couple of minutes." He shook his arms and shoulders. He flexed his hands and fingers. Now fully awake, he found himself very much annoyed. Picking up the ax, he stood a piece of pine on its end and then hit it, splitting it. He did it again, and again. It took a few moments, but soon he had an armful of timber. He entered the house. "Where would you like the wood, dear?" he asked.

"Leave it there in the kitchen," she said, "then join me here, would you?" She gestured toward the couch, which had served as his bed the previous evening.

"I'll be right in."

The thing was, he hated taking direction from a woman so different than him. It wasn't that she was female — he'd adjusted to the emerging roles and interests women had brought to the Comstock. Businesses and brouhahas — both had served to establish the equality of women, particularly women like Emma, in places where men used to make the decisions. She now *ran* the mission, not just worked at it. Her husband Henry, for all of his criminal interests, couldn't hold a candle to the lady. Someday, he'd told his friends in Virginia City, Emma Nauman would be running for a state office, and if Nevada politics didn't yet permit that, she'd change the public's thinking on the matter.

No, it wasn't that she was a woman. It was that she was a woman so *different* than him. *I don't know that she even attempts to understand me,* he thought, putting the wood pile down by the open screen door before pulling a couple of thin, sticky pieces from the stack to start the morning cook fire. He blew carefully into the stove. There were enough embers from the previous night's fire to immediately ignite the kindling. He closed the door to keep the cold out. She came into the kitchen.

"I got tired of waiting."

"No kidding," he said without turning around. He pulled three bigger pieces of wood from the pile and pushed them into the stove. "Emma, we should talk." She sat down at the table where they'd had supper the night before. He turned and faced her. "I'm not happy unless I'm doing what I care about. I need that to be okay with you."

"I know."

"I need you to know that bad guys bother me, and probably will always bother me. And while I don't harbor an un-Christian grudge toward them — I'm really a good and kind man, I think, maybe even a Christian man — I'll not have them pushing good people around in the community where I live."

"I know."

"And I'll not allow them to trouble other people with petty crimes and inconveniences if it's within my ability to call them on it. I care too much to allow that."

"I know you do."

"So if that means I've got to be about some business now and then, if it means that I need to pummel a few crooked men into closure or submission, for the sheriff or the marshal, or just because I can't stand it any longer ..."

"I know."

"... then I hope you'll be okay with that. It's just who I am, Emma. And to be frank, I don't want to be any other kind of man." He stood there a moment, a piece of wood in his right hand, his left hand hooked onto his front pocket not knowing what else to do with it, before pulling a chair from the head of the table and sitting down. "I don't mean for any of this to upset you."

"I know."

"So, we're good with all of this?" he said, leaning the piece of wood up against his chair before folding his hands in front of him, waiting.

"I guess we need to be," Emma said, "I don't mean to be such a bother." She looked down at the table for a minute and then took his hands into her own. "Look, William, I know who you are. And I loved you that way. And if continuing to love you means that I have to like your guns or your guts or your gumption ..." They both began laughing, the alliteration being too much to stand. "... then golly!" she said, "I'll give it a go."

"Really?" he asked, smiling.

"As best as I can tell."

"Then let's have breakfast." He kissed her full on the lips. He liked that. He waited a few moments before continuing. "After we eat, I've got to clean and oil my guns before riding into town. It's time for me to pay Orrin Hickman a visit."

"In Carson City?"

"Genoa. It's a fine December morning, a day after celebrating Jesus' birth, don't you know. I want to see what a Mormon has to say about meeting his savior."

"About the savior?"

"About meeting him sooner instead of later. Because, dear one, I'll not see another gang of inbreds and troublemakers on this side of the Sierra Mountains," he smiled, "until we make a few of our own."

Chapter 13

HENRY NAUMAN

Henry Nauman believed he was dead. Not in the literal sense, of course. He knew himself to be thinking, breathing and inordinately interested in the sort of things that would bury most men. But in terms of relationships, he'd left a good number of people wondering what had happened when he fled Nevada's capital for Hangtown a year and half before.

Some people believed the former Presbyterian lay minister and missionary was six feet under. He'd left suddenly and without explanation. It wasn't the sort of thing Presbyterian missionaries did unless something untowardly happened. Some figured Nauman had simply gone on with the rest of his life, albeit somewhere else.

Others, strangely enough, actively *hoped* something *had* happened to the man.

His wife for instance, the kindly, it-couldn't-have-happened-to-a-nicer-woman-but-it-did Emma Nauman, who was now running the mission she and her husband had founded thirteen years ago, before he'd been found to have collected a gaggle of hussies. "And there are more things you'll want to know," Ronin had told his friend, shortly after her husband fled Carson City on a stage bound for Placerville.

Emma and Henry Nauman had left a small, backwater town a few miles west and south of Pittsburgh in hope of doing something more meaningful with their lives. Not that their small farm didn't have a future in the southern West Virginia shadow of Steubenville, Ohio. Not that it wasn't exactly as God intended it — Emma's words, not his, you understand. He'd never been able to manage much god-talk. Emma took care of that, and quite naturally, to raise funds for instance, or to communicate with the folks back east. Their journey hadn't been easy. They'd been obliged to join multiple wagon trains to get through Iowa, Nebraska, the Wyoming and Utah territories, and then finally Nevada which was really, in those days anyway, an extended part of the Utah territory. When they hit the Sierra Mountains, they stopped in what was then called Mormon Station or Genoa — he thinking they'd weather the worst of the snows on the eastern slope before heading on toward Sacramento, she surmising pretty much instantly that the only really green valley they'd come across in their drive west — protected by snow-capped mountains on the California-side and stubby pinyon pine and sage-covered hills on the eastern side — was in fact home. Not that she asked. Her Savior told her, she said. Jesus, it had been hard.

When Henry left the mission ten years later, he was happy to get out of there. There were so many Indian children in the couple's care that he'd chosen to sell a few. And the good Christian folks he'd hoped to sell them to? They would have done those kids real good, if you went in for that sort of thing. Church people seemed to.

Henry Nauman's heart was elsewhere. It wasn't in the ministry. Emma knew. He wanted to be a businessman. Try as he did, he was never been able to make the kind of money he wanted to, enough to make up for living there among all those people — Paiutes, Washoe, Shoshone and some brown skins he'd never heard of except for the occasional sit-me-downs with Indian parents who wondered how their children were doing, living and learning there at the mission. He didn't particularly like meeting with the children. It was more Emma's thing.

He'd hoped to make a genuine living there in Carson City. So much was going on, what with Peter Cavanaugh constructing the capital building and their hauling all of that sandstone from the prison quarry. Then there was the start-up of the Carson City mint. Boom years, bust years, it didn't matter. There were always opportunities for a good businessman, he figured. Not that Emma felt that way. "You work for Jesus," she said, which was a mite uncomfortable he thought, given how he wanted to live his life not Jesus' life.

He chose the city, like the biblical patriarch, Lot — Abraham's nephew, who wasn't ever Abraham's equal if the scriptures were to be believed. Like Lot, he wanted to circulate among the city folk rather than rural folk. "It's where the opportunities are," he said. "There's fundraising to do," he told her. "Missions don't grow on trees," he pointed out. It was in the Bible, he was pretty sure, though he didn't really read it much. That was Emma's thing, too. It didn't pay to have two people in a marriage doing the same thing, else one of them would be wasting his or her time, he said. That *wasn't* in the Bible he said, though it ought to be.

So one day, after seeing one of his favorite people in the city — a shapely but squeaky red-headed girl named Ally, he'd never really gotten her last name — he packed up and headed over the mountains before the snows came, knowing he'd be a little late for the strawberries but just in time to pick through the Placerville gold fields.

Hangtown had become a hub for the area's mining camps, though it didn't offer much yellow earth anymore, having been well picked over after gold was found in 1849. "The California Gold Rush" and "Dry Diggins" it was called, later "Hangtown" and later still "Placerville" — it all blended together in Henry's mind at the time — the city's reputation for gold still lingered. So when he and the bosomy girl picked the last bone off the bird in that Ormsby Street bar, he was finished with the old and looking forward to the new. *Jack's Bar,* he seemed to remember, *I wonder if it's still around?*

Henry Nauman sat high up on the seat as the Salt Lake City bound train came over the hills from Truckee into Reno, and wondered. *Should I keep on going or should I stop?*

Nauman took hold of his black, patent leather suitcase — the only thing he'd gained by moving to Placerville, everything else having played out. He was probably a mere ghost in Carson City by now — times so quickly change — not that he was interested in finding his way back. Emma certainly was in his life. The marriage had never been a good one, what with her desire "to do something wonderful for Jesus" and his hoping to make a buck or two along the way, if Jesus didn't mind. Maybe it was better to let the past be the past.

His hands wrung the tiger-wood handle of his suitcase like it was laundry day and there was drying to be done. There was the issue of the children he'd sold, or didn't sell. He imagined it depended on how one looked at things, and who was left to testify, not that he wanted to get involved with the same roughnecks again. The Crestwell brothers and the Clancy family were a cruel and punishing bunch to be sure.

Pulling the suitcase to his chest, he drummed his fingers on the iron bar of the seat in front of him as the train came into the station. A heavy set woman looked at him smartly, as if he had threatened to drink from her coffee cup or had suddenly asked to kiss her on the lips. A quiet, non-descript waif of a child sat next to her, smiling. *Boy or girl,* he wondered?

But on the other hand he thought, standing up to get his hat from overhead before peering out the window to see who might be standing on the platform, maybe he could find that bosomy woman again.

Chapter 14
A STILL VOICE WITHIN

Familiarity has a strange power in most people's lives. Pulling us away from the unfamiliar — the good maybe or even the worst — the desire for comfort yanks at the very base of our being. It whispers seductively and adamantly into our ears, "You don't want to do that. Do something, go somewhere, be with somebody familiar. Change means danger," it says. "New dreams and destinations only bring frustration and fear."

It's not that Henry could hear the still voice within — he had long ago stopped listening to the inner promptings of his spirit. The competing voices in his head had long since captured his heart, conquering the healthier of life's songs within. He'd been given a few, all of us have. The choices he'd made — to make love to another person's wife, to sell the dreams of little Indian children, to double-cross his family and friends in an effort to make some green or gold, the color of the money didn't matter — produced a symphony of discordant voices within him. The only real choice Henry Nauman had was to silence a few.

"Pick one," he'd said to a hastily-chosen barroom friend in Placerville the night before. He didn't realize he was talking about himself. "Don't sit there wondering what to do," he counseled, unaware of his own need to choose. "Pick something and do it," he said. It was natural for Henry to give other people advice. It's what Presbyterian pastors do, even if they're not fully ordained. He wasn't, though Emma and his West Virginia church treated him like he was, paying him money to send missionary reports, whether they were true or not. The man suddenly punched him in the face, which was a total surprise since he thought his Saturday night friend was thinking of leaving his wife, the choice being easy. When he picked himself up off of the floor of that Hangtown bar he decided he'd had enough. He went back to the room he was renting above the Jackass Inn next to Helstner's Hay Yard — where the hanging tree used to be before the hotel was expanded — sat down on his bed and said simply, "Hell with it." And that was that. A week later he was on a train to Anywhere, U.S.A. thinking it had to be better than El Dorado County, California. And some places are, of course. Others only promise to be.

Nodding to the fat woman in front of him and her child, a girl he figured, he held his hat and suitcase and stepped off the train. And seeing a freighter heading to the Ormsby House in Carson City, he begged a ride.

"You can take the V & T," a clean-looking blond-haired young man said, pointing to another track. "It'll take you up the grade into Virginia City where you can have a nice meal and maybe get a room. You could head to the capital in the morning," he added, pulling a crate of lettuce off of the platform and putting it into his wagon. "That's what I'd do, mister, though you're certainly welcome to ride along with me if you like."

"It's a memory thing," Henry Nauman said. "I've got plenty at my age," he continued, thinking of the years Emma and he had spent at the mission, just a little ways outside of Nevada's capital city. Not all of them were bad. They'd built themselves a house there when he was but twenty-one years of age.

"Well, come along then." The boy grabbed the bag. He was about the same age. "You used to live in Carson City? It's a lot slower now than it used to be."

"That right?"

"Got a few folks concerned, if you ask me, not that I know about such things — people wondering what's going to happen if they don't find any more silver, or gold for that matter. Clothing stores, restaurants, some of them are closing. Folks are moving to Montana or points south to do their digging."

"Silver and gold will never be what they used to be, son. Are you heading to the Ormsby House directly?"

"I am."

"Happen to know a man named Jack, in a bar down the street?"

"Actually, I do," the boy said, laughing. California people were so strange. Take them out of their surroundings, plop them down in the middle of the American West, and they'll ask you for sure if you know a particular dusty cowboy or seen a certain brown cow. "I mean, if you're looking for the man who used to run whores on Curry Street, I know him."

"Well, actually I am, young fellah, though I hope you haven't found yourself in the grasp of such a woman. It's not the way of heaven, you know."

"Imagine not," he said, chuckling. He pushed Nauman's valise into the back of the wagon, between a large crate of chickens and a fresh box of California carrots. "Not recently," he said. "Truth be told, not ever," he said, laughing. "Mister ..."

"Nauman, my friend. Henry Nauman. I used to be the director of the American Gospel Mission at the edge of town."

"The Indian thing?"

"Yes. You know it?"

"I do not, though I've met a woman with the same last name as you who lives out that way I believe."

"One woman at a time, my friend."

The boy looked on, blankly. "I don't understand."

Nauman smiled. "This Jack fellow, does he still work there on Curry?"

"He does not. He's up a ways on Carson Street."

"Then you can drop me there, if you don't mind. I have a business proposition for him."

The boy offered his arm. Nauman took hold of the seat instead, and pulling himself up, sat down smiling. "This woman you mentioned ..."

"Yes sir." The boy pulled a sheet of canvas over the Ormsby House provisions and fastened it down before running around to the other side of the wagon.

"You know her?"

"I do not, sir. But she is a beauty to be sure — brown hair, green eyes and quite a figure, if you don't mind me saying, though her bosom could be a little bigger."

"They could all be bigger, my friend — every one of them."

Chapter 15

THE RANCH

Ronin lifted his handgun from his left holster with the thumb and index finger of his right hand. It was an awkward movement at best, but he didn't want Hickman to get the wrong idea. He placed the .45 caliber single action Colt on the kitchen table between them, the barrel of the firearm pointing forward, making it clear that each of the chambers was loaded and that he wasn't afraid. "Orrin, I'm just saying, if you continue to pursue your evil ways, there could be lots of trouble. You're an old man, my friend. Why not let bygones be bygones?"

"They're not my bygones to let go of," Hickman said quietly. The two had started out in a much better place, swapping stories of people they knew in eastern Nevada and talking about the earlier history of the church in Salt Lake. When Ronin raised the question of whether he believed the Danites still existed, Hickman sidestepped. His smile disappeared. "I can't undo another man's curse."

"You can let it be," Ronin said. "If it's not yours to undo then maybe it's not yours to act on."

"Who said anything about acting?" Orrin Hickman rested his right hand on a large Bible next to him. Ronin suspected a concealed pistol within it as soon as he sat down. There was a weight to the book as he nudged it to one side. He tapped the top of the book, tracing the letters "Holy Bible," to let Hickman know that he knew and to suggest an alternative course of action.

Hickman's Genoa home was genuinely stunning. The single story, cedar-clad ranch home ambled along the base of the mountain at the end of a lane near a small, white community church. The fact that it was made of wood instead of block or brick suggested that the owner had placed his faith in God and didn't fear fire. Mature bushes and trees formed an indefensible space around the home but blocked the Sierra winds. "Zephyrs," he'd learned to call them when he first arrived in Nevada in 1877. Hickman had come much earlier than that. The state was barely a territory, and Mormons were the territory's first white settlers.

Hickman came to the front door when he called and extended his right hand. "Welcome to Zion," he'd said, an obvious biblical reference to Jerusalem, specifically to the area where an ancient fortress stood. The more mystical writers in the Jewish tradition had argued an even deeper meaning. It was not only the name of a geographical area, the word pointed to an unchanging and immovable reality. The reference wasn't missed.

They were sitting alone in a darkened green and yellow kitchen when he became aware of a younger, angrier man who had pushed himself back into the kitchen's far corner. Slender, fit, his face whittled by a bad attitude and even worse weather, the young man's hat tilted forward hiding his eyes. Ronin figured him to be a hired gun.

He looked deeply into Hickman's eyes. Hickman seemed to be a principled man, but there was a certain sadness to his demeanor, as if he was living someone else's playbill or had only recently come to realize that what he had hoped for in life might never be his to live.

"You don't need to do this, Orrin."

"Who said I was doing anything?" the old man insisted. "I'm but one voice among many." The younger man uncrossed his legs and leaned forward. He looked up slowly.

"Mister Ronin."

"Nice to hear from the peanut gallery."

"I believe Elder Hickman has made himself clear, don't you think?"

"Yeah, I don't know," Ronin stuttered for effect. "I don't understand much about these things, being a former minister and all. I just …"

The man interrupted. "You don't understand or you don't hear, reverend?" Ronin slid forward in his seat, moving his right hand to the top of his strong-side holster and lifting his gun, his movement hidden by the kitchen table.

"Well, son, I'm afraid I don't know your name. But at my age it might be both," he said, smiling. He held the stare until the young man laughed.

"There's no need for that, Horace," Hickman interjected. "I'm sure Mister Ronin is only trying to get his point across. Listen, Ronin. What I want is to be faithful. It's what every Saint in this town wants. Twenty-some years ago an esteemed friend of mine cursed the people of northern Nevada because of a bad business deal. Floods and fires have been the only result. God will not be mocked."

Ronin nodded.

"While I'd hoped to live out my days ranching, I can't let the need for Blood Atonement go unmet."

"Blood Atonement? I'm not sure I understand."

"Let's put it this way. What folks did to Orson Hyde twenty-two years ago, what they did to countless others folks too, well, someone has to pay. If you don't mind me saying, Mister Ronin, you look like a man who might understand that."

He smiled.

The angry man in the corner suddenly stood up and grasped at his gun. Ronin pushed the heavy oak table into Hickman's lap and fired his gun first. The shot tore the holster off the man's waist, spilling his gun onto the kitchen floor. The old man — surprised that a someone so close to him had not only fired a shot but now had five more potential shots pointed at his belly — lifted the cover of his family Bible and began to reach inside. "Don't," Ronin said. "Don't make me. Please."

The angry man — Horace what's his name, dressed in black like a Halloween costumed Grim Reaper, sat back down — his hands on his head, his gun still on the floor. Hickman folded his hands on top of the table. Ronin picked up the Colt he'd earlier placed on the table from the floor beneath him, walked calmly into the corner and kicked the other man's gun over to where he had been sitting. He picked them up and pushed both of them back into his belt. Looking at Hickman, who was easily a man in his seventies, he understood. It was a matter of pride and prejudice. The elderly Mormon Saint was an unmoving mountain, no more able to change his mind than nearby Jobs Peak could change its manner.

"A man is as a man is," he used to argue with his religion teachers, "even grace can't change that." Culbert Rutenber, the best intended of the Episcopal school's professors, always took exception.

"A living Jesus means that men and women can revolutionize their lives," he said enthusiastically. "In the power of Christ, they can change them for the better." But people don't change, Ronin figured. Over the years he'd concluded faithful people — despite all the religious talk and discipline — seemed to change even less than others.

"Listen," he said, his gun still leveled at the two men. "I'm going to back out of this room. And I'm going to keep this ugly piece of iron in my hand pointed toward both of you until I'm gone. If either of you move, if either of you flinch or twitch or speak in such a way as to make me nervous, I'm going introduce you to a mutual friend."

"Friend?" Hickman asked.

"To the baby Jesus, who was probably hoping for a different end to your life than this."

"How can you be sure, Mister Ronin?"

"Indeed." He backed out the kitchen door onto a snow-covered porch.

Chapter 16

TUMBLE TIME

Ronin hadn't even put his foot in the stirrup when Hickman's hired man barreled out of the house. He hit his horse with such force — a heavy slap with the palm of his right hand — that Jackson reared up with a fearful scream and galloped for the tree line. Ronin's foot was momentarily caught in the stirrup, dragging him a couple of dozen feet. "Goddamnit," he said, when he was able to slip free, and stumbled to get his balance. The son of a bitch was soon on top of him.

"Just like that?" the man yelled, his face in Ronin's face, his fist jacked up next to his collar, pushing, punching and grasping to get a hold. His breath smelled like sugar and prune juice. *Jesus.* The ex-preacher tucked his right leg and threw his left leg and arm over and into the young man's ribs, knocking him a couple of feet into a carpet of pine needles and snow. His left foot now on the ground, his left hand also, he propelled himself forward, mounting the man like he would the back of a horse, tucking his heels underneath the guy's buttocks. He hit him twice — a right cross to establish dominance, followed by a left straight jab. *One, two.* The combination shuttered the man's eyes and broke his nose, which erupted like the geyser at Yellowstone. A super-heated column of blood exploded upward from the man's proboscis. Ronin thrust his gloved hand onto his attacker's face and pushed his head to the side. "I don't want you to die, you slimy Mormon son of a ..."

"He's no Latter-day Saint," Hickman called from the porch. "He's a simple man from New Jersey who needed a job. Let him be," the old man said, a double-barreled shotgun in his hands. Ronin paused.

"You're too far away, Orrin. Drop the barrel and I won't fire."

"You won't fire?" Hickman said, laughing. "Who are you talking to, son? I wasn't born yesterday. I'll cut you in half from the porch as sure as I'm a man of God."

"If you were a man of God, Orrin, you'd drop the barrel a bit and let me talk, before either of us take an action we'll regret."

Hickman paused. He'd seen the man's gun play earlier. It could all end there, forty feet from his Genoa home — he with a bullet to his chest or his head, the Gentile with a handful of birdshot in his belly, and then what? Would God raise up another man, with the same temerity and fearlessness that sat in his breast? One of the last of the living Apostles, a Saint who had no living peer, a man whose actions were depended on not only by the church, but by the Living God himself — what good would it do if he were to be killed in a moment such as this? He lowered his gun.

"Mister Ronin," he shouted, "you and I will talk in a bit. But it won't be now. And it won't be here. I'll promise you that. Whatever mercy is left in you, please allow my man to live."

Ronin looked at the man beneath him. Twenty years old at best, but cut like a fighter and hell-bent to die like one. "Don't move," he said, leaning into the side of his neck until the gunman passed out. "Alright, Orrin, I'll let your man live. But on one condition."

"What's that, Mister Ronin?"

"That you and I will meet again, before any more craziness happens. There are a lot of people upset already. They're not all sitting in church, if you know what I mean."

"I do," Hickman shouted.

"Then meet with me, my friend. Let me see what I can do to make things right. You know that's my heart."

"I do."

"Do we agree?"

Hickman thought for a moment. He'd make no serious commitment to a Gentile dog. "Be wise as wolves," Jesus had said, or something like that in the *Gospel of Matthew*. "I'll meet with you."

Ronin resituated both of his guns. "Hickman, you're a good man, more or less."

"Some days, some days not."

W. W. Ronin rolled off of the man, leaving him in a pile of pine needles underneath a tall tree. Hickman began walking toward him. They crossed twenty feet out from the house. "You know it might not go well when we meet again?" Hickman suggested.

"It doesn't matter," Ronin said, turning around and backing toward his horse. "Jackson!" he shouted. The horse loped toward him. He put the animal between him and the old man. "One way or the other, peace is what I'm interested in, my friend."

"I am not your friend," Hickman called, kneeling down by his man. "Nor this man either," he whispered while tapping his friend's cheek.

Ronin hoisted himself up into the saddle. "Here's how I see it, Hickman." He pulled his horse around so that it was pointed down toward the valley. "I live in this place. I intend to make my life here, my friend ..."

"I am not your friend ..."

"You said that already." Ronin's horse began to prance and circle. "So this I know, old man ..." Hickman winced. Age was a blessing. He would not be talked to that way, certainly not by a man who missed the boat spiritually, who despite his training had so little understanding of the eternal realms and truths that motivated better men. He tapped harder on his friend's face. "I will not sit by silently and see my community changed by people like you. I will not allow the peace to be disturbed by such bullshit or bloodshed. I will not permit ..."

"You will not permit?" Hickman bellowed, the man beneath him beginning to stir.

Ronin continued to interrupt. "I will not permit a man from your church, or any other church, to lift his hand or handgun or rifle or what have you, and do people harm. Not here. Not now. Not you. Not never. Am I being clear?" Ronin shouted back.

"Clear as the day is long," Hickman said, "and dead as the night is dark," he whispered to his friend, who was now sitting up and wondering what the hell had happened.

Chapter 18

HORACE BROWN

Brown wasn't the most popular name in Britain. Smith likely was, or maybe Jones, Williams or Davies even. But it had a sort of ring to it, more or less, and Horace Brown hoped he would make something of it, given that his name didn't amount to much, or the three generations of Brown men who had been born with it before him. And it wasn't like each of them hadn't tried.

When Horace *the First* left Britain for the New World, the boat trip was free given that the English Parliament had decided as early as 1597 to transport its vagrants and rogues "beyond the seas." In total some 50,000 people were similarly dealt with over the years in an effort to repair the Commonwealth's criminality. Most were men without any skill or trade, though some were women. All of them were destined to become servants or slaves or worse.

Horace *the Second* didn't fare much better, narrowly escaping the petty thievery of his father to become a shoemaker of all things, in time a cobbler of custom footwear in a day when left or right didn't matter as much as one's finances or fit.

Horace's father was a shy man except when it came to the use of his tools — a set of knives his father had put to unmentionable use — an awl, a hammer, stretchers and burnishers. Once, in an unusual outburst, Horace *the Second* heaved a heavy iron at his son when he learned he was heading west instead of staying in Patterson, New Jersey to apprentice. The moment was never forgotten by either man, his dad dying of heartbreak as Horace was his only son in a lineage that had only produced boys as far back as anyone could remember. Horace *the Third* — an employee "not a servant" he was always careful to point out — couldn't help but think of his dad's action as anything other than cruel, though he was a creative man and the best of the bunch, if anyone should ask.

Horace *the Third* wanted so much to be better than his dad or granddad, though there was little hope he'd ever amount to much. So when it became clear that he couldn't be a cowboy — it was dirty work and strenuous too, and who could stand the heat in Texas anyway — he found the verdant valleys of northern Nevada a reasonable and rewarding home. The Latter-day Saints, save their peculiarities, were the best friends he could ever have. The Gentiles suspected he'd come from disreputable stock, at least three generations of it in fact, coming to America when the states were simply colonies in some English person's crown. But the Saints loved him just the way he was. "Like Jesus does," they said.

Horace *the Third* made his money as a gunman, hired out to businessmen or women who needed something done. And like his grandfather, he didn't have half the sense of his dad to settle down and do something different than the English Crown expected of his kind. But he'd found his calling in helping Orrin Hickman be the man he thought *God* wanted him to be. He'd "handle the dirty work," he promised, hoping that maybe it would get less dirty over time. But it got more so, and in it Brown saw the opportunity to build something of a reputation. Not as a pirate or robbery man — criminality more common at the time, and some of it quite lucrative — but as "a shootist in service to the church," he said when he first mentioned it to the old man, who was so old he could either be his father or his grandfather. He didn't know. He'd "pick up the pieces," he said, meaning he'd pick-*off* those who were making trouble for the few Mormon ranchers that could be found in the valley or beyond.

"There may not be enough work here in Nevada," Hickman responded, suggesting he should turn an occasional eye toward California or Utah, "where there may be more work to do," though he didn't know whether Hickman was trying to help him grow in his chosen career or go, not that it mattered. He liked Nevada best of all of the places he'd been: Texas, California, the Arizona and New Mexico territories and other places along the way. The Silver State was more home than any place he'd ever lived. It was sunny in a special sort of way, inside and out, and when the rains came, or the occasional snows, they didn't linger long.

"What hit me?" he asked his mentor, the Apostle Elder Prophet Orrin Hickman. He knew he didn't have the titles right. *Who gives a shit,* he thought. He wasn't one of them, but they were kind and true and faithful to their words. And the money was good. The money was *real* good.

"The Gentile reverend W. W. Ronin hit you, my son." Hickman pulled a poultice from his left eye where Ronin had last planted his right fist. "Bet it hurts."

"Hurts like a mule, Elder Hickman. Did he hit me more than once?"

"Only once, Horace. But you held up. If it hadn't been for him sitting on top of you, you'd probably have brained him. But as soon as he got the upper hand, he didn't let go."

"I feel like a train hit me, sir."

"Might have been, son. Let me help you up into a chair."

For being an older man, Orrin Hickman was a strong as two city folk, "maybe three," he liked to boast. The ranch had its helpers, of course. When the hay was in, Saints up and down the valley took turns getting the work done. No man worked alone, even the most successful or wealthiest of the Mormon ranches understood the nature of God's economy.

There needed to be a gathering place, for instance, a village of sorts where the faithful could live and work together in harmony. Genoa had been that and Hickman was proud to have been a part of it. The Saints needed also to appreciate their lives. They were stewards of everything that had been given them. With God's help, they would make the earth a more fitting place to be. It was up to them to do God's work. Thirdly, they needed to live frugally, cooperatively and with unity. Brigham Young had said it best, though in his later years he didn't seem nearly as smart. "Except I am one with my good brethren, do not say I am a Latter-day Saint. We must be one," he said. "Our faith must be concentrated in one great work — the building up of the kingdom of God on the earth." Hickman had taken Brigham's words seriously, caring for the people who had been left behind, who hadn't fled back to Utah when the threat of federal troops came. He'd stayed the course. He'd fought the good fight. He'd lived for only one thing in the last twenty-some years of his life — that he was doing what God wanted him to do. And finally, there was the value of equality. "If we are not equal in earthly things," Joseph had said, "we cannot be equal in obtaining heavenly things."

Orrin Hickman had kept all of these spiritual principals soundly in his heart. It was the way life ought to be lived. While Horace Brown was not one of them, some day he might choose to be. Then he could look back on those days when he was treated like the man God was calling him to be — a brother and a true friend.

"You'll see the rascal again," he told Horace Brown *the Third* as he leaned against the kitchen table while sitting in the same chair Ronin had sat in less than an hour before. "And when you do …well, when you see him, you can express your surprise and interest."

Horace looked down at his shirt, "black as the night" he'd told the man at Koppel and Platt's clothing store, a few spaces down from the Ormsby House, next to John Fox's bookstore at Third and Carson streets in Carson City. And the proprietor, despite being a Jew, understood.

"You want something dark and dangerous looking," Joseph Platt said, before turning away to laugh. Not that Horace Brown noticed Platt laughing, because he would have killed him right there, right where he stood. But it was exactly what he'd hoped for, dark buttons and all. And now it was ripped. He'd express himself for sure.

Chapter 19
CARSON CITY

Ronin didn't know why he hadn't hauled Brown's ass to jail, not that he was a lawman, not that he ever wanted to be a lawman. The pay was piss-poor and the reputation, more often than not, little better than the night watchmen who used to rattle Carson City's doors at night. Still, free wasn't anywhere a jackass ought to be, not if he was going to cause trouble again. Letting Horace Brown lay, crumpled as he was at the base of Orrin Hickman's porch steps, and Hickman for the most part at liberty also, leaning over Brown like an old man wondering what had happened to his jackass son, didn't seem to be wise either.

The two of them were definitely up to something.

Hickman had practically said he was, inferring that some folks had their own mind about setting things straight, whatever that meant though he knew there was a lot to be set straight. Still, the wrong done so many members of the Latter-day Saints' church after they'd been called home — "Help, federal troops are coming!" or whatever Brigham Young had said to make reasonably-minded Mormons give up their valuable ranches and homes and sell what they could to buy guns and head back to Salt Lake City — was a long time ago.

No one should carry a grudge that long. What is it with religious people?

Ronin pulled up on Jackson's reins when he got to the crest of the hill looking west toward Jacks Valley and wondered whether he should stop by the house or head straight into Carson City. *It sure is beautiful.* He gazed north toward the lumber yards and imagined he could see the flume he'd barely survived riding from

Lake Tahoe. "There's no reason to do that again," he mumbled, thinking of the Chinese man who had pushed and pulled kept him in check after he had stumbled into his arms. Emma had been there just after he'd arrived. The damn doctor, too. *That was yesterday. Today is today.*

"Yup," he said, and Jackson began moving again.

He would have done well had he stayed in the parish. A bigger one by now, though Episcopal bishops couldn't be counted on to think like regular folk. They'd keep you tied up in the tiniest hellhole if the money wasn't good, or the parish wasn't growing, or someone said something about whoever or whatever. The next thing you'd know the bishop thinks it's good for you to stay where you are for a couple more years. "God isn't finished with you yet." *Whatever.* Despite the obvious game of it all, he'd probably have behaved well enough to get a bigger church in a larger town a little farther west, though he couldn't think where he would have wanted to end up. Carson City was nice. It might have worked out there.

He kicked Jackson's flanks to pick up the pace.

Maybe he'd grab a late breakfast with his friend, or see what Shubael Swift thought of Hickman's words. *And what the hell is with a hired gun,* he wondered? "The day of the desperado is over," he'd told Dustsucker the evening before, not that his friend agreed.

"The country will always need people like you," the deputy argued. "Like both of us, actually. It's not like the West is going to get all civilized all of a sudden. You can't hang it all up," his friend said, referring to his gun belt he figured, given that he had to pull it from a cabinet to run to Genoa and brace Hickman. Not that bracing him helped any. "Sooner or later, professional police officers *will* tame the frontier, Ronin. I have no doubt about that. But there will always be exceptions."

He knew Dusty was right. Still, looking over at Emma, it was real clear that whatever the country needed, she didn't think it needed *him* riding around making things right. Not now, anyway, not since they were talking about starting a life together and maybe having some little ones. They'd talked since that, of course. And he'd made a point to make sure she understood that he was back and forth on the matter, though most of the time he knew where he stood. "I'll handle what needs to be handled," he told her.

"And nothing more?" she asked.

He didn't know how to respond to that.

He'd have to find something to do if he didn't make his money "fixing things," he said. She was quick to point to the mission children, of course, and the ranch. And there were things she hadn't told him yet. He knew of her interest in the suffrage movement, for instance. There was a whole lot of talk about government doing this or doing that. He wasn't used to political chatter. Assemblyman Curtis Hillyer, she said, had resolved to amend the Nevada Constitution to allow women to vote in 1869, and it had passed both houses, she pointed out, though it had ultimately failed. He wasn't paying attention. And another Assemblyman, Oscar Grey, she said, brought it up again in 1873, but it had been indefinitely postponed. And now seven or eight years later, things didn't seem at all different, she continued. He wasn't able to follow everything she was sharing.

He had his own sense of what was right, right for him anyway, not that he always wanted to say. Whether women could vote or run for public office, well, the question just wasn't on his to-do list right now, though if it were he'd probably vote in favor, not that it would matter. It seemed Emma could hold her own. Most of the women he knew could do the same, though the men he knew didn't think so. Not that he cared what they thought. He had his own business to take care of. And much of the time, that didn't make much sense to her.

Dusty was outside the courthouse when he arrived in the middle of town. He nodded as Dusty greeted him and took hold of Jackson's reins to walk over to the livery. "I don't keep him there anymore," he said, smiling. Dustsucker looked up and remembered. Ronin was out at the house now, and Jackson too, of course. He was no longer staying at the Ormsby House. He was with Emma now.

"You're right. I'm sorry. Where do you want to go?" He offered Jackson's reins back to his friend.

"I thought we'd get a quick lunch, Dusty. And then maybe hop on over to see Shubael to talk about Orrin Hickman. I went out to see him this morning."

"I thought you would."

"Well, I know things seemed a little confused the other night. But Emma and I have worked it out."

"You think?"

"I'm hoping. 'A double-minded man is unstable in all his ways,' you know."

"How's that?"

"The Bible, Dusty. It's in the Bible. *James,* actually."

"Then I hope it's something you'll listen to. I hate seeing you go back and forth all the time. It isn't good for a man."

Ronin laughed. "Where do you want to eat, Dusty? It's my treat!"

Deputy Slade smiled, like there was no tomorrow and patted his belly. "Well," he said, "there's a new place on Carson Street run by a guy named Jack."

"That sounds wonderful."

Chapter 20

SHUBAEL SWIFT

"Sure beats a log jail, doesn't it?"

"Mister Ronin, how are you?" Shubael Swift rose from the wooden bench out front of the Ormsby County courthouse and extended his hand. "Hard to believe this used to be a hotel, right?"

Many of the capital's buildings had seen double duty over the years. "Hell of an improvement over that Mormon pile of logs John Blackburn had to use," Ronin quipped.

"It sure is."

John L. Blackburn was the city's *first* sheriff, "High Sheriff" to be exact. His tenure ended in 1861, when a gambler named William Mayfield plunged a bowie knife into his back, killing him. Subsequently, the county paid Carson City founder Abe Curry more than $42,000 to shape a courthouse out of Curry's Great Basin Hotel. An additional $6,000 built the city's first professional jail. Ronin was no stranger to the building.

"I heard you were back in town. I was hoping I'd get to see you sooner than later."

"Your man came to see me."

"I know he did," Swift said, tipping his hat back to see more clearly. "We were just talking about you this morning, in fact. Slade said you were willing to look into things. And I said I was happy about that. You boys want to sit a bit?" Swift moved to the north side of the bench so as to allow the two of them to sit down. Ronin shook his head.

"We were headed to lunch, Shubael, when William here suggested we peek in to see if you wanted to come along. And here you are."

"And here I am," Shubael said, laughing. Pulling a silver watch from his vest, he began to smile. "Hell, Marcus, it's hardly 11 o'clock. It's not time for lunch yet, not for a couple of couple of hours."

"I know. I was just thinking ..."

Ronin interrupted his friend. "Actually Shubael, I was thinking that the three of us might want to visit a bit about your man in Genoa. I was down there this morning, and to tell the truth, it didn't go all that well."

"It didn't, huh?" Swift grinned. "I didn't think it would. When Slade here told me you were going to put the fear of Jesus into him, I said to myself, 'Myself,' I said. 'What's a former preacher going to tell a good church-going Mormon man about Jesus that he doesn't know already?' That's what I said to myself."

Ronin fingered a stack of books sitting on the bench. Swift's predecessor hadn't struck him as much of a reader. Swift had a dozen or more volumes spilling out of a Folgers Coffee bag. "It looks like you might enjoy a good cup of coffee, Shubael. Sit with us a while?" He picked up one of the books. *Mormon Wives: A Narrative of Facts Stranger Than Fiction,* by Metta Victoria Fuller Victor. He lifted a second book, *Male Life Among the Mormons* by Maria Ward. "Any good?" he asked.

"Second in a series, I think."

"Huh," he said, letting his finger trail down the spines of the others. *Eagle Plume, the White Avenger: A Tale of the Mormon Trail,* by Albert W. Aiken. *Gold Dan: The White Savage of the Great Salt Lake: A Terrible Tale of the Danites of Mormon Land. Mormonism Unveiled* by Orvilla S. Belisle. "You sure seem to be studying up on things, Shubael. Expecting some trouble?"

"I am, Mister Ronin. And not knowing whether you'd have any first-hand knowledge of this cult, I thought I ought to do some reading."

"Cult?"

"Well, sure. They're hardly Christian, the way they treat their women. The fanciful stories of talking angels and golden tablets, and Indians that used to be Jews and such. I never heard of such things until Hickman started yakking about the Great Salt Lake. Hell, it doesn't take a smart man to know that a Paiute has never been to Jerusalem!"

"No, I imagine not," Ronin responded. He'd noticed that some folks didn't trust their Latter-day Saint neighbors. But he hadn't met anyone as upset about the Mormon Church as Sheriff Swift.

"Shubael, I'm not the smartest guy on the block, to be sure. But folks around here believe a lot of crazy things. Hell, every Washoe Indian I know thinks there's a giant bird that lives at the bottom of Lake Tahoe. Don't get me talking about Presbyterians and Baptists …"

"What's wrong with Baptists?" the sheriff asked.

"Nothing. Forget I said anything. I'm just saying they're people just like you and me. No better. No worse. I'm sure we'll work things out. It's not like there's a couple of hundred Mormons living in Genoa trying to figure out how to take over the state's politics."

"Used to be."

"Old news, Shubael. Surely you don't believe that. You certain you don't want to come along?" The old man paused. Shubael Swift had been sheriff from 1869 to 1879 — five two-year terms. He was a popular man, having his hand in the city's fire protection service as well. The city had three volunteer fire companies. One of them was named "the S. T. Swift Engine Company." It would be one hell of a funeral when the old man died.

"Oh, I don't know, Ronin. I'm sitting here enjoying an unusually warm winter afternoon. And the cottonwood trees — hell, I don't care if there are leaves on them or not. They're just about the prettiest things God ever put on the earth. I'd just be jawing at you."

"Well, maybe jawing is what we ought to do, sheriff. Did you know that Hickman has himself a hired gun?" Swift's mouth dropped.

"A shootist?"

"Best that I could see."

"Did you meet him?"

"I did."

"And?"

"I broke his nose," Ronin said, laughing.

"You broke his nose?"

"Yeah, after I shot him."

"You shot him?" Swift looked at Dustsucker, who shrugged and looked back.

"Did you kill him?"

"No." The ex-priest stood there, his hands in the pockets of his duster, smiling.

Shubael smiled back. "Mister Ronin, maybe we ought to visit," he said. "Things sound like they're going to get worse before they get better. I want to be included."

"Didn't mean to exclude you, sheriff. Things went south pretty quickly."

"That's what I'm saying." Shubael Swift stood up, buttoned his duster across his gun belt and walked toward the men as they were stepping off of the boards onto Musser Street. Ronin turned around.

"You don't want to take your books with you?" Ronin asked.

"Hell, I don't need no books. I'm staring at one up-to-date son of a bitch. You'll tell me what I need to know, son. And then we'll figure it all out together."

Chapter 21

IT MUST BE LOUISE

Two week's worth of groceries and other supplies took the hill well, coming up out of Washoe Valley and then down again into Nevada's capital. The young man confidently guided the two-horse team in a manner that kept his wagon safe and his passenger comfortable and happy.

It's great to be home, Henry Nauman thought as he tugged at the knot of a red paisley print tie he had found in his jacket pocket. "Not too strong, is it?" he asked. The boy shook his head. "It matches, right?" The boy nodded. "A gentleman shouldn't ramble about looking like he's spent the whole day slopping pigs or digging behind the barn, I always say."

If there was any chance he might be recognized — and he wasn't sure how he felt about that — he wanted to look tidy. He might come across Ally, for instance, "the big-breasted, happy little red head," he used to say when she was the object of his affections at a bar on Curry Street. There were other women he had known, biblically-speaking of course, and being a former missionary for a small Ohio Valley Presbyterian Church, he didn't want to look like he had come out of a coal mine in West Virginia. It was important that Henry Nauman looked sharp. The former lay missionary for the Presbyterian Church turned businessman had always been that way.

"You know, Gillom," he said, grabbing hold of his hat, "you could be a handsome young man if you wanted to be." The dusty-haired boy in his mid to late teens was judiciously applying a hand brake to smooth out the wagon's ride on the road east of the V & T Railroad tracks. "I mean, you're still a young man, even if you do live with your mother. Women like that. Well, not the mother thing. You get as old as me you have to work a little bit harder to be appealing to the fairer sex. You know what I'm saying?"

The boy smiled. Henry Nauman didn't look much past 40, he figured, though he was an unexpected and scrawny rider, talkative too. They'd covered just about all the news that was news by the time they hit Franktown. After that, it was all downhill the boy thought, given that he'd never met a real live missionary, though he'd seen a few of course, over the years at church. He generally rode the road alone.

"Benefit of clergy," the boy said, when the man offered to pay. He figured that a free ride was expected, the way Nauman had looked at him, like he was somebody to be welcomed, or appreciated or at least recognized. But when the man began talking about all the women he had known in northern Nevada — naming cooks, seamstresses and servants he'd met while doing his daily deliveries — well, Gillom wondered if he should have charged the man double for cattin' around so.

"Pardon me for asking," he said as they passed the first of the tiny wooden houses that had defined Nevada's capital prior to the sand and stone buildings going up. "Is it normal for a missionary to ... to ..." The teenager stuttered for a moment, unable to decide how to say what he wanted. "I mean, is it okay to have an interest in so many ladies?" He winced as soon as he said the words. His mother would have smacked him.

Henry Nauman laughed. A thin man, about 5-foot-eight or so and skinny as hell, he counted himself lucky to get anything at all from women, Emma having been the grand exception, though living with her hadn't been that much of a joy. *There was a woman though, if she could have just lightened up a bit.* "Son, one thing I've learned from the Mormon Church is that when God gives you a gift, it says a great deal about God's intentions. Not that I'm Mormon you know, but if he gives you one woman, for example, I don't see why he wouldn't be inclined to give you two women, or three or more." Nauman began laughing. He was a likeable fellow, though *really* scrawny.

Gillom shrugged. No one had ever explained women to him like that before. It didn't remind him of any Sunday School he'd ever been to, Mormon or not. They were Methodist, though he wasn't sure.

"Are you married?" the man asked.

"Not yet, sir."

"Do you have someone you're seeing?" he asked.

"There's a lady I'm hoping to," Gillom replied. "As soon as I get me a better job, I'm going to ask this girl to be my wife."

"Now hold on, son," Nauman exclaimed. "I'm not talking about multiple *wives*. Hell, even a Latter-day Saint can tell you that multiple wives isn't always God's best plan. I'm talking about friends son, special friends. You're going to want a couple of them," he said before pausing.

"Oh."

"I'm talking about Monday, Tuesday, gosh it's Wednesday so it must be Louise kind-of-friends ..."

"Oh!" he said, once he realized the missionary was talking about sportin' girls. "Well, sure, I've got a few favorites," he said, thinking of some of the girls in Dayton and in Virginia City, though he had never been with one. He'd only said hello. His mother would beat him if she knew.

"Well, son, good for you. And how about you sharin' some of those women? I mean, I might not find the woman I'm looking for at Jack's, and if I don't, well, I don't want to go too long without ... well, you know."

"I do, sir." *Missionaries aren't all that much different than the rest of us*, he thought, though he'd never gotten that impression in his mother's church. "I might be able to help you with that," Gillom said. He was always looking for a way to make money. "Tell you what I'm going to do," he said, offering as big a smile as a teenage boy ever did, inside or outside of church. "I'm going to drop these things at the Ormsby House, Mister. Then I'm going to come looking for you north on Carson Street. And if you need some help, I mean if you're finished at the bar and looking for someone to have some fun with, then we'll figure it out together. I'll get you what you need," he said. "Fair enough?"

"Fair enough," Nauman replied before pressing a couple of silver dollars into the boy's hands. "That's not just for the ride, son." Gillom pulled up on the reins in front of a tiny building along the boardwalk, north of Telegraph Street. He didn't tie up. He didn't need to as Nauman was half-way out of the wagon by the time the horses stopped, a suitcase in each hand and a large over-stuffed carpet bag stuck underneath one arm. A tall, gray-haired man was painting a sign outside one of Carson City's smaller drinking establishments. "Jack's Bar," it said in ten-inch red letters. And underneath, in black and gold, were the words "A Saloon Since 1859."

"That's a bit of a stretch, isn't it, Jack?" Nauman said, as he stumbled up onto the boardwalk, putting his suitcases down.

"Excuse me, sir?"

"The year, Jack — you haven't been open that long."

"I'm sorry, sir. Do we know each other?" the older man asked.

"Jack, we do not, though we've done some business over the years."

"You look familiar," he replied. It was as practiced a response as any, and he'd become quite good at it.

"And you look sober," Nauman continued, "which is probably why you don't remember me." He stood there smiling, waiting for the old man to recollect. "Do you recall the redhead with the shapely breasts?" he asked. And just like that, something within the old man snapped. He remembered her alright. And now he remembered him — same corner, same window, same table, same jokes and God, how could a man forget what a pain in the ass the local Presbyterian clergyman had been? Henry Nauman was back in town. The son of a bitch would soon be looking for his favorite barmaid, who was long gone and he sure missed her. She was maybe working up at Lake Tahoe, he didn't know and he didn't care, good Catholic that he had become since then, repenting of all his sins, real sins and some just imagined. True to his wife he was now, both of them taking the sacrament every Sunday at Saint Teresa's. But this slimy son of a bitch was a dead man if he was going to bring old times up and maybe look to court another impressionable young woman in his saloon, even if he wasn't interested in the girl. And he'd crown him a good one with the closest chair or bottle if he was thinking of bringing Ally around again. It'd be a handful of trouble for him and the missus. He'd figure a way to do it, too.

"It's nice to have you back, sir," he said, gritting his teeth. "Can I help you with your bags?"

"Well, Jack, you sure can. I sure didn't expect that from you." Henry smiled. "You always seemed sorta, well, self-absorbed."

Jack smiled. "Life has its way of surprising all of us," he said. "Every one of us gets what is coming to him."

Chapter 22

GILLOM ROGERS

Gillom pushed the lever forward on the family wagon so that a wooden chock rested firmly against the driver's side rear wheel. He undid a strap from one of the metal tie rails used to hold the wagon's load in place and pulled Nauman's twisted brown corduroy jacket free. "It's an odd place to stow a coat," he'd said when the missionary asked permission to toss it in the back. But with the wind and all coming through the valley, a good amount of dust had been stirred. And Nauman, anxious to look presentable, had folded it inside out rather than have it soiled by all the sand and dirt.

"It'll do," Nauman said, though Gillom saw the man shiver once they hit the shade of a mid-day cloud leaning up against the Carson Mountains.

"Mister Nauman," he shouted as his passenger disappeared into the saloon. "Shit," he said, sliding off of the scalloped wooden seat the horses boarded at his mother's rooming house on Mountain Street had been chewing. "Goddamnit," he said, catching his left pant leg on the tie rod as he attempted to step down. "Now what am I going to do?" he complained, though no one was listening.

No one ever listened to Gillom Rogers, not in his mind anyway. Not his mom, the kindly Bond Rogers, or so her friends said, Nor his dad — though God could only say what had happened to him dying the way he did and so suddenly that nothing good or nurturing could be remembered or said. Nor the sheriff, whom he had met on a number of occasions, none of them friendly, but that was the sheriff's job he figured. Not even the talkative deputy lodged in his mother's back room, Marcus T. Slade, though he was never able to ask what the 'T' stood for. He pulled his pant leg free and, holding the man's jacket in his arms like it was a newborn calf, touched his boot against the door to Jack's Bar and pushed it open.

His mother didn't much like his cussing so, nor the sheriff nor the deputy nor anyone else for that matter who lodged with them on the west side of Mountain street, up against some cottonwood trees and a fallen-down stable that sat nearby. "If those people had money," he'd told his mother that morning over a short stack of pancakes, "they'd pay extra to have their horses tended to."

"They do," Bond Rogers said.

"I mean somewhere else, where their horses can be taken better care of," he said before his mother pointed out that it was his job to watch after their mounts, and whatever other livestock they had brought with them. One time, a man had brought a couple of goats with him, trailing his carriage like he was going to set up housekeeping somewhere. It turned out that their guest simply liked fresh goat milk and didn't much trust what he could get at the house or hotels nearby.

"Mister Nauman," he said, holding the jacket out like it was a newly pressed suit, "I've got your coat here."

"In fact you do, young man."

Nauman took it from him, and pressed a coin into his hands. "Can I buy you a beer?"

Jack looked over from a selection of bottles behind the bar, where he'd been wondering which of the jugs and carafes would best brain the dumb fuck. *Brown glass or green?* He was thinking green. "Hold on, son," he said, turning to face the bar. "How old are you?"

"Old enough to kick your ass, Jack."

"Really?" Jack responded, wondering why a saloon owner had to put up with such talk. It simply wasn't Christian. "Well,

I guess if you're old enough to talk like a man, you're old enough to drink like one," he said, reaching for a brown bottle, but not before briefly pausing over a green one. "You want it in a glass, son?" he asked, not that he cared. Generally, he tried to, but not if folks were going to be rude — to hell with them then.

"He'll have a glass, Jack," Nauman said, taking the bottle with his own and grabbing a bowl of peanuts.

"Did you know that peanuts are not a nut?" he asked the boy, who was wide-eyed as hell, because he was going to get to sit in a real-live bar and have a real-live beer, which is something he hadn't done since before his father had gotten sick, not that his mother knew. It was such a good memory. He treasured it so.

"I did not," he said, because he didn't know.

"The peanut is more a vegetable than a nut. It's a bean, actually."

"I didn't know that, sir."

"Not many people do," Nauman said, looking over at Jack, who was hefting glasses left and right, as if weighing their contents. "It's a legume. I believe that's the word. The oldest specimen goes to Peru I'm told, though they're found practically everywhere. I believe I'd like to taste a peanut in every country of the world, my friend." Jack raised his glass.

"That would be a hard thing to do, sir," Gillom said, "though I imagine you'd be the person to do it if anyone could," he added when he saw Nauman's smile fade.

"That's a kind thing to say, young man. To your health," he said, clicking the boy's bottle with his shot glass.

The proprietor brought a clean glass to the table and set it before the young man. "Can I order you both some dinner?" he asked, looking first at the man he would surely brain before the evening was through, and then to the boy who he guessed he had seen a couple of times around town.

"Not for me," Gillom said. "What time is it, sir?"

"Well, I don't know," Nauman said, "though I imagine it's about lunch time. Stay with me, won't you? We'll discuss my earlier proposition …" And it was at that very moment that W. W. Ronin, his friend Dustsucker and Sheriff Shubael Swift shuffled into the saloon.

Chapter 23

MORMON CHURCH

Every Latter-day Saint there felt the same way. A long time ago they had been shafted, not by the federal government — Brigham Young and John Taylor had made damned sure of that — but by the people of Carson Valley, the Eagle and Washoe Valleys as well.

When the wagons pulled out of Genoa at the end of September in 1857, the Saints had only ten days' notice that they were needed in Salt Lake. Properties were unexpectedly sacrificed as the faithful readied 150 wagons, many of them filled with gun powder, so they could resist and punish the federal troops threatening Salt Lake City. Those that remained behind — Gentiles mostly, but some Mormons as well — reaped the benefit of that loss. In the social and political vacuum that resulted, some men made lots of money.

"It might not have been your folks who were hurt by the apostate slime that remained," Orrin Hickman declared about mid-way through his sermon. "It might have been your neighbor's folks, or no neighbor's folks, but mark my words. As sure as God is in heaven and we are on earth, some people took it in the ass."

Hickman's vulgarity was uncommon for Mormon Church leaders, and was a rarity for the barrel chested man who had secretly borrowed and spent all he could "to help other Mormons go home." The preacher winked. "I'm talking about their wallets, of course." He grinned. Narrow Mormon lips broke into large toothy smiles. Bad-mannered but rarely uncouth, the self-declared Elder and Revelator for the Latter-day Saints in northern Nevada, Hickman was never at a loss for words.

"I'm telling you what you already know so that you can be a part of God's great plan," he said, glancing behind him at a half-dozen Mormon gentlemen assembled for the event. "These men know what I'm talking about," he said, "and they want to be part of it. Hotel owners, restaurant cooks and servers, soldiers who have fought for their country ..." Hickman had a way of stretching a middle vowel until every eye looked up and every ear begged to hear more. "These are your friends, your family, your neighbors and folks you *want* to know," he continued, "not the vermin who expect us to forget that *God's* people were cheated, and that a half-dozen years of travel and travail, looking for a city set on a hill, hoping for a pearl that wouldn't need to be cast before the world's swine, should be swept away like a bad memory. Oh, no!"

The Mormon prophet leaned into the kitchen table, so that he could see all the way into the living room and bedrooms that were filled with faithful women and men. "These days are an opportunity, God says, to climb a new mountain, to make a new right, to tell the *world* that the faith that Joseph Smith bore onto *his* Calvary tree in Carthage, Illinois, is *still* alive, *still* at work, *still* a force to be reckoned with and reckoned with we shall be!"

Applause filled Hickman's large Genoa home. "We are a sweet-smelling savor," he continued, "to the Eternal God above, who loves us and calls us to be his people in this place. Can we do this?" he asked. "Should we do this?" He paused. "Can a man take salvation into his breast and not do what God wants done?"

Hickman's congregation was small, by Protestant and Roman Catholic standards. But it drew from a 25-mile radius, a boast that most of Nevada's religious communities could not make. Eight miles to Lake Tahoe, maybe fifteen or so to Carson City, another ten or more to the Washoe Valley, the faithful were not shy about camping at Hickman's ranch to get a dose of the truth. And they were getting it that night.

"I want to introduce you to a man who was sent here to help us. You may not know him — he wasn't raised in our church nor did he grow up nearby. But he knows *you*. He knows you to be a proud and faithful people, who haven't forgotten about the sacrifices that brought us west. He knows *you* and the Saints that preceded you out of Fayette, New York to Kirkland, Ohio, to Nauvoo, Illinois, to Council Bluffs, Iowa and finally to the Great Salt Lake —a grand Old Testament-style exodus to find what God is now bringing us to."

Hickman took a sip of water and looked out into the adjacent rooms. "God knows we weren't meant to stay there. We were sent out two by two, and in bands of twelve to spread the good news that God is in this land. Let me tell you a secret." He began to whisper. "While he isn't one of us yet, he'll be one of us someday, because God has raised him up!" He picked up the volume and pace as people applauded. "God has raised him up!" The applause grew louder and louder as Hickman spoke. "Like old King Cyrus, God has raised him up, a Gentile too, to end our captivity and bring us to a new land!" Folks began to hoot and holler, and stand in their excitement. Hickman motioned them to be seated.

"But listen, my friends, Horace Brown doesn't need to take us to a different place, no. Like Cyrus of Persia, he'll simply end our Babylonian captivity and allow us to return home. You ask me, where is home? I'll tell you. It's right here, on your neighbor's ranch. It's right there, on your neighbor's farm. It's that house that used to belong to your ancestors — that corral that used to belong to the first settlers in this state. It's that patch of land that God first called our people to — wrestled from the Indians at great cost, nurtured by the strong backs of our people and watered by the sacred sweat of their brows. It's time to take it back!" he said. "It's time to take it *all* back!" he shouted. "It's time to take every piece of it back!" he screamed, so loud that some held their hands to their ears as others raised them to the heavens and shouted the sacred name, "Hallelujah!"

"Brother Brown," Hickman continued, "and I call you that because God is calling you that, my friend. Tell us what we need to know. And then lead us in prayer."

Horace Brown stood up. A tiny man with a steely glint in his eyes, Brown was dressed entirely in his new favorite color, black — shirt, pants, tie, broad-brimmed hat. If it wasn't for the six-gun on his hip, he would have looked like one of the brothers. His face, with its blackened eye, said he was a killer.

"We're about to have us a Blood Atonement, my friends," Brown said. "I'll leave the teaching about Blood Atonements to Elder Hickman, but you all know what I mean. Now, I'm not much for praying, but I'm not against saying a few words over the men and women who will prevail in this place. There's a good thing coming for all of you, to be sure. And there's some dying that will go on as well to get us to where we are going. We'll all do our part. You may not be one for a gun. That's okay. There are others nearby who have demonstrated their gifts and abilities in that way. But, God has called you … I guess. Elder Hickman has called you, to be sure. And when the battle begins, you must take your place. Do I have an 'Amen?'"

The construct was awkward and more Methodist that anything, and the Saints seemed confused. But Brown had heard the words before and thought them appropriate. "Can I have an 'Amen?'" he asked again. And with that, each and every man and woman present signaled their heart-felt agreement.

Brown paused to look out into the farthest spaces of the house — two bedrooms, a living room and dining area, the kitchen, too. It was a big house. He took a crumpled ball of paper out of his pocket and began to read slowly, awkwardly like a new reader or a child just asked to read before his parents. "I will go before you," he said quietly, "leveling their heights. I will shatter the … bronze gateways," he read, "and smash the iron bars. I will give you the… hidden treasures," he continued, "the secret hoards that you may know that I am the Lord." Horace put the paper back in his pocket and smiled, before reciting the words, "Isaiah 45:1-3."

"Thank you, son. You make me proud." Horace Brown smiled and returned to his seat. "Before we pray son, I want to say something to you in front of all these people." Horace nodded. "You are our Messiah, Mister Brown — our Cyrus. Do you know the ancient meaning of that name?"

"I do not."

"It means 'hero,' son."

There would be a new tomorrow for the Saints in the Carson Valley and beyond. God would deliver them, to be sure. And those God would deliver, he would make rich.

Chapter 24
JACK'S BAR

"Son of a bitch," Dustsucker blurted out. "If your mom knew ..."

"Deputy Slade, let's not get all upset. There's no reason to drag my mom into this."

Gillom Rogers knew his mother would be troubled by his having a beer in public. She didn't seem to mind his sneaking one behind the stables, and maybe she didn't know. But if she knew he was downing one in a saloon on Carson Street? Well, there'd be hell to pay. Then there was the matter of the groceries for the Ormsby House that were still in his wagon. She'd not stomach his idleness, either. "I was just getting a drink with my friend here before I pushed on to the hotel. I haven't been here but a moment or two."

Slade looked at the boy with a well-tuned eye. "Gillom," he said, "my pappy used to say, 'A man is never more truthful than when he acknowledges himself a liar.'"

"I believe Mark Twain said that, Mister Slade."

"Samuel Clemens, son."

"Whatever, Mister Ronin."

"Gentlemen, why don't you join us? Gillom here meant no harm."

"And you are?" Ronin asked.

The former director of the American Gospel Mission, just south of Carson City, didn't know what to say. Not one to normally sit silently, he did just that, with a sort of "I shouldn't have said that" look all over his face. The sheriff saw it, Slade did too, being lawmen and all. Ronin wasn't far behind in noticing that

Henry Nauman had turned into a mouth-breather, a sure give away that what he was about to say or do wasn't in anyone's best interest other than his own. "I'm ..." he paused, looking at the tin star on Shubael Swift's chest. "I'm ..." he said, thinking it was best to perhaps make up a name. "I'm ..."

He was scrolling through a list of possibilities when the boy with the wagon raised a half-full glass of beer and said, "Why friends, I'm surprised you don't recognize him! This is Henry Nauman. He used to live in these parts. In fact, he was the founder of that Carson Valley Indian mission ..."

"Eagle Valley, actually," Henry said without thinking.

"Of course," Gillom Rogers said, smiling. And that was when W. W. Ronin went for his gun.

Ronin dumped his 4-inch Colt out the backside of his holster about the same time his deputy friend shouted, "No!" grabbing at Ronin's gun hand with his right hand while reaching for his own gun with his left in a sort of Hickock-style draw, twisting the 7½-inch hogs leg from his cross draw holster and leveling it. He hesitated and then heard himself shout, "We need to take him alive!"

Sheriff Swift had no idea what was happening of course, other than the two men who had invited him to lunch were now involved in a donnybrook of sorts, a dispute with someone he didn't know, but a man clearly intent on getting out of the place as he was lurching for the back door when Jack's green glass bottle went cascading by the man's head. A brown glass bottle followed, and then a half-a-dozen bottles of beer, whiskey and gin after that, sending the former lay missioner from a small Ohio Valley Presbyterian Church scurrying across the floor and out into the alley beyond.

Ronin pulled his gun hand free, glaring at his friend who had his eyes fixed on the young man from the house on Mountain Street where Dustsucker lodged. "Slade!" he shouted.

"What?"

"What do you mean what? Come on," he yelled as he piled out the back door onto a small street that butted up against buildings on the next street. Nauman was gone. Walking back into the bar, he found his friend sitting at the table with Gillom Rogers and the sheriff. "Want to tell me what that was about, putting your hand on my gun?"

"I'm sorry, Ronin. I just didn't want him dead. Besides, there's no warrant out for him, not to my knowledge anyway."

"For who?" Swift asked.

"Henry Nauman, sheriff, the son of a bitch who organized the kidnapping of all those kids a couple of years ago."

"Allegedly," Dustsucker interjected.

"Whatever," Ronin said, glaring.

"Sure there is, though I don't recall the name. And if there isn't, there ought to be."

"Exactly," Ronin said, pulling out a chair and sitting down. He looked at Gillom. "Son, how about you tell us where Mister Nauman is staying in town."

"Mister Ronin, I'm so sorry. I had no idea he was a wanted man. I mean, he was kind of peculiar, but there's no law against that. And with all of the women he's had, I guess I got sort of distracted."

"Women?" Ronin asked.

"Well, sure," Jack said from behind the bar, causing everyone to turn around.

"Are you Jack?" Dustsucker asked.

"I am."

"Same guy that used to have a place over on Ormsby Street?"

"Sure as Christ. Welcome to my restaurant." The three of them looked around. Glass was scattered everywhere. A bottle full of brushes sat next to the front door, tins of paint beside it. The man had been a painter before he had become a bottle thrower.

"Heard you had a nice sandwich, Jack. Glad we happened along."

"Me, too, my friends. Sorry for all the glass and such. I remembered that pickled piece of shit from the old place. He used to pick up a gal named Ally who worked for me at the time. Pissed me off then and pisses me off now. So I guess I was sort of happy to see the two of you draw down on him. Shame you missed."

"Yeah," Ronin said, still glaring at his friend. "Now what are we going to do?"

Shubael stood up. "Do you know where he's staying, son?"

"Sheriff, I do not. And I surely would tell you if I knew. I'd do anything to make sure my mother isn't going to hear about all this misadventure."

"I can't promise you that, son." Swift turned to face his deputy. "Slade, I'm going to head back to the office to see what I can dig up on this Nauman character. You and Ronin can brief me on Hickman after you finish here. Hopefully I'll have something for us by the time you're done."

"You bet, sir. Mind if we stay a while to talk to young Gillom here?"

"I do not. And when you're finished, bring me back a turkey sandwich, with some coleslaw. You have turkey, Jack?"

"Sheriff, we have plenty of turkeys here on Carson Street. I'll be happy to carve you up one for lunch."

Chapter 25

IAN SLAVIN

Ian Slavin hadn't counted on heading to Carson City in December. He had hoped to find work at the Depot Hotel in Elko, given his unexpected contribution to the peace and harmony of folks in Wells after the capture of the Livestock woman and the little miscreant, Tony Latigo. Once the criminals were on the train with Deputy Dustsucker and Ronin, he figured the Depot Hotel's owner would see his potential value and pony up a position that fit his talent and needs. But James Clark, the elderly owner of the hotel, thought differently.

"Eighty rooms upstairs, give or take, a billiard hall, a barbershop — don't you have something for me?" he asked.

"I didn't think it was a good idea when Ronin mentioned you to me the first time, son. Then with all that gun play ..."

"I think I more than made up for that, don't you?"

"Son, a tiger doesn't change his stripes. A leopard doesn't lose its spots. I don't cotton a man that drinks and I won't have anyone standing on my steps waving a gun. I'm sorry," the old man said. All trussed up with a starched collar, frock coat and tie, Elko pioneer James Clark looked like a Protestant clergyman, which was part of the problem, he figured, given that Slavin was a Mormon, not that anything had ever been said. Still, it wouldn't surprise him.

"Sir, you own the best hotel in town. Hell, the railroad and stage lines stop at your front door. You sure you can't help me?"

Slavin had started his professional life wanting to be a lawyer, much to his father's disappointment. But when his money ran out, discontinuing his professional studies at Hastings College — the first law school on the West Coast, he was proud of saying, though saying so didn't seem to get him any jobs or earn him any money — he turned to gold. He hadn't done well at that, either. After his experience helping the deputy from Ormsby County and Ronin, he thought something might come of it. He was hoping so, anyway.

"Mister Clark, the Reverend Ronin said he'd talk to you."

"And he did, son, not that Mister Ronin would ever want to hear you referring to him as a reverend. And I listened, I really did — like I'm hoping you're listening to me. Ian, you don't belong in Elko, not that it's any of my business, you understand. You ought to go back to school, back to California. That's where you belong."

Slavin hung his head, having hoped against hope that Clark would give him a second chance. And he would have stayed there — head down, kicking at the dirt and feeling the pain of a man who had nowhere to go and no way to get there, when Jimmy Clark dropped a hundred dollars into his hand. "That's my thanks, son. That's also my way of saying your home isn't in Elko. It's elsewhere. And son?"

"Yes?"

"I believe in you." It was enough to bring a tear to his eye.

He missed the first couple of trains after that, deciding to see a few people before he left, Mattie, for instance, and the two men from Lamoille — Maverick and Pixley. He caught a train the following day to Virginia City, where he inquired from the U.S. marshal the whereabouts of his new friends. Augustus Ash told him Carson City, after pouring him a beer and celebrating the capture of the two criminals wanted under his Ash's warrant. "You're a good man," Ash said before Slavin asked if he could put that in writing in the event he went back to law school. Maybe that was where his life was headed, he said before shaking hands with one of Virginia City's leading businessmen, the owner of the Bucket of Blood Saloon. The man gave him a sandwich and a pickle, of all things, before pointing the way to the Virginia &

Truckee platform on D Street so he could catch a train back to the capital city.

Virginia City, Gold Hill, Silver City, Dayton — the little towns along the way seemed like the dark side of the moon to him, or at least what he imagined the moon to be. Dirt, craters where dirt used to be and more dirt piled high and ready for the fool who thought good metal might be found in those hills. He was so done with the years he had lost in the Rubies and elsewhere. Slavin had a badge to return and wanted to make sure he thanked the man who loaned it to him, fulfilling an easy dream that he might become a lawman, or a Pinkerton he had said before Ronin read him his rights before God and everyone else who would listen. "You don't need to work for a man, son. Not a corporate man. And you don't need to be beholding to a man for the rest of your life, wishing you had chosen to do something different. Don't join anything, before you figure out what it is you want to become." Ronin's advice rambled, to be sure. But it was heartfelt, and that mattered. It reminded him of his father's last words. "Be happy."

He had a badge to return all right, Dustsucker's badge, though the deputy didn't like him calling him that. But hell, they'd done their very best not to die in Wells that night, with all the bullets flying and Sheriff Tom Kelly sitting there in the midst of it tied to a chair of all things. And they'd done it together, so he figured the intimacy wasn't too much to impose. And when he caught up to his friend, he'd probably stay a few days to see the capital before heading back over the mountain to talk to the school's founder, Serranus Clinton Hastings, who had built apartments for the poor and had been the school's personal benefactor before admitting he couldn't do more for him without Slavin doing something for himself. He was ready to do that, by God. He was ready to head back to church, too.

So when he did get to town, he went right to the sheriff's office at Carson and Musser Streets. And Dustsucker asked him if he didn't mind attending a church meeting before heading out of town. "I guess not," he said in sort of a confused sort of way, thinking it was odd for a Gentile to encourage a Latter Day Saint to go to a meeting. But when he explained that a man named Hickman was moderating a loose congregation of Mormon ranchers and other converts, who are thinking of dropping a bomb into Carson City's social order, well sure, he said. He figured he owed him that. It was about one o'clock in the afternoon when he located his friend in a little saloon on Carson Street, and went in to report what he saw.

Chapter 26

RANGE WAR

"Call it what you want," Jack was saying as Slavin came to the door, "Hernando's Hideaway, Angelo's, the Y-Not Saloon, it doesn't matter to me. This bar has had many names over the years. And just because it's got a new owner or location, doesn't mean I can't call it what it's been — a saloon since 1859."

"Whatever," Ronin said as the fresh-faced almost-an-attorney pushed the saloon's double doors open and lifted his hat.

"Gentlemen — and I use that term lightly."

"Funny."

"Ah, come on Mister Ronin, aren't you glad to see me?"

Ronin looked up. "I was hoping you were on a train to San Francisco to attend the university."

"I am. I am. I said I'd do a favor for Dustsucker here first, and I did. Now I need to report."

Ronin looked across the table. "You knew he was here?"

Dustsucker smiled. "I did, William. I figured I'd tell you at lunch when we caught up. I asked him to attend a prayer meeting at Hickman's the other night."

"His being Mormon and all ..."

"Exactly. So how did it go, young man?"

"It was real interesting, to tell you the truth, sir." Slavin pulled a stool away from the bar and pushed it up against the table.

"Sit on a regular chair, would you?" Ronin said. "I don't like looking up to a man unless I have to."

"Geesh, Mister Ronin. You get up on the wrong side of the bed?"

Dustsucker put his sandwich down — thinly sliced roast beef, Swiss cheese, a tomato and onions on a dark bun — and laughed. He wiped at some mayonnaise on his chest. "He doesn't know what side of the bed he's supposed to sleep on yet, Ian." The boy looked confused. "He's with Emma, son. Remember?"

"Oh," Slavin said. Gillom smiled.

"Stop your grinning, you guys. You don't know anything about it, and don't need to."

"Of course not." Everyone smiled.

Ronin began tapping the table with his trigger finger. "So what do you have for us?"

"Well, Mister Ronin, as I said, it was real interesting. Hickman is a decent preacher, if you ask me. Has a real rhythm to his speaking, keeps you interested and all that. Not like the church back home."

"No, I imagine not." W. W. Ronin had never heard a Mormon preacher, but he'd yet to meet a Mormon man who was transparent enough to tell his own truth in the pulpit rather than parroting someone else's. "So, how many people were there?" he said, looking over at his friend.

"Twenty or so, I guess. He filled pretty much every room. The front room had a dozen people in it, the kitchen maybe six or eight, and then both bedrooms had another half-dozen or so. So I guess more like 30 people were there."

"Men and women?"

"Yes."

"And?"

"Well, they were hootin' and hollerin', that's for sure. It was like a Baptist prayer meeting I saw one time in San Francisco, though not as cold of course, and not like anyone was in the water."

"Of course," Ronin winced. Simply put, some thoughts could go on too long. And young people ought to think twice before sharing some of theirs. "Your point is?"

"My point is that Hickman is a pretty charismatic leader. I mean, if he tells them to pick up guns, they're going to pick-up guns. If he says, 'shoot those people.' Well, they're going to do some shooting."

"Jesus, man, would you get down to it? What was the meeting about? What did he say?" He looked at his friend. None of this Mormon stuff was looking good.

"He said they had been wronged. He said it was time to make things right. And that some people might actually have to die. Wait, he didn't say that — his hired gun said that."

"Horace Brown?"

"That was his name."

"And he said?"

"He said that it was okay if folks attending the meeting didn't want to fight. He knew of others who did and that it wouldn't be a problem."

"What wouldn't be a problem, Ian?"

"Their joining them. It's time for 'a reckoning,' he said. And 'it needs to be soon.'"

"Anything else?" Dustsucker asked.

"Well, maybe this, Dusty ..."

"Really? He's calling you Dusty now?"

"... if this man isn't lying, and there's others who might join these 30 or so people in Genoa, you're going to have one hell of a range war, you know?"

Ronin looked over at Gillom and then down to the floor. There would be some good people who would be needing some protecting if all this was real. And if Hickman was anything like the Mormon militiamen that had fought years ago, there would be a profound amount of suffering on everyone's part. Not just those wanting to right a wrong would be hurt — He held nothing against the wrong-minded, it was so easy to believe a lie — there would be many others hurt who were simply wondering what the hell was going on.

"Another march through Georgia," he mumbled to himself.

"What?"

"I'll explain later, Dusty. Son, you hanging around these parts for a while?"

Slavin grinned. "If you want me to."

Ronin grimaced. "I not only want you to, I need you to. Because one of the first places those people are going to hit is the mission."

Chapter 27

THE AMERICAN GOSPEL MISSION

Ronin had Jackson back in the corral just before sundown. Emma met him at the gate.

"How did the visit go?"

"Not too bad," he said, watching her dry her hands on her apron and dress before reaching out to him. She pulled his arms toward her and embraced him. "You smell good," he said.

"I'm making cookies. Chocolate cookies."

"Chocolate chip?"

"Is there any other?" she teased, as she pirouetted and began to walk toward the house. She looked over her right shoulder. "You coming?"

"Soon as I put my stuff away."

"Let one of the men do that." She gestured toward a couple of hands who were walking toward the corral from the barn. "You come and sit down, and tell me about your day. I'm curious about your talk with Hickman."

He pulled his rifle from its scabbard and handed Jackson's reins to one of the men as the other began to loosen the cinch on his saddle. "Mister Ronin, you look tired," one of the men said, as he put the cinch up over the saddle's seat.

"I am. Some days I don't know why I bother."

"Why is that, sir?"

"Because no matter how hard I try, there always seems to be a jackass loose to shake things up." The men laughed.

"You will be staying the night?"

The question caught him as odd, given that he'd been staying at the American Gospel Mission since he'd gotten back from Elko. He'd kept the room at the Ormsby House just in case. But all things being equal, he preferred the quiet of the school after dark and the company of the woman he loved.

"I will be, Pedro, until I hear otherwise," he said, smiling.

"We are all in the same boat, señor."

"Indeed." The one constant, he thought, was that a man's life was in large part determined by the woman he was with.

When the once-reverend W. W. Ronin said "yes" to serving as the pastor of a mission church in Wichita, Kansas, he didn't realize his words had begun a marriage of sorts. His spouse — the bride of Christ in those parts, a congregation of less than 30 souls — had been an awkward and demanding wife.

It wasn't the sacraments and sermons that sometimes led to dark nights, sitting alone in the room the church had provided "for our beloved pastor." He loved the opportunity to talk with people, formally, informally, it didn't matter. If he had to break some bread and pour some wine as a way of getting to that, he was more than willing. Fact is, charity and mercy came easy for him. He'd seen the elephant and understood that much of life — despite the organizing doctrines and dogmas of the church that were meant to make life more meaningful — was painful at best. But caring for people who weren't willing to care for themselves? It made him crazy to see so little come from his efforts to grow mature men and women from the seeds God had supposedly planted within each of them. Some nights he'd lie there in bed and all he could think of was being somewhere else.

One morning in particular was forever stuck in his memory. He'd gone into Wichita to see a member of the church's vestry. Church business, he figured, "in and out," maybe a quick "how's the ankle feeling?" or "what's going on with your mother?" He'd be back in his room before noon to start on his Easter homily. Three and a half hours later, after an ear-bending recitation of the faults of each of his parishioners, he had decided to leave the pastoral ministry for a run with the Pinkertons. *A man's life is determined, in large part, by the woman he is with,* he mused as he picked up his pace toward the front door of the house. Which is to say, home comes to no man who isn't careful where he's spending his time. He rested his hand upon the door latch.

"And the Lord said unto Abram, 'Get thee out of thy country, and from thy kindred, and from thy father's house, unto a land that I will show thee. And I will make of thee a great nation, and I will bless thee." The passage from the twelfth chapter of *Genesis* practically pushed him out the door, when he decided to leave the ministry. It was only a couple of days later that he left his Father's house — the St. John's Episcopal Church in Wichita, or "East Jesus" as he had come to call it — after a grueling game of croquet with the Ladies Relief Association and headed west. In the eight years he'd traveled, he never looked back.

"Emma?" he called. "You in the kitchen?"

He peeked around the wall where the sofa sat, and not seeing her, headed into the bedroom instead. "Emma?" And there she was, sitting on the edge of the bed, her blue prayer shawl gathered up around her shoulders. "What's going on?"

"I've been thinking of Henry all day," she replied before looking up. "I can't shake the feeling. It's as if he's not dead, but alive. And more so, it's like he's back, padding his way up toward the corral and house and coming into the front room. Am I crazy?"

How can I tell her? And yet, someone needs to.

"Emma, I want to talk about today, to be sure. I had no intention of being gone so long. I'm so sorry. But I have something more important to say, and it *is* about Henry."

"Oh, no ..."

"He's alive, Emma. A couple of hours ago, I saw him in a city saloon." And with that, Emma Nauman — the self-established paragon of virtue and everything that is right in the world, a woman who needed her life appropriately structured and aptly ordered by whatever doctrine or dogma her faith declared true and necessary — promptly fainted. When Ronin was able to wake her, she was shaking.

Chapter 28
BACK TO THE ORMSBY HOUSE

"You can't be here," she said. It was the first thing she said, despite his cradling her in bed and waiting for her to stir. "You can't," she repeated, pulling at his arms and pushing him away. "Not if Henry is alive. It's not right ..." The words kept pouring out of Emma, despite their not making any sense.

Of course he could be there. Her husband had abandoned her. Emotionally, financially, physically he had left her, many years before the son of a bitch actually left the house. The Bible's exhortations to living a holy and righteous life be damned. There wasn't a person anywhere who wouldn't understand his remaining there. Maybe not in the same bed — neither of them talked openly about that, and they were being chaste for God's sake, for the most part, anyway. The man was a wanted criminal. And if it turned out that he was not, he wanted him nonetheless. Someone needed to pay for the mission's sins, for whatever part people played in the emotional conspiracy that had resulted in children being taken from the site a year and a half ago.

"Emma, please calm down. You'll be okay. It will all be okay." He patted her head and smoothed her hair. "Your husband, if I can call him that, will soon be arrested. Shubael wants to question him, and I've got my own intentions."

"William, you can't go around hurting people! Not anymore — we agreed. And you certainly ought not to be picking on my ex-husband, or husband, whatever."

"You're going to call him that, after everything he's done? All the women, all the excuses and pretensions to be a minister in the Presbyterian Church ..."

"Lay minister, William."

"Whatever. All the misbehavior and God knows what else that led up to the Clancys and the Crestwells using and abusing those kids? You're comfortable with that?" He sat up. She crossed her arms and turned away. *This is why I never got married.* "So you're just going to invite this piece of shit back into your life and let me go, is that it?"

He waited, and not hearing a response, slide his legs over the edge of the bed and onto the floor. He walked out into the front room.

"William, I don't know what to do," she said from the bedroom.

"No, that's clear," he said, sitting down in the chair by the stove. "You do *not* know what to do." A starry December night peered in the front room's windows, a silent witness to their argument.

Fact is, W. W. Ronin was the product of parents who couldn't live together. His mother in Pennsylvania, his father in Tennessee — Ronin split his time between the two of them depending on when and why. He'd never accepted his mother's explanation for the separation between them. Clearly, they didn't get along. And as much as they tried to hide it — "Your father needs you down on the farm," "You could go to a school back in Pennsylvania, there's one close by," "Someday we'll find someone to buy the house and then we can all be together again" — he knew there was tension between the two of them. Over the years, things said and unsaid had produced a grown man who didn't know how to think of women without giving up all sense of control. He was not going to be that man again.

"Emma," he said. "I'm going to head back to the Ormsby House."

Silence.

"I'll be out of here tomorrow morning, dear."

More silence, and then ...

"Maybe you should leave tonight."

"Tonight it is, then."

The once reverend W. W. Ronin got up and gathered his things from the bedroom as Emma pretended to sleep. He pulled his bedroll from the couch, his books and journal from a nearby table and met the stable men at the front door. "I'll send someone by in the morning for everything. I'm out of here."

Ronin wouldn't stay where he wasn't wanted. That had always been his rule. Living with a woman was hard enough. And what didn't come naturally needed more muscle than he was presently able to muster, given the Hickman case and the bizarre return of his intended's husband. *One thing at a time,* he murmured. Emma would have to wait. He pushed his brass-bodied Yellow Boy rifle back into its scabbard and attached the scabbard to his horse. Pedro handed him the reins. "You and Jackson are leaving sooner than you thought, señor."

"There are three things that are too wonderful for me, four which I do not understand ..." The words came from the 30th chapter of the *Book of Proverbs.* It had been a long time since he had he quoted them..

Pedro smiled. "...the way of an eagle, the way of a serpent upon a rock, the way of a ship in the midst of a storm and the way of a man and his woman."

Ronin laughed. "You are a religious man, Pedro?"

"Sometimes."

"Does it help?"

"Occasionally."

"Does it help you understand your wife?"

"No, señor."

He pointed Jackson toward the gate and nodded. "I'll be back..." Jose and Pedro were holding onto the corral fence. They nodded. "... or maybe not."

"This may not be your home, señor," Jose called out, "but you are always welcome here." W. W. Ronin smiled, pulled his hat low to cover his face and kicked Jackson's flanks. He headed home to the Ormsby House.

Chapter 29

BREAKFAST

"So that's it?" Dustsucker asked.

"As far as I can see," Ronin answered. "Who knows what will happen after Shubael arrests the man."

"I'm talking about you and Emma."

"I know." Ronin was covering, but it was none of Dustsucker's business. Sheriff Swift had his attention on something else, given the way he was staring at the Ormsby House door.

"Excuse me boys, would you?"

Ronin looked over his shoulder and found a couple of volunteer firemen looking back. He whispered to his friend. "Is he able to handle this, I mean with everything he's got going on? I've never seen someone so busy with other things."

"Seems so," Dustsucker said. "Those boys are from the Warren Engine Company just up the street."

"I thought I recognized them. Listen, what I'm saying is with everything else, maybe you ought to take a little more responsibility in this Nauman thing. He wasn't even sheriff when it happened, you know."

"No, he was not. But he's a popular man and he's used to juggling a lot of balls. And my head will be one of them if I do anything to undercut his responsibility or authority. Shush now, he's coming back. You and I ought not to be talking like this."

"I'm just saying …".

"Yeah, I know."

"You boys hear any of that?"

"Sorry, sheriff. We were talking about other things. We didn't hear a word."

"Well, Mister Ronin, those were some of the boys from the Warren Engine house on Musser, and they say they've seen our man ..."

"Nauman?"

"Exactly. Seems like he's got no sense that he might be wanted in these parts."

"And he is, right?"

"Yes, deputy. Sheriff Hill swore out a warrant before he left and it was sitting in a tall stack of papers on my desk right next to this, Mister Ronin. Interesting, huh?" The sheriff handed him a wanted poster with a likeness of Anthony Latigo, the Elko midget.

"Your point?" Ronin growled.

"No point, except to say that he's on his way to the state prison today. If you look out the window in the next few moments you might actually see him."

Ronin glanced toward Carson Street and then back to Sheriff Swift. "And the woman?"

"Alvira Fae Livestock was a twin."

"I'm well acquainted with that fact."

"Well, she survived her sister who was killed during a gunfight on C Street, in the main commercial district in Virginia City."

"Yes, I know."

"Well, Latigo was the shooter. The sister's death was accidental. The bullet was apparently meant for someone else."

"It was meant for me."

"Oh." Swift looked surprised. "Well, she's being tried separately. And I guess we'll see what happens. The woman isn't normal, Ronin, if you know what I mean, not that I'm an expert on such things." He picked up a piece of buttered toast from Dustsucker's plate. His deputy barely hid his annoyance.

"No, she's not," Ronin replied. "Incidentally, the sister, Ellie Mae, was a good woman."

"More or less," Dustsucker said, pulling his plate closer to his vest, reaching for the remaining triangles of toast. He dipped the two of them it into the last of four fried eggs.

"More or less?"

"I don't mean anything by it, William, just that she was involved in all that hocus pocus stuff. You know, crystal balls, card reading, talking to the dead and so on."

"Yeah, but then you're a Roman Catholic. I don't see the difference. You pray to the Saints, don't you?"

Slade dropped his toast and put his hands beside his plate. "I don't pray much at all, Ronin. You know that. My parents were Roman Catholic. I don't know what I am."

"I'm just saying."

"You're doing a lot of saying, if you ask me."

"Did I interrupt something between the two of you?" the sheriff asked.

"No," Ronin groaned. "I'm just a little put out."

"You can say that again," the deputy said, lifting the lid off of some strawberry jam. The jar said "Sacramento." It was the only word visible on the label as sugary brown preserves had stained most everywhere else. Dustsucker took his spoon and began to stir the jam, smiling.

"Dusty, that's not your coffee."

"Gosh guys, I'm sorry. I must be distracted too. I'm thinking of other stuff."

"A woman most likely," Ronin replied, wondering if his friend was thinking of Emma, the bed between them not even cold yet.

"Gentlemen, I thought we were going to get some work done. Can we let whatever it is between the two of you rest? I want to talk to you about what I heard about this Nauman character and share with you some thoughts Mister Slavin and I had last night about Hickman and his friends."

"You met with Slavin after we went to bed?"

"Mister Ronin, I'm the Ormsby County sheriff. You can figure that I do a great many things you don't know about. And some of them are probably not any of your business. Are you ready to talk about what is?"

The former reverend nodded. The tone wasn't welcome, but the lawman was right. He was the unfocused one. And if Hickman was going to be stopped and Nauman was going to be brought to justice, he needed to think of only one thing.

"Excuse me, sheriff, for just a moment?" The sheriff nodded. "Dusty, do you have an extra box of shells for your Winchester?"

"I do. Why?"

"I believe I'm going to need them."

Chapter 30
SOUTH ON STEWART

Henry Nauman crossed Telegraph Street running. Hitting the railroad tracks, he gave fleeting thought to standing on the train platform and waiting for a train to head east. Where didn't matter, as long as Sheriff Swift, his overweight deputy and their angry-looking ex-clergy friend didn't catch up to him.

Frankly, he was surprised that anyone recognized him.

He'd never really hung out in town, except to visit Jack's Bar on Ormsby, or was it Curry Street? So much had changed in the year and a half he was gone. Nor had he bothered to meet any of Carson City's ministers or managers, despite the promises he had made to his wife to take care of the fundraising in return for her handling the mission staff and children. It was better that way, he figured. And the thought that he'd start a business in the capital city? Well, it appeared to him that there were plenty of businesses already — book stores, clothing stores, barbers and bankers. Folks seemed to have the local economy all sewed up. He decided early on to move, there being so few opportunities. It had just taken him a few years to work things out.

Truth be told, he'd intended nothing ill to happen to the children under his wife's care. Hell, most days he shuffled their name cards with a silent prayer that something good would come their way. The kids weren't exactly dirt-eaters. He'd run across a few such Indians in his travels since then — "clay-eaters," "sand-lappers," persons who ate dirt as a regular part of their diet or discipline. But their habits as Indian children seemed just as destructive. In California once, an Indian man had handed him something called "acorn bread." He had it halfway into his mouth when the man explained it was made with acorns, potatoes and clay, of all things. The dirt helped keep the local delicacy down. No, the kids were better than that.

Fact is, he felt like he was doing them a favor. Getting the kids out of his wife's backward-thinking mission and into the world was a good thing. He'd seen the damage done to the traditional Paiute and Washoe territories by the influx of white Americans pursuing a new place to live, worse still the gold and silver in the new places they were living. Since the first white man had seen the Silver State, Indian ownership of space and resources had been compromised. Not that they thought they owned it, but still. The white men did. Those Indians that resisted the western expansion died. So too, those that ignored it. Emma had one thing right — accommodation to the white man's way of life was the only workable strategy. Not that it was fair. And not that it was lovely.

Nauman had run right past the V & T railroad station and headed south on Steward Street when it occurred to him what he might do next. If he was in fact recognizable, and if there was a warrant for his arrest or a possibility of being questioned by the county's legal authorities, his time in Carson City was limited. There'd be no opportunity to find his buxom friends, Ally and others who he'd become acquainted with to pass his afternoons and evenings. "Business, honey," he used to say, when it was really "monkey business" he was after. There'd be no time to wet his wick either — Gillom's recommendations of people to see and places to visit would go to waste. There was only one woman he needed to see, to tell him what was going on and to clear his name if that was needed. That was Emma, his beloved wife. And given that it was breakfast time, he knew where she could be found. She'd be in the kitchen.

It's an odd thing, to consider a place home when in fact you no longer live there. But that's exactly what Henry Nauman felt toward the mission residence just south of the city. Not that he'd ever raised kids there, his kids anyway. And not that the time he'd spent there with his wife had been all that warm or wonderful.

He used to think the problem of their marriage was in fact his. He couldn't feel his emotions like other people. He hadn't been true to his wife, like he was supposed to be. He wasn't able to put his trust in people, like he imagined most people could, never having asked anyone about it but being raised with two parents who seemed to prefer each other to the company of others.

He used to imagine that if everything had been equal — he'd gone on to satisfy his entrepreneurial urges instead of pursing the lay ministry of the church, they'd stayed in West Virginia in the close shadow of Steubenville, Ohio and Pittsburgh, Pennsylvania beyond that — they might have made a decent go of it, she the homebody that she was, he the rancher (not a farmer) ranging far and wide for the family's health and happiness. Now, he didn't know.

It was poor form to think that Emma was responsible for his being such a dolt, the inexcusable moral dullard that he sometimes imagined himself to be. Still, if he'd had some help being a better man, a happier man, a more home-driven man, a truly God-honoring man, he might have been a better man. And that would have been good.

He reached the Carson-Tahoe Lumber and Fluming yards when he realized that Emma might not be as pleased to see him as he would be seeing her. Hundreds of millions of feet of timber had been hauled out of the Sierra Range east of the city via the Glenbrook railway and a 12-mile wooden V-flume that ended just in front of him, a little south of the Carson City Box Factory. The yard was a morgue for Lake Tahoe's tall stands of pine, hemlock, fir and other trees. And if the yard was a morgue — as some folks were fond of saying — Virginia City's mines were the grave yard. A million or more board feet of timber lay in front of him, more than a mile and a half wide.

He stepped carefully, given the abundance of tracks and timber piles, and thought about walking around the mess rather than through it when someone called out, making it clear he wasn't welcome stumbling through someone else's business. "I know Mister Bliss and Mister Yerington," he thought of saying, though he really didn't know them and the noise of the steam engines and other machinery would have drowned out his response anyway. He tipped his hat and waved his hands instead before turning north to follow the main road. What if Emma didn't want to see him?

Shortcuts could be treacherous in life, he reminded himself without thinking that the very desires he had focused on in his life — making easy money, having inordinately good times, creating pleasurable alliances and other self-serving relationships — were shortcuts as well. He had side-stepped the traditional paths that brought a man peace — fidelity to one's wife, a family to delight in and appreciate — and before he knew what had happened, he'd bypassed the very roads that would have deepened his sense of self and home, and ended up elsewhere.

He stopped at the lip of the lumberyard, if there was such a thing — there seemed to be no end to the roads or canyons that led to the place where he was standing. The mission was still a mile or so down the valley and it was getting warm. Maybe he wasn't welcome there anymore, he thought, having first imagined a warm greeting from the boys in the barn and an embrace from the warm-hearted woman he'd left behind when he climbed over the hill via a stagecoach to Placerville and God's good future, not that it had been all that bright. But it had been his to follow at least. There was nothing wrong with that.

He leaned on one leg and then on the other, his hand up against a lonesome pine tree, before finding a place under a couple of bushes and sitting down to consider what he'd do next. Hearing a man coming toward him, humming, Henry decided to wait a spell before making a decision.

Chapter 31

WHERE THE HEART IS

"So let me understand what you're saying, sheriff. Ian Slavin walked into your office and sat down and told you that Happy Hands had seen a man resembling Henry Nauman, sitting on a rock south of the city last night? Is that what you're saying?"

"Not exactly. What I said was 'a man identifying himself as Henry Nauman' had a nice long chat with your friend Happy Hands."

"And how is Slavin involved in this?" Ronin asked.

"Well, I assume he knows your friend, I guess."

"No, not to my knowledge," Ronin said. Swift looked over at his deputy, who was shoveling the last piece of egg — "Sunny side up please, runny as you can make them" — into his mouth, having begged an additional piece of sour dough toast from Vic Goodwin, the hotel manager. He shook his head as well.

"Well, I don't know then. I just know that when Slavin came to my office around midnight, he had talked to the Indian and they had decided the man was up to no good."

Ronin stood up and grabbed his rifle and began walking toward the front door.

"You don't want to know the rest of the story?" Swift shouted.

"Don't need to, sheriff. I know exactly where Nauman went and I'm surprised none of us thought about his going there. I'm headed to the mission."

"Geez ..." Dustsucker wheezed, throwing his napkin down on his plate and standing up. "We should have thought of that."

"You coming, sheriff?" Ronin called from the doorway.

"I doubt that you'll need me."

"How's that?"

"Slavin said your man had only warm feelings for the woman at the mission. More so, he said your friend was heading there with him."

"Happy Hands?"

"Is there another?"

"There are very few, sheriff, I have to give you that."

W. W. Ronin pushed his hat back on his head. "Can we grab those shells, Dusty?"

"You bet. I'll head to the office. You get the horses. We'll head out there directly."

"No time for that," he said as he turned to run across the street. "Meet me there," he shouted over his shoulder. "If Nauman and Hands are still at the mission, I won't need them anyway."

Ronin skipped up onto the boards at Third and Carson Streets, out front Benton's Livery, and pushed his way past a couple of horses. "Boys, I'm going to need my horse," he shouted. Benton was alone in the back.

"Hold your horses, Ronin. I'm working as fast as I can. The boys are off." A likeable man, Benton had been a surgeon during the Civil War but had served with the other side. The two men — despite their different services and situations — occasionally held each other in mutual esteem. "Where you headed off to now?"

"South, Mister Benton, to the mission ... I'll get him."

"No, you won't. Wait right there — Jackson's on my dime." Benton moved quickly toward one of the stalls where regular boarders were kept. He pushed a small carriage out of the way. "They're good people down that way. I was talking to my pastor the other day, and we were thinking we ought to do something to help out. Say, Ronin?"

"Yeah?" he said, tapping on door frame while looking south on Carson Street.

"I happened to notice that woman's husband last night. What's her name? Emma? I brought a stage in from the lake, kind of late. So I happened to be out in the street waiting on it. Tourists, you know, wanting everybody to be safe. Anyway, I thought her mister was dead, or missing or something …"

"Yeah, me too."

"So you're headed out there to talk to him?"

Ronin looked up. "Why do you ask?"

"Well, there's always been something strange about the man. I used to see him catting around over on Ormsby Street, a woman on each arm. You know. And I used to wonder, what kind of an outfit is it that tolerates their people doing such things. You know what I mean?"

"Sure, Jim. But I really need that horse …"

"I know. I'm working on it." Benton rolled up the sleeves of his white shirt before pulling Ronin's saddle off of its stand and throwing the cinch underneath. "I'm just thinking …"

"Well …"

"I know, we're all pretty much the same, pastor says."

"Oh, I don't know …"

"What I mean is, we're all looking for the same thing, you know."

"What's that, Jim?"

"Listen, I just own a livery, a stage line, an icehouse. You don't have to be smart to do what I do. I'm just thinking, if this guy's home was the Carson Valley, why the hell was he wandering so far away?" He placed a bit in Jackson's mouth and tugged gently on the straps of the bridle before leading the horse around the carriage to where Ronin was standing. "What do you think?"

Not quite forty years of thinking about such things began to congeal in Ronin's heart and mind. "Home is where the heart is, Jim. That's all I know."

"Exactly, Ronin. It isn't a place, is it?"

"Nope, and it's isn't another person, either."

"That's for sure," the New York native said, smiling. "And it ain't a business, though I surely appreciate yours, my friend." Benton had been born just over the Pennsylvania border, in rural Steuben County, south of the Adirondack Mountains. He was as Yankee as a Yankee could be, short of being born in New England.

"I like to say home means Nevada, Jim. Right now, anyway."

"So it does. Be safe, my friend."

Ronin nodded, pulled the reins to his right, and started south on Carson Street.

Chapter 32

THE 1871 PRISON BREAK

Horace Brown didn't know when the information he held would be helpful, but he knew someday it would be. In 1871, the largest prison break in the West freed 29 dangerous men from the Nevada State Prison in Carson City. And Brown knew that some of them — robbers, thieves and murderers — were still hiding in the capital city. They might be willing to take up arms again if it meant being paid, at least he was hoping so.

Brown understood what it meant to be a wanted man.

He'd never been to the big house per say, though some of the county jails he'd stayed in were large enough to gain a reasonable reputation. But he figured prison couldn't be much different than the jails he'd seen. Sure, the food might be worse and it might be more difficult to have visitors. But captured was captured. If a man's liberty was taken away, it wasn't much different whether one was sitting in a county jail or prison, working on a Chink-driven rail crew — he'd known a few — or being bossed around by a mean-spirited wife. Not that he'd been married, of course. But there was the shapely helpmate of a certain Mormon railroad supervisor he had known.

Brigham Young, she said, thought he should have been included in the ceremonies when the two competing transcontinental railroad tracks met at Promontory Summit in Utah. When laborers were needed, the LDS Church provided them. And when the tracks were completed, Brigham Young and his Mormon minions were owed millions, just like their Mormon brothers and sisters in the Carson Valley years later. Being a Latter-day Saint wasn't easy. Being married to one didn't seem any easier.

Brown fingered his side arms to make sure they were secure and covered as he came to the lumberyards south of Carson City. He turned his horse north toward the city, and in the eastern shadow of Carson Range passed a wee little man sitting underneath a cottonwood tree. "Hey," he shouted.

"Hey back," the man said, though he didn't stop. The squirrely son of a bitch looked haggard and confused, and wasn't of interest to him given how he was already dealing with old man Hickman's moods. One day, he'd be breathing the fiery vengeance of God upon all Gentiles living in the nearby valleys and probably points north and south of there — he'd not yet said. The next day, he'd spend the whole day in bed, like the crazy, wheezing geezer he was quickly becoming. *If it wasn't for the money ...*

He'd been lucky to be sitting in a bar on Carson Street thinking about what he'd do next when he heard the barkeep whispering to a couple of patrons. The proprietor, it turned out, had been involved with planning the prison break. In something like seven days, they'd figured out how to cut into a plaster ceiling and bust their way into the personal quarters of the prison warden. The poor man's wife and daughter were visiting, talk about coincidences. The warden, Frank Denver, grabbed a gun to defend himself. If it hadn't been for a prison trustee and a chair, the barkeep said, Denver would have found himself dead. "He was a lucky man," the barkeep said before looking Brown's way. He immediately took to looking at his beer. The Carson Street bar had become a frequent watering hole for him over the last couple of months while staying in Genoa. The Mormons didn't like him drinking. It was far enough away that they didn't know, and he met the most interesting people there.

"You remember grabbing the guns and the ammo," the barkeep said to his friends over coffee one night. "You remember how shot up everyone was. It was a miracle of God, I'm telling you, that none of us died there," he said. "That's why I'm a Catholic today," he said. *Jack a Catholic? Who would have guessed?* Horace didn't care if the man was religious or not. He'd not grown up that way and never had a problem with people who were. It's just that he'd never met a true believer before. Sure, Hickman and a few others were making some obvious sacrifices to be a part of Hickman's looney bin. There were guns to buy. Horses and powder would be needed if they were going to rain terror on folks. But how funny was it that people didn't notice that Hickman wasn't planting anything for the spring? He was leaving the fields fallow, as if the church's Most Worshipful Master, Prophet or King — whatever he was — wasn't expecting to succeed, like he was planning on dying. *Horace Brown the Third is not going to die. Not here. Not now.*

The way he had come to understood it, the convicts in that 1871 prison break secured their arms and ammunition from the prison's own armory, and left through the prison's main gate. Every guard suffered some sort of wound. Several prisoners as well had been knifed or shot. The owner of a nearby hotel was caught up in the gunfire and killed. They were tough men, to be sure. Twenty-two of them had fled east. Two headed west toward the mountains. And five crossed the railroad tracks toward Empire City. In a little over a month, 18 of the original 29 convicts had been recaptured. A couple of years later, they found another one. But ten of the prisoners had never been heard of again, unless he was looking at a couple of them at Jack's Bar.

"Can I help you?" Jack had said a couple of weeks ago, catching him looking their way.

"Not today, friend," he said with a smile, thinking there might someday be a day. And sure enough, the other night when he was meeting with Hickman and the other Saints, it occurred to him. If the Mormons wouldn't rise up with guns, he maybe knew some people who would.

Horace got off his horse outside his favorite tavern on Carson Street and tied up to a hitching post. *Today might be that day*, he thought to himself as he patted his mount before pulling his Winchester from its scabbard. He looked up at a freshly painted sign — "Jack's Bar," it said, "a Saloon Since 1859." If Hickman needed gunmen, Horace Brown *the Third* knew where there might be some. At least, he knew a man who might know some, and that was probably enough.

Chapter 33
NOTCHES

"So what you're saying is that you want me to contact some of these men — and I'm not saying I know any of them — and ask if they want to get involved with some Mormons hoping to bring about the second coming of Christ. Is that about what you're asking?" The man behind the bar asked.

"Look, I was hoping to catch you before you locked up for the night, I'm just wanting you to think about it," Brown said while reaching past his glass to touch the barkeep's forearm.

"Don't grab at me, son. I don't know you."

"Of course you do, Jack. I've been coming in here for months now." He pulled his hand back to his beer and fingered a stale stack of crackers.

"Listen, I'm just saying I don't *know* you, friend. What makes you think we're buddies?"

Horace tugged at his coat — intentionally, unintentionally, Jack couldn't tell. A quick look showed a set of nickel-plated Colts in quick draw pouches, hanging on a belt that looked as if it had seen better days. There were scratches and tears along the front of the belt that looked as if they had been purposefully scribed into the leather. Their possible meaning didn't escape Jack's grasp. "Jack, Jack," he said. "These friends of yours, aren't they tired of running? Aren't *you* tired of hiding out in this hole..."

"Are you talking about my tavern, son?" Jack looked down the bar toward the door, where an empty green wine bottle sat. It wouldn't take much, the son of a bitch.

"No, of course not." Brown smiled. "And I'm not talking about any religious obligations — Jesus coming, anything like that. Nobody likes an angry Mormon. But I've got no trouble with Mormon money. I'm just saying, your friends might not have any trouble with Mormon money either."

"We're closed!" Jack shouted to a couple of ne'er-do-wells who had begun to push against the doors. "Stupid piss-ants. Can't they read? Look... what did you say your name was?"

"Horace Brown, Jack. Whore...ass...Brown." He sounded it out, so that the proprietor understood. It wasn't Henry, or Hades or Hackey. It wasn't Hardy or Hector. It was Horace — Horace Brown *the Third*, he said.

"You need to get a new name, friend. I mean, if those notches on your belt are what I think they are. Something that isn't so funny." The gunman winced. "But be that as it may, I'm not promising you anything. I'm going to talk to a couple of my friends, cowhands mostly. And if they know someone, I'll pass it on. Does that sound good?"

"And yourself, Jack? You tired of hiding out in this..."

Jack waited. He grabbed the empty wine bottle and put it behind the bar. It wouldn't take much. *A pop upside this yahoo's head and it's good night. A couple of pigs in Chinatown would take care of the rest. Even the baby Jesus would understand.*

"Listen, you've got a fine establishment here," the gunman continued, "and I've enjoyed every afternoon and evening I've spent in it. I'm just asking."

"Son, and I mean no disrespect. You strike me as a man who gets things done." Brown beamed. "If I know anyone who wants to throw in with you, I'll let you know next time I see you."

The front doors rattled again. "Come on Jack! You open or not?" the voices called. Jack picked-up the green bottle from the sink in front of him and tossed it at the door. The bottle shattered. Horace Brown — "Big Bad Brown" he sometimes imagined being called, though he wasn't all that large a man, and nicknames were more for pretenders — pulled his gun, just as a matter of reflex. But not having anyone to shoot, he put it back into its pouch. "Let me take care of this, Jack. And then maybe you'll trust me more."

Horace Brown *the Third* slid down off of the white pine barstool and skated across the sawdust-covered floor until he stood in front of the doors. Without warning, he pulled his right foot up to his chest and stomped on the lock. The doors flew opened, knocking two midnight whiskey-seeking cowpokes onto their December asses, their mouths open. Brown swaggered as the barkeep let loose a string of expletives beginning with the words, "You stupid son of a bitch..."

"You got more?" Brown yelled, looking down at the men sitting on top an unexpected late-night dusting of snow. He dug his thumbs into his belt, his hands unintentionally forming a triangle that pointed to his male anatomy. *God, I love this stuff,* he thought as he tapped the front of his pants with his hands. His index finger counted the number of notches on the right side of his silver buckle, a gift from a gal in Utah, not that she mattered anymore.

"We got nothing, sir. We just wanted a couple of drinks."

"You boys already look like you've had a couple of drinks," he said, thinking he sounded like a certain Utah railroad supervisor, who was now dead and gone not that he mattered because he'd never wanted to marry the woman. The stupid jack-a-lope never had a chance. He never should have drawn on him, even if he still had his pants down around his feet he was faster and surer than any Jesus-loving Mormon man could ever be. And what if he had accidently shot his wife, kneeling in front of him? It was no big deal. Brown grabbed the man closest to him, and pulled him up by his red flannel shirt. "Time to get moving, fool."

"We're out of here, sir. Thank ... thank you," he stuttered. Brown smiled and turned to face his friend.

And quiet Jack what's his name — nobody had ever asked him what his last name was, and he wouldn't have told them if they had — picked up a second green bottle from behind the bar and hefted it Brown's way. "You stupid moron!" he shouted. "You broke my fucking door."

"Wasn't much of a door if a simple kick broke it," Brown said, ducking. The bottle hit the flannel-shirted fool square in the forehead and knocked him out. Horace Brown saw it happen. And Jack did, too, before looking Brown right in the eyes and beginning to laugh.

"Maybe we ought to work together, Whore...ass...Brown" he said, putting his hand on a third bottle, a green one this time, just in case.

"Maybe we should," Brown said, raising his thumbs to his vest, and drumming his fingers on his chest in a sort of self-satisfied way. "I think, and it's just me saying this of course so what do I know, but I think we'd all have a dandy time."

Chapter 34

HENRY'S GONE

Ronin tied Jackson to the front porch post and rapped on the screen door. It was almost January, but Emma liked to "air out the house" a couple of times a day. It wasn't unusual to find the front door open, but then it was pretty late. "Emma?" he shouted.

"Ronin, is that you?" she called from the back room.

"Can I come in?" he asked. A couple of days prior, he would have simply walked in. But things had changed. He had spent the last few hours wondering how much and for how long.

She fell into his arms, shaking. "He was here, William. Henry was here."

"I know."

Happy Hands walked into the living room from the kitchen. "Good evening, my friend."

"Kind of late for you to be here, isn't it?"

"I was about to say the same thing, William. What took you so long?"

"I came as soon as I heard," he replied, stroking Emma's hair and back. "I'm sorry I wasn't here, Emma. The man's wanted. Did he hurt you?"

"I would not have allowed that, William."

"I'm surprised you allowed him to come at all, Hands. How is it you didn't grab the son of a bitch and haul his ass to the sheriff's office?"

"I was under no obligation, William — nor are you." The Washoe holy man looked at his friend as if there was a point to be made, not that either man knew what it was. The tension was palpable. "This is his home, you know."

"This *was* his home, Hands. The hoosegow is his home now, and people want to see him there."

Emma pushed at Ronin's stomach and chest until she stood free of his embrace. "I don't need to hear this from either one of you right now, if you don't mind. I'm upset enough." She walked over to the couch and sat down. She folded her head into her hands, crying. The two men looked at each other. Ronin gestured toward the door with his head, and then sat down in a cranberry-colored wingback chair across from her. The chair was new.

"There's a warrant out for his arrest, Emma. That's all I know. I didn't mean to stir things up between the two of us."

She looked up and saw Happy Hands with his fingers on the screen door. "You're leaving?"

"I am, my lady. You're safe, now. That's all that mattered to me. Ronin, if you need me, I'll be in town."

"Where?"

"I don't know, one place or another. I'll check with you at the hotel tomorrow morning. Will you be there?"

Ronin began to answer when he saw the look on Emma's face. "I'll stay the night here tonight. I'm sorry for jumping at you. I'm not liking any of this right now. Between Nauman being back and the Mormons wanting to start their own state or whatever, I'm not sure what to do. It's all feeling a little too close for comfort right now. Emma, do you mind if I stay?"

"I'd *prefer* you did."

"Then I'm here for the night. Let's say breakfast at Mullers, mid-morning, okay?"

"Mullers it is," Happy Hands replied. "We'll have a pastry."

The words sounded funny coming out of Happy Hands' mouth. In the six or so years he'd known or heard about the holy man, he'd come to expect surprises. One moment he was sure Happy Hands was a heathen. The next moment, he was acting like a Christian Saint. "Excellent, then. We'll be more comfortable there than the St. Charles or the Ormsby House." Both hotels catered to a higher class of people. And while they might have to fight a few loggers for a table, the food would be better. Dustsucker, who was enamored with Muller's wife's cooking, would be happier there too. If Dustsucker could have married a meal — and Mister Muller, the baker, wasn't already married to Missus Muller, the cook — he'd have bedded Muller's wife.

Happy Hands pulled the door closed. Ronin grabbed his Yellow Boy from behind the door and walked over to the rocking chair by the fire. Emma was already asleep on the couch. He looked at the winged back chairs set in front of the large window looking out toward the Sierra. Were they new or old? Perhaps they were something the Naumans had brought with them from their home in Ohio. And why there, where Emma liked to sometimes stand and pray? *I'm gone two days and things are already changing.*

He pulled the rifle onto his lap and swung the lever down, ejecting a cartridge. The 200-grain flat nose .44 rim fire would do what he needed up to about 100 yards. Anything over that, he'd have to depend on Slade's and Slavin's Winchesters. He bunched his sleeve up in his right hand and rubbed at the brass receiver until he could see himself next to the loading gate. The rifle had been with him a long time, replacing an earlier Henry he'd picked up from a Union soldier during the war. It took a different caliber of ammunition than those used in his side arms. There had been a few times when he'd gotten confused, attempting to finger a .45 caliber slug into the right side of the rifle, and vice versa, dropping a .44 rim fire into one of his Colts. He always caught the mistake before things had gone too far.

If he wasn't so attached to his handguns, he might have gone with a different caliber. A .44-40 for instance, in the 1873 model Winchester and in his pistols. But some things didn't need changing, he figured while looking at the chairs. Other things, of course, did. Besides, with the shiny brass receiver, the wood fore end and a long octagonal barrel, the rifle looked both new and old. *The way things ought to be. The damned thing would even shoot upside down.*

He pulled at the pouch of rifle cartridges on his side. A half-dozen Henry rim fires rattled within. *I wonder if the sheriff has talked to any of the troops in Dayton?*

"Is Happy Hands gone?" Emma asked, raising her head from the couch.

"He left a few moments ago."

"You want to come to bed?"

He thought for a moment. Being with Emma was, most days and most evenings, one of the most pleasant things in his life. But the baggage it seemed to come with was not. "Emma," he said.

"Yes, William."

"Let's leave things as they are right now. I have a few things on my mind and I want to be clear-headed when it comes to you."

Chapter 35
ENCOURAGEMENT

Hickman picked up the pile of playing cards and attempted to shuffle them. The action was an unfamiliar one, his not being a man given to gambling. But his captain had left them there on the table and the curiosity of what some men found so inviting, even habit forming, had finally gotten to him. He peeled the two halves of the deck back with his thumbs, anchoring the cards to the kitchen table with his third and fourth fingers, then let go. Multiple clumps of cards hit the table in an unsettling and unsatisfying thump, reminding him that the world's ways were not Christ's ways, and he did not belong to the world. He was "in it, but not of it," as the scriptures said. He belonged to Jesus.

He threw the playing cards into the kitchen sink and called into the front room. "Horace, you finished yet?"

Brown put down his pencil and cursed quietly. "Goddamn," he said, hoping he'd kept his voice down so that Hickman couldn't hear him. "Almost," he shouted, licking the point of the pencil and pressing it against the paper so as to write another name. "I've got three or four more people to put down before we compare notes. You done with your study yet?"

Hickman patted a leather bound *Book of Mormon* next to him and looked around for his Bible. He'd told Brown he was working on a suitable message for the new recruits Brown had promised, though he'd not seen any sign of them. "Order is next to godliness," he told him, though he wondered if the gunman he'd just named "Captain of the Lord's Host" had any real depth, having never led a band of men to do anything save a couple fellows here and there, he said, who had been helpful in his work.

What kind of work his new captain had done was unclear, but Hickman wasn't asking. "Beggars can't be choosers," he said. He thought the sentiment was well known, until he noticed Brown's blank look in return. Jesus, they had their work cut out for them.

Hickman pushed at the open edge of the *Book of Mormon's* cover until the volume fell open to *First Nephi*, chapter three.

"And it came to pass," the scripture said, *"that I, Nephi, said unto my father: I will go and do the things which the Lord hath commanded, for I know that the Lord giveth no commandments unto the children of men, save he shall prepare a way for them that they may accomplish the thing which he commandeth ..."*

Hickman had been sitting at the table for an hour, looking through a narrow window into a wooded Genoa garden and wondering what to tell the new recruits Brown had in mind. And while he wasn't a fan of just letting the holy pages fall where they would, sometimes good thoughts came from letting the Bible or the *Book of Mormon* open that way.

"I will go and do the things which the Lord has commanded," he whispered. "And God will prepare a way for me," he murmured, before folding a sheet of paper into the book and writing across the top of the paper, "Encouragement." If God would meet him there — leading a group of Gentiles against other Gentiles, because his Saints were seemingly too timid to take up arms, at least at this point, then maybe God would move as well — the Gentiles toward God's free gift of salvation, and the Saints toward a willingness to work harder for theirs.

A few years back, he'd met a former bishop of the LDS Church in Cedar City who was then living in Nevada. He'd been a party to the Mountain Meadows Massacre in 1857 and had even testified against the Mormon judge and Indian agent who were convicted and later hung for the event. The massacre had left the skeletons and skulls of approximately 120 Gentile men, women and children scattered across two miles of green Utah prairie.

He said he hadn't really been involved in the event, save to take a shot or two at immigrants from Arkansas, which he later regretted. He'd been a big part of saving some of the smaller children from being harmed, he said, and seeing them adopted by Mormon families in the area. But what Hickman found to be most interesting was the man's attestation that a Paiute tribe had joined Mormon militiamen in the massacre.

Klingensmith had been a private in the militia and was still pretty broken up about the event when they talked while taking a break during a business transaction in southern Nevada. Church folks had dressed as Indians, he said, hoping to be able to blame the massacre on others. It was a particularly difficult time, he said, given the federal government's intent to invade Utah — and so no one was really thinking clearly. He asked the man what it was like to work with heathens. Had he hoped to convert them? he asked. The former bishop replied, "Some had already found the Lord through the Church," though he wasn't sure how much of the Lord they'd actually found, given that they'd walked off with most of the cattle and personal belongings of the dead. Other stuff had been gathered into the ward's tithe storehouse for distribution. But he had been hopeful that something good had come out of such an awful thing.

"I know the Church will kill me, sooner or later, because of what I have done," he said. "It's only a matter of time." Klingensmith's body was found in August in a mining pit near Pioche. Mormon papers lamented his role in testifying about the event. Gentile newspapers took their usual tone, asking that the Mormon religion be disbanded.

"You done yet?" Hickman yelled into the front room. He'd found what he needed in *First Nephi*. It would do. The exact words of what he would say would come to him when he needed them.

"I've got one more name to write down, Orrin. Then we'll compare," his new captain replied, who Orrin was still praying for because he hadn't yet repented or been baptized, and if he kept calling him by his first name he'd have little opportunity to do so before he sent him on ahead to meet the baby Jesus. There could be a whole bunch of heathen that might find Jesus Christ if things between them were successful. And he'd be ready to tell them that God had given them the vision and strength to do what they needed to do, even though they were still sinners. The wrongs would be righted. And though a good many people might get hurt, God's people would be glorified.

Chapter 36
BLOOD SACRIFICE

Aside from looking like a professional baseball player, with all the bottle throwing and such, Jack seemed less than enthusiastic about his overture to hire Jack's criminal friends to serve as a sort of Mormon militia. It wasn't as if the Mormons couldn't do it all alone, he figured.

Horace had sat with Hickman, briefly at first, in between the violent contacts he'd made elsewhere. He'd put a bullet in a man's ear once, for instance, because the individual hiring him wanted to make sure the victim "heard the bullet coming," rather than sneaking up on him like some "classless son of a bitch" and shooting the guy in the back. "If you're going to be a professional," his employer said, "then act like one." Brown had subsequently learned to be tidier in his profession, asking where and when a client wanted their jobs done. Clearly some people preferred it that way.

More recently, he'd been sitting with Hickman regularly, listening to the stories of Mormon "men of thunder" who in years past had defended the Saints in Missouri, Illinois and Utah. "It was a violent time back then," Hickman said of the '30s, '40s and '50s, when Mormon men and women were being murdered for the simple fact that they were just that. "Not so much now," Hickman added, a bit wistfully, "though there have been some occasions."

When their mid-Thursday afternoon conversations turned toward religion, Brown was surprised to hear Hickman speak of the need for a "blood atonement," he said, pointing to a Mormon religious doctrine initiated more or less by the Prophet Joseph

Smith and later by his successor, Brigham Young. Smith and Young had a clear preference, Hickman said, for shooting a man in a capital crime rather than hanging him. "Even better, one should cut off his head," he said. "Spill his blood on the ground, like a sweet smelling sacrifice. God is pleased, if it's deserved," he said.

When he first heard Hickman suggest the thought, he was mid-way through a steaming cup of Mormon coffee — a roasted wheat, bran and molasses beverage, which prior to meeting Hickman Brown had thought disgusting, but not so much now. He spit it out and had to apologize. It seemed so much of a surprise, even for Hickman's character.

"The hanging of Judas Iscariot was not a suicide, my friend," Hickman continued. "It was an execution carried out by Saint Peter," as if the biblical reference, real or made up, could explain why a man might want to witness a body lose all of its blood. He'd seen too much of that to be comfortable with the thought, and had never grown used to watching the sticky red stain spread out beneath a man's head or heart until the very body the man had inhabited had no more blood to give.

"The decapitation of sinners is the law of God," Hickman argued. "Brigham Young said that. It's probably the only thing Young ever said that made good sense," he said, being no fan of the stream of the Mormon prophets and apostles who had led the church after Joseph's Smith's demise at the hands of a mob in 1844.

"You're still angry about that, huh?" he'd asked a couple of weeks back, only to be met by Hickman's death stare. Apostate or not, Hickman was a true believer and would be a formidable foe if the two of them ever had to square up.

He leaned forward until he fell out of the davenport in Hickman's front room and walked into the kitchen, where the Prophet and Revelator was praying. He waited until he was finished. "Listen, so here's what I've got," he said, though he wasn't sure he had anybody really lined up, not in the sense that Jack the barkeep had checked back with him after their first conversation a couple of nights ago. "If it goes the way I think it's going to go, we'll get all ten men to pitch in."

"Pitch in?"

"Like a baseball, Orrin. Like the Boston Red Stockings ..." He was searching Hickman's eyes when he concluded the reference was not understood.

"I don't know what you're talking about."

"I'm guessing Charles Jones will emerge as the leader, having already led the men some ten years ago."

"I thought that bunch headed south toward Mono Lake and killed a pony express rider, or something like that?"

"That's the story, a couple of other men and a few horses as well. How do you know so much about this, sir?"

"I've been in this valley a long time, son. And Mono Jim, the Indian tracker they killed? He was a friend of mine, more or less. I put up the money for the men's return."

"Well, time seems to have done what money couldn't do. I believe they're no longer in California. They're here in the Carson Valley, or just north. And I'm certain, if my friend has his way, every one of them will want to help us."

"You're believing that or you're certain of that?"

"I'm believing that, sir."

"Well, normally Mister Brown, those words mean the same, biblically speaking that is. 'Faith is the substance of things hoped for, the evidence of things not seen,' *Hebrews* 11:1. But we're going to want more than that, Horace. We're going to want a promise, son."

"A promise? I don't know what you mean."

"It's a retribution, son."

Horace stuttered, attempting to repeat the words. In the end, all he could do was to say them over again.

"The blood of the prophets cry out for payback, for vengeance. 'And thou has shed the blood of a righteous man, yea, a man who has done much good among his people. And were we to spare thee his blood would come upon us for vengeance.' *Alma* 1:13."

Horace blinked. Pushing his hat back, he crinkled his brow. *Scripture,* though he had never heard it before. "So …"

"So… we'll need every one of these men to swear the same things the brothers have promised in their endowment ceremonies."

"I'm sorry, Elder. You know I don't know about any of that."

Hickman laughed. "In time, son." Hickman took a step toward his captain. His eyes were wide, his fingers shaking. He leaned forward and began to whisper. "My throat be cut from ear to ear, and my tongue torn out by its roots," he rhymed, while drawing his right thumb across his throat.

Brown flinched.

"My breasts be torn apart …" He put his right hand over his left chest and began to shake his head. "… my heart and vitals torn out and given to the birds of the air," he said, "and the beasts of the field." He began to draw his thumb across the middle of his body as if disemboweling himself. "… my body be cut asunder …"

"Okay, okay. I've heard enough," Brown said, "Whoa!"

"These are the words that Joseph said during the temple endowments, my friend. We have repeated them here every week."

"Listen, Mister Hickman. I don't think these guys will want to say anything like that… but we'll ask, okay?" Brown took a deep breath and turned to go back into the front room. Hickman returned to his chair.

"Horace?" he asked.

"Yes, sir?"

"I have my speech ready. When the ten men arrive, bring them into the front room. I will tell each of them what they will need to do."

Chapter 37

BOND ROGERS

Bond Rogers wouldn't tolerate a hooligan living in her Mountain Street boarding home, despite having entertained at least one man of dubious character in years past. In the end, J. B. Books, an aging gunfighter who was looking for a place to die, had been more than a handful to deal with. Rogers however, known to be a person of great faith and principle, proved to the very end to be compassionate and gracious.

She would not be so kind when she learned of her son's late-night carousing with a former missionary in a capital city bar. Not only was Gillom underage, he was Methodist. And Methodists — disciplined and enthusiastic followers of the Lord Jesus Christ — didn't sit in such places, let alone imbibe when they did.

The First Methodist Church in Carson City, like many of the other churches in Nevada's capital, was quarried out of the sins of many, having been erected practically single-handed by the Reverend Warren Nims out of prison rock in 1867. He was thought to be "a brave and prayerful little man," the *Morning Appeal* said at the time, though Rogers had never met him. She was no Methodist pioneer, but she was an enthusiastic adherent to the church's services and teachings. And she believed in building on "a sure and certain foundation."

"Mister Nims?" Gillom asked, a couple of years back when his mother first used the phrase. Gillom was certain she was speaking of the church's sandstone exterior.

"Negative," she replied, having just finished speaking eloquently about the pastor's construction efforts and the spring-less seat of his stone-laden mule cart. "A sober life," she said, while pouring out the remains of a bottle found in one of her downstairs rooms. "We are to do all the good we can, by all the means we can, in all the ways we can, in all the places we can, at all the times we can, to all the people we can as long as ever we can." And she said it in one breath, too.

The previous week's lay minister — a heavy-set man in his fifties who was traveling the circuit through Reno, Washoe City, Virginia City, Dayton and points subsequent and in-between — had taken more than a few breaths to share the saying widely attributed to Methodism's founder, John Wesley. When he was finished, Gillom noticed, he was gasping for air, which wasn't nearly as bad as the Methodist pastor in Gold Hill who had recently died gasping for food, having chosen to feed his family their last remaining morsel, instead of asking his church for a larger monthly allowance. His mother's examples had been efficacious, as Gillom had been binge eating and binge drinking ever since.

His hands began to sweat when he noticed the deputy sheriff opening the front gate and walking past his mother's roses. "Sorta late for you to be out for a walk, isn't it?" he said to Slade as he climbed the steps onto the front porch.

"What are you talking about?" Dustsucker said.

"You being out and all."

"I'm always out at this hour. I started as night guy and I'm still a night guy, Gillom. What's got into you?" He shook his head.

"I'm nervous, okay? Ever since you found me with Mister Nauman. Well, I just figured you'd be saying something to my mother sooner or later."

Dustsucker laughed. "Gillom, that's not my style. I told you she'd be upset, I didn't say that I'd be the one to upset her."

"Then you haven't told her?" he asked.

"I have not."

"Are you going to tell her?"

"What did I just say?" Slade raised one eyebrow as Gillom's mother pushed open the porch door.

"Well Marcus, how are you this evening?"

"It's quite a night ma'am," he stuttered. The relationship had never been easy. There wasn't anything in Slade's life that he imagined his land lady would like, though she'd occasionally left a tart or freshly baked piece of pie in his room. He'd thought nothing of it, until Ronin had mentioned it might be one of the ways that Rogers was trying to break the ice. He figured something would happen between them sooner or later. "I mean, it's quite late already, ma'am. What are the two of you doing up?"

"Well, Mister Slade, it's this Mormon thing. It's got everybody upset."

"Mormon thing?"

"Yes, you surely know what I'm talking about, Mister Slade." She held her hands against her apron, one covering the other, the top one tapping as if she was nervous or upset. A piece of pie dough was stuck next to the apron's pocket. Flour dust was everywhere.

"I know there's some concern about a group down in the Carson Valley," he said. "But I hardly think that's something you need to be concerned about, ma'am. It's a dozen or more miles away."

"It's sixteen miles, Marcus. You ought to know that. You're the deputy sheriff."

"Yes, ma'am." He put his hands into his pants pockets so that he wouldn't fidget.

"Then you know that what happens in Genoa or Gardnerville, or even Alpine, is just a few minutes away from happening here."

"Well, not hardly ma'am. They may be only a few miles away, but there's a big difference..." She interrupted.

"Miles, minutes, I'm not talking about measurements, Mister Slade, I'm talking about Mormons. What is this about a big meeting at the Kent House?"

"You mean the hotel?"

"You know exactly where I mean."

"Yes, ma'am. Well," he paused, "what have you heard?"

Bond Rogers' eyes grew gray and cold. "That's not what I asked you."

Dustsucker looked at Gillom, who shrugged his shoulders.

"No ma'am, it isn't." He took a deep breath. He couldn't think of a single individual he knew that liked being scolded. "I heard there was a meeting, ma'am, if that's what you mean. A couple of ranchers, nothing more ..."

"Nothing more? Nothing more?" she asked, the words each time a little more extreme.

"Ma'am, it's late, and I need to get to bed."

"We all need to find our evening's peace, Mister Slade. Gillom, what are you doing up, anyway?" she asked, turning his way. The boy shrugged and went into the house, the screen door slamming behind him. Dustsucker thought he saw the boy look back and smile as he walked down the hallway to his room. "See what I mean, Mister Slade?" she said. "Everyone is out of sorts with this Mormon thing, even the youngsters."

"Ma'am, he's not all that young anymore ..."

"Don't tell me how young he is or how young he isn't, young man. Who are you to talk to me about my boy? What you can tell me is what you're going to do about the Mormons. I'll not have town ruined by a bunch of polytheists married to a mindless bunch of women ..."

"Polygamists, ma'am, not that all of them are. And I don't believe the Saints living in Genoa are married to multiple wives, anyway."

"I meant what I said, Mister Slade. Polytheists, each and every one of them. Multiple gods, you just ask one. Each one has their own planet. And then there's the matter of their marrying multiple wives. Did you know that Joseph Smith married more than thirty women? What kind of prophet is that? And Brigham Young married more than fifty women!"

"Yes, ma'am."

"You knew that?"

"No, I mean I did not."

"I'll not have it, Marcus. I'll tell you what. What kind of a man needs more than one woman? And listen," she said, without taking a breath, "if you men can't solve the problem, we women will."

"The problem, Missus Rogers?"

"Of Mormons meeting at the Gardnerville Hotel, swearing on Bibles that they'll do whatever that demented old Mormon man says. I'll talk to him myself, Mister Slade, if that's what it takes."

"If that's what it takes to do what, ma'am?"

"If that's what it takes to settle the city down again."

"I'm sorry, Bond. I'm totally missing your point. Again?"

"Since the last time there was a Mormon uprising, Mister Slade. Don't you know anything?"

"Yes ma'am," he said, as he sat down on the cedar bench he'd made for the widow last Christmas. He gave it to her so as to say thank you for holding his room in the midst of all the adventures he and Ronin were having. The sheriff had kept his job open as well. Of course, he didn't expect anything in return. Maybe he didn't need to give her anything.

"Marcus, are you listening to me?"

"Bond, is this about my not making you a Christmas gift this year?"

"Mister Slade, this isn't about the baby Jesus. It's about the people who say they hold him dear, and what they're going to do to the rest of us if they get organized."

"Organized?"

"Aren't you listening? A lot of cruelty has been shown their way, Marcus. And it takes no imagination to think that some of them might want to give some of it back."

Chapter 38

PRACTICE

Ronin ejected six shells from his Colt and slipped the gun back into its holster. It was the last day of year. Snow had settled into the Sierra the night before, leaving the scent of sage in the air and the subtle hint of a December rain. For the hour, just past six, the wind seemed brisk and promising. He pulled at the edges of his jacket until he could button it. "Son," the ex-preacher said, "I don't remember you shooting this good. I really don't."

"You gave me quite a lesson in the Rubies, Ronin. And I guess some of it stuck with me."

"Well, I guess some of it did," he said laughing, before putting his gun hand on Ian Slavin's shoulder and pausing to think about his words. He looked into his eyes — *so much promise.* "You know I'd still prefer you went back to law school. You seem so enthusiastic when you talk about that place."

"I am, and I probably will. I've just got to settle a few things first," he said. He slid the ejector forward to inch out a stuck case. It fell into his left hand before rotating the cylinder to make sure it was clear. "Fact is I really care about school. And I want to do good by my parents. That's what they want. But there's a piece of me that has to prove something first."

"Prove something?" Ronin reached under the left side of his open coat, pulling the longer of his two Colts from a cross draw holster and tossing it into his left hand. He flicked the loading gate open with his right thumb.

"Well sure. Doesn't everyone?"

Ronin lifted a half-dozen cartridges from his belt and looked at the boy before sliding them into his gun. Here was a man still acting like a boy. He smiled. "Son, not everyone has something to prove. After a while, a man simply is what he is. I imagine the same is true for women."

"Guess you've been doing some thinking about that, haven't you?" Ian said.

He grinned. "Indeed I have, but how about you? What do you need to prove?"

Slavin set four tin cans on the top rung of the corral fence and looked about for two more. "I don't know. I think I wanted to do something else for a while. But I didn't make any money at it. And then I couldn't seem to catch anyone's attention in Elko for anything else ..."

"Ever occur to you that you might not be meant to do anything else?"

"Meant?" Slavin asked, turning around. "I didn't think you believed in that sort of thing."

"I guess I don't," Ronin said, thinking of the years he'd studied the Bible and listened to his teachers speak about God's good plan for people's lives. "Not like I used to, anyway." He kicked an empty can Slavin's way. "I'm just saying, some things feel good to a person. Some things don't. Seems to me that people ought to pay attention to the things that do. Life's too short to make yourself live someone else's life."

"My mom's?"

"Your mom's, your dad's, whoever's life it is that you're trying to live. Who told you that you should do something other than lawyering?"

"It was the money, Ronin. I told you that. It ran out."

"So get a job. Start a business. Borrow a few bucks from a friend. It can't be that hard."

Slavin moved away from the fence. Ronin drew his short iron and shot from his hip. A can went flying. He dropped it back into its holster, and pulling the longer piece from his left hand, spun around to his right. He fanned three slugs into a fence post before taking careful aim and thumb-cocking shells into the next three cans. He tossed the empty gun into his left hand as he dumped his strong-side iron back over the top of the holster and fired once more. A single can remained, wobbling. He looked at his friend. "Opportunities don't last forever, Ian." The can fell backward onto the ground.

The boy stood there, impressed. "Listen, Ronin, first you ask me to stay, then you tell me to leave. Which is it?"

Ronin shook his head as he began reloading both guns. "That's exactly my point. You can't be listening to other people's business. You can't be running around wanting to please other people. There's only one person you need to please."

"God?"

"Not hardly, Ian. God doesn't need your contributions."

"Then who?" he asked.

"*You*, boy." He turned the long Colt around in his left hand and dropped it into its holster as he slipped the shorter Colt, both now loaded, into its strong-side pouch. "Come here." Ian walked over to where he was standing as Ronin re-buttoned his coat. He watched him pull his leather gloves from his pocket, pick up the empty box of shells and pause.

"What?"

"Promise me this. After we put a few of these bad boys to bed, you'll take a long look at things, maybe head to the lake for a few days. Give some consideration to leaving Nevada. Home means Nevada for me. It may not be home for you."

Slavin sighed. "Okay, I promise." They started walking back toward the house. The sky began to sprinkle, in a December mist sort of way. Ronin pulled his hat down over his eyes.

"It's chilly."

"It is that."

"Listen, son. The kids are out this morning on some sort of hike. While I build a fire or two, how about you tell Emma and me about Hickman and the Mormon Church? I get the impression he's not exactly a straight arrow."

"He's an apostate, Ronin. The word is Greek for ..."

"Yeah, I know. "The word means, 'defector.'"

"Right," Ian said. "Orrin Hickman lives on the edge of the Church. He's someone who has fallen away from the truth."

"The truth? In whose opinion, son? Who says what the truth is?"

Slavin turned toward his friend before stepping up on the porch. "Ronin, I thought you knew this stuff. The Prophet says what the truth is."

"Ian, the Greek word is used only twice in the New Testament. It means to fall away from God. It has nothing to do with falling away from men."

"Well, I can only tell you my experience. In the Latter Day Saint Church there isn't much of difference. You do what the Prophet says, or you're ..."

"Apostate."

"Exactly."

Ronin put his arm around Ian's shoulders, as Ian reached for the screen door. "Well, there's your issue," he said.

"My issue?"

"Yup," Ronin said. "If you would start thinking for yourself, you might not be a Mormon anymore. And you'd more than likely be back in law school."

Chapter 39

NO FREE LUNCH

"Charlie, calm down, would you?"

"I can't help it. The fact that you told that crazy son of a bitch that you knew the ten of us makes me just want to punch your face in! What kind of a friend finks on his buddies?" Charles Jones, a grizzled, raisin-skinned survivor of the 1871 prison break, had the owner of Jack's bar backed up against the mirror he'd just lettered on. "No free ride," it said, suggesting that credit was something to be remembered and that a complimentary lunch was nowadays out of the question.

"I didn't say any such thing, Charlie! I suggested that I *might* know where a few of the guys were, not that I *definitely* knew. Hell, I don't know anything. I'm just a barkeep. And anyway, I didn't talk about *you*. Put me down and I'll make you a baloney sandwich. Free of charge."

Jones extended an index finger and poked at Jack's chest. "There's no free lunch, man." He allowed his feet to dangle, but kept his hand on Jack's shirt, knotting up the freshly pressed cotton cloth into a fist-sized ball.

"Ow, Charlie! You don't need to keep poking me like that." Jones had delivered five thrusts, one poke per word, denoting the exact number of fingers he had in his right fist, which he was about to deliver to either the goddamned mirror or Jack's face. He didn't care which.

"Listen, you dummy. Nobody knows who we are, or where we are, or what we're doing, or what we're going to do, you stupid piece of shit. And that's the way it needs to stay." He paused, looking over both shoulders to see if anyone could hear him. No one was there. "If you have a problem understanding that …"

"I've got no problem, Charlie. I'm just trying to help out. I know you guys don't have a lot of money …"

"Which guys are you talking about?"

"No one, Charlie, I'm just talking about you. I just figured *you* might want a few more bucks than you already have …"

"I do okay, Jack."

"Of course you do, Charlie. But smithing has got to be hard, and with everyone leaving…"

"Leaving?"

"I mean, with the mines closing and all …"

"Nobody's closing any mines, Jack. They're just not opening any new ones."

"Yeah, that's what I meant…"

"There's a good three or four thousand people here in town who might take exception to your poor talk, Jack."

"Of course, they might. I didn't mean anything by it. Maybe there will be a comeback. You're right. I just meant that if you wanted a little extra money for the New Year and all, well, you might meet this man and see what he's got in mind. That's all I meant."

"And you didn't say anything about the other nine of us?"

"Honest to God, Charlie. I'm a good Catholic. I tell you something, it's the truth."

"Jack, you just offered me a free lunch …"

"So?" he said.

"So your sign says 'no free lunches.'"

"Nah, Charlie. It says no free rides. Honest. That's different."

He let his feet drop and pulled the bar owner to one of his tables and pushed him into a chair. He leaned in, placing both of his hands on the chair's arms. "Jack, listen would you? I'm not trying to scare you. I'm not trying to hurt you. I am simply trying to figure out what it is you told this slick young gunfighter."

"I didn't…" Jones put a finger to Jack's lips. The barkeep stopped talking.

"I'm hoping to discover whether you told him that you *knew* us."

"I told him I *might* know you."

"And?"

"And that I'd talk to you, I mean *if* I knew you…"

"Jack."

"What Charlie?"

Jones started to count to ten in his head. If there was any chance that his friend told anyone that the ten of them were in Carson City, hell that any of them were in Carson City, he didn't know what he'd do. Well, he'd leave for sure — head down to Bishop, maybe, or Bodie — nobody goes to Bodie looking for trouble, or maybe Montana. But he might have to silence the lips of a man he'd come to appreciate the last few years. And that would be unfortunate.

"Jack, I'll tell you what," he said. "You put me in touch with this dandy. You don't tell him who I am. You don't infer or connect me with the prison break or anything like that. You just tell him that you know someone with a gun who might be interested in joining a few other someones with guns, and we'll see where it goes from there. How's that sound?"

"That sounds good, Charlie."

"And listen, Jack."

"What?" Jack began to relax, as Charlie took his hands from the chair and gave him a little more breathing room. Charlie pushed his hat back on his head. He almost looked friendly. He even smiled.

"Jack?"

"What?"

"Don't call me Charlie anymore."

"Okay. What do you want me to call you?"

"Call me Joseph, if you like. It's a good Mormon name and it might make me some money."

"Okay. Anything else?"

"Yeah," Joseph said, putting his hands on his gun belt and pulling his strong-side holster around to the front of his leg, so that it rested closer to his right hand. "Get me some twine. No," he grinned. "Get me a leather strap."

"What the hell for?"

Joseph pushed the back of his hat up, so that the front almost covered his eyes. "I don't know this Horace Brown, you jackass. When I meet him, I might want to use my gun hand."

Chapter 40

THE MOVE OF GOD

"The fact is, it's not the speed of your hand that counts most, Orrin. It's your mind that has to be fast. You can't be standing there wondering about breakfast or thinking about lunch. And you can't be deliberating on whether or not you should shoot a man. If your gun has cleared leather, it should already be going 'Bang, bang.'"

"You sound like you know what you're doing, Mister Brown."

"I don't believe you would have hired me if I didn't."

"So when we see our targets, these Gentiles we've marked for death, we just shoot them. Handguns, rifles — it doesn't matter. Is that right?"

Hickman hesitated. Perhaps the old Danite wasn't up to the task. Most men getting ready to kill a handful of people would understand. "Sure," he said hesitantly. "If the shot's clear, you take it. No second thoughts. Second thoughts are what you have when you're making up the list." He paused. "Be resolute, I always say."

"That's a good word, Mister Brown. The early Saints have much to teach us, you know, pulling their ox carts west and walking literally hundreds of miles. In the midst of hardships and struggles," he began nodding, "they were resolute, too."

"Then you understand," he said. "If you've got to bend around a bush or climb a tree or get a little closer, then you'll want to wait until everything is in place. But there's no deciding anything at that point. What's been decided is decided. You see your target, the way is clear, you shoot."

"… until he's dead."

"… until he's not only dead in *your* mind, Orrin, but dead in *his* mind, as well."

"That's pretty cold."

"Killing is pretty serious business, Orrin." The gunfighter flipped the plough handle of his revolvers forward and dropped them into their holsters — two pouches, strong-side, guns facing backward. Hickman lifted his chin and pointed at Brown's black and tan gun rig. Silver conchos made from Carson City dollars sat on either side of a shiny new buckle. Nickel points ran along the belt's bottom edge. "My belt?" Brown smiled.

"Your guns, Horace. They sit backward. Is that normal?"

"That's how Wild Bill Hickok carried them. And he was as normal a gunfighter as a gunfighter gets."

Hickman's eyes grew wide. "You met Wild Bill Hickok?"

"Sure, him *and* Cody, though I don't know neither of them per se. I saw them act once, if you can call it that, in one of Buffalo Bill's Wild West shows — "Scouts of the Plains," in Rochester, New York."

"Well, Mister Brown, I had no idea you were a man of culture."

"I'm not. But I knew I wanted to meet the man who created the American West. I grew up on those stories. Cody was a genius, and an Indian hater."

"Horace, we all grew up that way." Hickman leaned across the kitchen table and looked into the front room, where a dozen or so Saints were gathered for prayer and study. They'd been meeting in Hickman's home for a dozen or so years. Some had worn out the seat cushions kneeling on the floor for the evening's prayers. "Is this a good time to begin training the troops?" Hickman asked.

Jesus, if this is Hickman's army, then the good Lord himself needs to find a rifle. "As good a time as any," he replied. "Is this it?"

"Is this what?"

"I mean numbers, sir. My impression was there were more Mormons willing to fight than the handful you've got in the front room."

Hickman counted a dozen able-bodied men. "There are. But it will take these men to bring them out of their homes and into the Lord's service. 'His ministers are a flame of fire, Horace. Psalm 104.'"

"Of course, they are," he said. "Then let's get started." Horace Brown picked up his rifle and headed across the kitchen floor into the front room, until he stood in front of a large gray and brown granite fireplace. The rocks had been carried down from the mountains over the years, Hickman had pointed out. They were an offering to the One who had carried God's people from Palmyra, New York to Kirkland, Ohio, to Independence, Missouri, to Nauvoo, Illinois, and to the Great Salt Lake. They were "cemented together with prayer and suffering," Hickman said. No doubt many of the men in the room had applied shovel and trowel to the massive hearth.

"These are no small souls," said the Elder entering the room, as if intuiting Horace's thoughts. "They've built homes and farms in this valley, and in valleys north and south of here. Some of them, like myself, have seen the Gentile cheat them of their inheritance, and have had to listen to the Church's false prophets saying, 'Lay down your arms,' 'Make peace with these men,' and 'Do no harm, be the Indian's friend.' But they know the truth, Horace. It resides within them, just as it resides in you."

Hickman, a good foot taller than Horace Brown, rested a ham-sized hand on the gunman's shoulder. He tugged at him gently. "Look outside these windows."

Brown gazed westward toward the hills and the Sierra beyond, and then turned to face the marshes and mountains east of Hickman's ranch. "You have an outstanding view, Elder Hickman. You really do."

Hickman smiled. "I'm not asking you to admire my Nevada home, Mister Brown. I'm asking you to realize something very, very profound. I'm asking you appreciate the fact that men didn't make these mountains, Horace. But these mountains did make these men." He smiled. "You are part of a great movement, my friend. It's something bigger, better and more exciting than anything you've ever done before."

Horace Brown remembered for a moment the night he met Buffalo Bill Cody and Wild Bill Hickok in Rochester, New York. While the latter man seemed broken and drunk, spent beyond his years, speaking with them after the show was still the high point of his life. How could anything be better? He looked into Hickman's eyes, who was still looking deeply into his. Maybe his life was coming full circle now — the previous moment being seven years ago and the man he so admired turning out to be a mere shadow of what he had once been.

Something inside him felt stirred by these men, these hairy examples of what it meant to be American men — each of them tall and strong. *It can't be all that bad*, he thought, *meeting these Saints, training them to be soldiers in the Lord's Army. It might be a good thing. It might be exactly what his life needed.* "And what is that, sir?" he heard himself asking, his lips moving as if something inside of him wanted to hear more.

"The move of God, my friend — can't you feel it burning inside you? It begins tonight."

Chapter 41

JUMPY

Emma passed the sheriff's office without pause. If Ronin was going to post at the house overnight, she didn't feel any need to check in with Sheriff Swift, which is what he had asked her to do when she had complained about feeling unsafe, she and the children, given "the Mormon uprising," as Ronin had referred to it.

"I'm sure you're making more of the discontent among our friends in Genoa than is warranted," the sheriff had said, though his smile didn't assure her much. And why was Ronin needed if everything was "likely okay," words that struck her as a little funny coming from a professional sheriff.

The last few evenings at the mission were a little strange, too. The horses seemed anxious. They had awakened her a couple of times during the night. There'd been some unexplained noises coming from some of the out-buildings as well. She had been assured that someone would be available each night for the next week or so, or until things settled down in the Carson Valley. And what was there to report, anyway? "Sheriff Shubael, I've got a couple of anxious chickens." "One of the cows is no longer giving milk." "I'm not sleeping the way I usually do." No, stopping by the Carson City courthouse would be a waste of everyone's time. They had their job. She had hers. And there were groceries to unload as well.

It took Emma about an hour to get back to the mission. She'd gotten in the habit of taking her time on their monthly runs for supplies, and the afternoon was actually quite lovely despite what she was feeling. The smell of sage was in the air. Snow was blowing up in the mountains. Save for the December temperatures — which had been temperate, but still — it was her favorite time of year.

She pulled up next to the house, lifted two grocery boxes from the carriage and began walking toward the door when one of stable boys braced her with a concern. "Señora Emma," he said. He seemed jumpy.

"Yes, Manuel?" she replied. The boy took two boxes from the back of the wagon, stacked them and began walking toward her. He paused to look over his shoulder at a line of brush west of the front corral. "Son, what's bothering you?"

"There were men who came by, earlier today, ma'am. Mormon men, I believe. They had Bibles in their hands and were testifying about things I'd never heard before. I shooed them away, but they kept looking back at the house as they left."

"And you thought it unusual, Manuel? Perhaps they were just looking at you to see if you had changed your mind."

Over the years, she had come to respect the instincts and inclinations of some of the families employed at the mission. While Christianizing the children was necessary — she'd found the Washoe children, the Paiute to a lesser extent, and the few Mexicans friendlier toward the cultural graces that had become the civilized norm in American Indian schools — there needed to be some allowance, she thought, for those habits and dispositions that didn't offend faith or propriety.

"Manuel?"

He was looking at the tree line. "No, ma'am, this was different. In chapel, you have taught us to reject those who would bring a gospel different than the one we have received. 'They are accursed,' you said."

"I didn't say that, Manuel. Paul the Apostle said that, a very long time ago. He was one of the original disciples of Jesus, like you are of me, and I am of … well, the pastors in Carson City."

"Yes, ma'am. Well, they were preaching a different gospel. So I asked them — and I was mannerly, as you've asked all of us to be — to leave. They were upset. But some of the little children were listening, señora. I did not want them misled."

Emma enjoyed the Mormon scriptures, or more to the point, the Mormon stories. While she hadn't yet met a Saint who thought as she did about *The Book of Mormon* and the other writings they thought to be inspired, she hoped someday to meet Latter-day Saints who regarded their scriptures as inspirational, but not nearly as special as those books handed down to the Church as the B-I-B-L-E. Those books — *the Old and New Testaments* — had been given to the Church by the apostles themselves. She liked the others, to be sure — *Doctrine and Covenants*, even *The Pearl of Great Price*, parts of which she considered silly at best. But she didn't feel comfortable reading them to the children. It felt inappropriate, despite their being of some interest or value. *But then, what isn't?* she often wondered.

"You did fine, Manuel. Thank you. Tell me again why you are so nervous."

"Nervous, señora? I do not mean to appear so."

"I saw you looking over your shoulder a few moments ago, son. Do you expect them to come back?"

"Señora," the boy paused, "I wonder if they have left."

Chapter 42

MISSIONARIES

Emma suddenly felt anxious. She nudged the front door open with her left foot and gestured for Manuel to follow her inside. She walked by the front window next to the wood stove and rocking chair, where she often sat and prayed for her children and friends. She looked out beyond the corral and wondered. There'd never been a missionary visit by Latter-day Saints to the school, though there wasn't any reason to assume that such a thing would be out of the ordinary for particularly religious people. She'd left a few gospel tracts once by the door of the Roman Catholic Church in Carson City. A few weeks later, Father John Grace, the church's priest, tore the building down — supposedly to make room for a new church. She wondered if she had contaminated the previous edifice with her actions. "Manuel, did the men have horses?" she asked.

"They were on foot, señora."

She walked into the kitchen. If the men weren't seen with horses, they had either walked — which was unlikely, given the distance from town — or they had ridden their horses and hidden them. She put her box of groceries on the table. Manuel followed suit. "Leave the rest of the groceries in the wagon, Manuel. I'll get them later." She went immediately to the front door and locked it. She then went to the back door, and watching Manuel return to the stable with her carriage and horse, paused to wonder if she should call on his father to check on the children. Ian Slavin suddenly appeared at the kitchen window.

"Miss Emma," he said. She jumped. "You look upset. Is everything okay?"

"Mister Slavin, do not do that!"

"I'm sorry, ma'am."

She pushed open the back door to let him in and then barred it, top and bottom. "Ian, I know you must think all of this a bother, your being a Latter-day Saint and all ..."

"I'm not a member of the same Church as the others, ma'am. I'm a Utah Mormon. They are, that is, the Genoa Mormons are, well they are something less, ma'am."

"You call them 'apostates?' Is that the term?"

"We do. There are other groups, of course — the Reorganized Church of Latter-day Saints in Missouri, for instance. The Prophet's wife remained with them, rather than follow Brigham Young to the Great Salt Lake."

"Emma Hale."

"Yes, ma'am. There are some Reorganized folks in Washoe Valley." He pulled out a chair from the kitchen table and waited for Emma to sit down. He sat in a second chair facing her, took off his gloves and smiled.

She smiled back. "We should talk about all of that someday," she said. "But let me ask you a question first."

"Of course."

"One of the stable boys said that there were missionaries at the door today."

"That's not uncommon, ma'am."

"Except for all trouble in Genoa, I would suppose not. But given that..."

"Emma," he interrupted, "Latter-day Saints take their religion very seriously. If I wasn't casting about a bit, I might be on a mission myself, or back in school. I wouldn't worry."

"I remember you saying something about that to Mister Ronin," she replied.

"He and I have talked a lot about my going back to school."

"I wouldn't normally worry, Ian, except that the men who called on us didn't come on horses."

"Now that is interesting, ma'am. It's a good many miles for Mormon missionaries to be walking, and I don't know that there are any in these parts. Lock the door behind me," he said, getting up suddenly and lifting the heavy planks from the kitchen door. He touched the Remington single-action handgun at his side, tugging at it gently to make sure it would clear leather. "I'll go check on the children. Then I'll take a quick turn around the mission and grab my rifle. When I get back, we'll sit together until you get sleepy, or until Mister Ronin comes by tomorrow morning."

"He's coming tomorrow morning?"

"Yes, ma'am, it's New Year's Day. It's Sunday, and he's coming for breakfast. He says there's nothing better for breakfast that your pancakes and eggs."

"Let's hope we're here for pancakes and eggs in the morning, Mister Slavin. Or our good friend Mister Ronin will be very, very angry."

Chapter 43
THE LIST

When the Virginia & Truckee Railroad established service between Carson City and Reno in 1872, a new way of travel became commonplace for many in the capital city. The Virginia City rails had been laid three years earlier, making Nevada's tiny capital a sort of rural suburb of the Comstock's culture and mines. But when the northern extension was finished, linking the tiny V & T to the much larger transcontinental route in Reno, the "very crooked and terribly rough railroad," as the V & T had become known, became a smooth-running wood and steel corridor to the bigger world beyond.

By the turn of the century, like the short lines at Glenbrook and Incline Village at Lake Tahoe, the V & T Railroad would shift its focus from carrying timber and ore to area mills and mines to transporting tourists and other passengers. A man of vision, the coming change was not one Orrin Hickman had missed.

The Virginia & Truckee Railroad was making money, connecting with larger rail systems everywhere, and funding businesses, investments and utilities in dozens of other locations, states and countries. Soon people would be traveling the 31-mile northern route — past the nearly empty Washoe City, Franktown and Steamboat Springs — to connect with people and cities across the globe. And despite the slowdown on the Comstock, some 40 to 50 trains a day out of Carson City were paying impressive dividends to investors. It all had Hickman wondering. If $100,000 of V & T dividends were being distributed monthly, and hundreds, maybe even thousands, of people were traveling monthly, an interruption in the Virginia & Truckee Railroad's business might be felt worldwide.

"You don't think we could burn those buildings down, do you?" the Elder asked Horace Brown, who was sitting outside Hickman's house whittling a long stick to make a point.

"The roundhouse?"

"The shops, the roundhouse, the whole thing."

"Sure," he said, shrugging his shoulders. "The sandstone won't burn, of course, but everything else will. Have you been up there?"

"I work for a living, Horace. I don't ride the railroad."

"Well, I mean your people, Mister Hickman. The roundhouse alone has over 100 windows. They'd burn or break quite nicely. A good fire at the right time in each of the eleven sheds or arches would peel the paint off of every engine. That'd be expensive. And if you could set it so that the machine shop, the repair shop, the boiler and blacksmith shops, the locomotive and car shops and the foundry all exploded at the same moment — well, that would be something I'd want to see! It'd be one hell of a New Year's Day, if you don't mind me saying."

"That's what I'm thinking," Hickman replied, "though I don't know that we could get it all together by tomorrow morning. Do the trains run on Sundays?"

"Frankly sir, I don't know. Like Ronin, I don't ride 'em. But I'd be happy to find out."

"That won't be necessary, Horace. I sent a couple of men to the station earlier to look around. They'll grab a schedule and then we'll begin making plans."

"You know, Elder Hickman, they say the V & T roundhouse and shops are as nice as any in Sacramento. The bell from the Episcopal Church in Carson City was repaired there. They've got quite an expertise, sir."

"I don't give an angel's ass about the Episcopal Church in Carson City, Horace. In fact, let's put them on the list, too. What have we got so far?"

Brown picked up the tablet of paper he'd been writing on and began to read. "There's the V & T, of course."

"Right."

"And Saint Peter's Episcopal Church."

"Is that the church in town with the bell?"

"Yes sir. I mean they all have bells, I imagine. There's the Roman Catholic Church, a Methodist Church, a Presbyterian and an Episcopalian. The Episcopalian was the last of the four to be built."

"Blow it up. And blow up the Presbyterian Church, too. What else have we got?"

"Well, you suggested the mission."

"Good ..."

"... and the Ormsby House. Sir, are you sure you want to do the Ormsby House? They serve a nice steak."

"Do they serve liquor also?"

"Of course, sir."

"Blow it up. Oh, and Horace?"

"Yes sir?"

"It's come to my attention that one of our number has been seen at Jack's bar at the north end of town. Most of us don't drink, of course. We keep 'the Word of Wisdom,' as you know. Kirkland, Ohio. February 27, 1833."

"Sir?"

"The date Joseph inquired of the Lord about the use of tobacco and alcohol."

"Yes, sir."

"That wouldn't be you, would it?"

"Not any longer, sir."

"Well, blow Jack's bar up as well."

"Yes, sir."

"Beginning next week Horace, the whole damned world might change. And that because of the actions of a few, dedicated men."

"Yes, sir."

Hickman leaned forward. "What are you carving there, if I may ask?"

"A lance, sir. Some of your Mormon boys don't have any weapons."

"Not even rifles?"

"No sir."

Hickman looked incredulously at his captain. And what a captain he was going to be, particularly if he was baptized before the Lord's army was dispersed to do its work. "So you're going to teach them to fight with sticks?"

"I don't know what else to do, Orrin."

"You know what they say about sticks and stones, right?"

"'Sticks and stones won't hurt me,' something like that."

"That's my point, son. This is an important work that we do. We need to do it well."

"Well Elder, I don't know if this helps. But no one has ever said the same thing about spears."

A big smile came over Orrin Hickman's face. No more important truth had ever been spoken. And wasn't it like the Lord to put his faith in frail, ill-equipped people? Like tiny David of old, the Lord God was raising up a Mormon army to do a mighty work. Some of their number might not have the armor and swords they needed to take on Goliath. But they had the rocks to do it. He took a seat on the porch next to the captain of his army and chuckled over the double entendre. "Horace, you ever hear the story of David and Goliath?"

"I have not, sir." Brown picked at the point of the branch he was sharpening with a small knife, and then touched its edge with his palm. *Sharp.* Folding his blade and putting it in his breast pocket, he leaned forward to scrape the top edge of his spear on a small rock he had brought up onto the porch. A few others were stacked nearby. Hickman bent over to pick one up and began tossing it up and down.

"Well son, it was a long time ago, in a land far away. In ancient Israel actually, or perhaps Canaan — the scholars are unclear. The Philistines, one of Israel's most powerful enemies, had met the Israelite armies on a plain near the Valley of Elah. And every day, twice a day, the Good Book says, for 40 days, they trotted out their champion and suggested they settle their differences by single combat. Do you know what I'm saying?"

"I think so, sir. Two big armies were facing each other. One of them taunted the other with what I'm guessing was an amazing soldier."

"That's correct. He was a goliath. I'm talking about his size. In fact, that was his name. The Bible says he was nearly seven feet tall." Hickman smiled. "That's one big man, my friend."

"It sure is," Brown said, listening. "Elder Hickman," he asked, "is this a true story?"

"As true as I'm sitting with you, Horace, though there's a deeper meaning to the story, of course. That's why they call it the Bible, I guess."

"I wouldn't know anything about that, Elder. And the meaning is?"

"Well, I'm no bishop, or what I mean is, this Prophet and Revelator stuff is all new to me. The calling is that recent. But I'm guessing that 'forty days, twice a day,' and a larger man verses a smaller one — as David was not just a small man, about your size I imagine, but a young man as well — I'm guessing all that signals that the story is meant to tell a little more than just history. I think it's meant to share hope, for people like us."

"How so?"

Elder Hickman grabbed the porch railing to steady himself, and leaning forward again, took the stick out of his captain's hands. He hefted it above his head, measured its weight and pretended that he was going to throw it at something or someone. "Well, I'd not normally say that a spear is going to beat a rifle. And I don't really see how a spear is going to beat a train. But in God's hands, it's not the instrument that matters, son. It's the man."

"Because?"

"Because the Lord is on our side, son. And when all of this over and done, and our faith has been tested, and our cause carried far and far away, you're going to see that God is in this and that what we're about really matters."

Horace Brown smiled. There was something compelling to Hickman's manner when he spoke that way, something warm and maybe even logical in a spiritual sense. And the hope that they had only a small number of men, untrained men, unprepared and ill-equipped men to rain Hickman's havoc on the surrounding countryside — well, maybe that was the sort of thing God honored.

"Mister Brown, have you considered baptism yet?" Brown looked the old man in the eyes.

"I have, Elder Hickman. Would it be appropriate that I be baptized before all of this takes place?"

"It would be, son." Hickman practically clapped.

"Then when?" Brown asked.

"How about right now?" He looked out, past the edge of the porch into a glen of trees where a small snow-covered stream flowed gently by. It looked cold, to be sure. The future captain of the Lord's host, who was about to bring death to the Philistines in the Eagle Valley and beyond, looked at the stream too, and shivered.

"There?" Brown asked. "It looks... sort of icy, sir."

"Horace, you're absolutely right. The water should be deeper, anyway." Hickman smiled. "Son, when we push you *underneath* the water, we want to make sure every inch of you is covered."

Brown looked up. "Every inch, sir?"

"Baptism is a one-time only thing, son. We don't want to miss a single sin."

Chapter 44

THE TRAIN STATION

"This two-by-two stuff is utter nonsense," the grizzled, prune-faced gunfighter Charles Jones said, looking at his unnamed Mormon friend. "It would have taken me half the time to see twice as much if I wasn't here babysitting you."

"Elder Hickman thought you might need some focus, Charles."

The shootist raised his eyebrows. "You can call me Mister Jones, you son of a bitch. I've seen more of these parts that you'll ever see — I don't care how long you've lived in Genoa."

"Yeah, but you were in prison." The Mormon man's voice trailed off when he saw Jones tugging at the toothpick stuck between two blistered lips, rolled to one side of his mouth. "It's a biblical thing, anyway," the Mormon whispered, looking down at his watch. It was a couple of minutes past six o'clock, *dinner time.* "Jesus sent them forth, two-by-two," he continued to stutter, thinking it was important to be bold about one's faith. "He gave them power over unclean spirits. Gospel of Mark, chapter 6 verse 7." The Mormon's head was nodding, like the brush stroke of a man painting a fence.

"Are you still talking? And who are you calling unclean?" Charles Jones bellowed, whose only real distinction in life was leading the 1871 prison break in Carson City — the biggest jail break in the history of the American West — that and the fact that the 29 convicts who escaped were able to take with them several prison-issued rifles, shotguns and pistols as well as nearly three-thousand rounds of ammunition.

"I'm just quoting scripture, Mister Jones."

"I don't care what you're quoting," Jones said, pulling at his hat. "Say it to yourself, and say it quietly if you're going to be talking. I've got no interest."

"Yes, sir."

"Fucking Mormons," he murmured, before pulling his hat down over his eyes and stepping to the corner of Carson and East Washington Streets to read the building's sign. "Isn't this the train depot?"

Jesus, the Mormon said.

The V & T station sat at the busy corner of two city streets. Situated so as to provide a boarding area as well as offices, the long and narrow building was painted a bright California yellow, as if to say, "Yo, over here. This is where you catch your train!"

The Mormon shook his head. There was no question the Saints needed the expertise of these criminal men. A handful of them had met with Mormon neighbors and friends at Hickman's ranch the night prior. And while there were distinct differences between the two groups — the Saints believed in God and hoped for the restoration of their properties and the judgment of God on those who had wronged them, "the scruffians," as Hickman called them behind their backs, believing in nothing more than the value of money — there was one thing they all agreed on. They had the ability to do what was needed, more or less, and to see the effort through, for a prize no one seemed willing to discuss.

"If you are unable to quantify the amount of money God needs to set things straight, why should we risk our lives?" one of them asked before Hickman's boy shouted them down, saying they had no faith. *And what did God need with money, anyway?*

"Yes, Mister Jones. That's the train station," he said carefully. "And beside it you'll see some meeting rooms and offices," he offered, hoping not to anger the man whose reputation was well known even though his whereabouts had remained unknown for the last ten years. "Mister Jones?"

"Yes?"

"Come back here in the shadows sir, and tell me where you've been the last ten years. You don't need to stand out where everybody can see you."

Jones kicked a rock west on Washington Street before turning around. "You want to know where I've been? Why is that?"

"Sir, I'm only making conversation."

"I can see that," he said. "I've asked you to be quiet a couple of times." He wrinkled his brow. "And you've ignored my counsel..."

"Yes sir, but..."

"I'm not a man used to having my conversations interrupted, Mister... what did you say your name is?"

"I didn't, sir."

"And?"

"And what, sir?"

"Your name, what is it?"

"Davenport, sir. Israel Davenport, III."

"Well, Mister goody two-shoes, Davenport the Third, or whatever your name is — I'd advise you to keep your mouth shut so that we can do what we're out here to do..."

"But sir..."

Jones flexed his neck as he wound his head around in a circle. Scrunching up his lips, he squeezed his fingers into a ball and launched a fist forward into the Mormon's forehead. Davenport fell backward onto his ass and into the street and blinked. Once.

"I was just..."

"You're still talking?" Jones said. "Seriously?"

"Mister Jones," the Mormon continued, taking his hat off and rubbing his head. "I was just trying to say the V & T roundhouse and shops are over there." He gestured with his right hand before returning it to his face so as to wipe tears from his eyes. He began smoothing his hairline, rhythmically, front to back. "I'm just trying to help."

Jones looked. And of course the complex of buildings, erected by the father of Carson City, Abe Curry, sat there obvious as hell. The massive sandstone structures sitting as they always had been, dominating the northeast corner of the city, there all the time. And he knew there were trains going in and out, and shops. Hell, he'd taken a saddle there once, to get the leather re-stitched, and paused for practically a whole afternoon watching some men pour a church bell. He just hadn't put two and two together.

"So you are, son. My apologies." He offered his hand.

Davenport stood up and brushed the dirt off of his knees and backside. "I just thought it'd be a good thing if the two of us got to know each other, Mister Jones. I mean, given that we're working together and all. I meant nothing more. Should we walk over that way?" he asked, gesturing toward one of the arches.

"Son, look, I don't mean you any disrespect. I really don't. You can believe in all that Orson Hyde stuff if you want, that he didn't get his money, or that he and you and Lord knows who else were cheated of your possessions by people who don't understand your religion, let alone *like* your religion. And that the good Lord is going to pay everybody back with terrible earthquakes, and floods and God knows what else. I don't care," he said. "But we're not working together. We're just... together," he said, raising his eyebrows again.

"But..."

"Don't start butting me again, son."

"Yes sir."

"I just don't think your brooms and spears and little girly guns are going to finish what your precious Prophet, Elder Hick-man, has started. So you can believe in all that stuff..."

Davenport interrupted. "...that God will honor our efforts, no matter how weak, no matter how strong. That it's God's battle,

Mister Jones, just like Elder Hickman says it is. That he's going to see it all through. It's not up to us, Mister Jones. 'Without Christ,' the scriptures say, 'we can do nothing…'"

Jones held up his hand. Davenport stopped.

"I'm simply saying, Mister Davenport is it?"

"Yes."

"I'm simply saying, when everything is good and done, you all are going to pay me a good deal of money for something I've done, and the others have done. And you know what?"

"No sir."

"You can believe anything you want to, I don't give a good goddamn rip of Mormon ravioli what you believe, as long as I have the money in my hand your Prophet has promised."

"Yes, sir."

"Now write some of this down. I don't want to forget how everything is laid out. When we light the fuse — and son, you and I will do this — I want everything here to say, 'Goodbye, goddamnit. I've had a very nice time.'"

Chapter 45

THE PRESBYTERIAN CHURCH

It was late to be sure. But Alfred Helm was used to working the nighttime hours. The product of a New York dad and a Massachusetts mother, it was a given that he'd carry the Helm family's work ethic to the Utah Territory. When single-minded men and women carved the State of Nevada from it, he was one of the first to "step up," as his father used to encourage. He'd served the Silver State ever since, clerking its courts, chairing its committees, supervising the building of roads and dormitories, and as president and trustee of a couple of boards and agencies.

A few years after his wife Lydia died in 1867, he found a new wife, Flora, 26 years his junior. They had a child, Frank, and commercial interests — real estate, two hundred acres of mining claims, a couple of businesses. And they had the bills and debts to prove it.

"That's what Masons do," he murmured after letting himself in the back door of the Presbyterian Church's manse at Nevada and King Streets. "They stay up late. They get the job done. They do what other people should be doing, too."

The new pastor at the church wasn't expected until March, and while a series of supply ministers had kept the lights on and the spiritual flames burning ever since the Reverend Thomas Fraser took his leave in December of the year prior, there was the question of whether the church could use a little more money to build some possibilities for the next year.

Helm pushed a pile of papers, records of the church's subscriptions for the coming year, from on top of the minister's desk into a small leather pouch he'd brought with him. He'd update the congregation in the morning, though no one really expected to see that many people in church, given that it was the first day of the New Year. But pushing on when lesser people, or less committed people, quit or went to bed, was a mark of what it meant to be a member of Carson City Lodge #1. "Free and Accepted Masons, thank you," he often said as a way of measuring a young man's character if he was prospecting his interest. If they asked what the words meant — he wasn't supposed to invite a person to join, but saying interesting things about the lodge or Masonic order wasn't prohibited — he'd go on to share the lodge's motto, "Making good men better." If they simply smiled, he often talked about the church instead.

Helm looked around the room. He never quite understood why a minister would want to live in church-owned house. The manse was in pretty good shape, though they might want to tidy up the second story someday, particularly if the new minister was going to bring children. He moved over to a well-worn couch, looking toward Proctor Street, when he saw a shadow step into the bushes on the northeast section of the property.

It was a nice patch of land, a city block more or less.

The church was situated diagonally and east of the Methodist Church, whose devotees had begun meeting in Carson City a couple of years prior to any Presbyterians ever counting their sheep. Saint Peter's Episcopal Church sat a couple of blocks north. The Roman Catholic parish had a building one block east. And a local brewery — but no bar, thank God, what would the churches do with a bar so close by — was situated on the opposite corner one block south. While it wasn't entirely out of the ordinary to see people walking this far uptown so late at night, folks didn't generally stroll by the town's churches for fear that one of the pastors would get hold of them and subsequently delay them from a reasonable day's pleasure or business. Though Helm and his wife had made quite a few friends at the church, he'd made a good deal of money there as well.

Helm picked up an oil lamp from an occasional table next to the front door and pulled it open. "You over there," he shouted. "Get on with your business. You don't belong here."

It was never really clear to Helm or to the others gathered at the Presbyterian church who belonged or didn't. Not that they didn't keep roll. "As it is in heaven..." one of the last ministers had said, hoping to instill a little more order in a congregation that sometimes lacked order *and* ardor. "...so it should be on earth," he said. The remark had left a couple of people cold, as most of the pastor's sermons seemed more meddling than ministerial. And it was never good "to should" on people, particularly church people, who would sometimes bite back when least expected. Still, they'd made an effort since then— methodically crossing some people off the rolls for lack of attendance or contributions after a few years' time, but leaving others on hoping that they would someday come back. They'd kept Orion Clemens, Mark Twain's brother, on the roll, for instance. He'd left in 1866 after the death of his daughter Jennie and being unable to develop a successful law practice. Clemens had served as acting governor and secretary of the territory at one point, though he couldn't get elected to an office once Nevada became a state.

Helm had communicated with Twain once, or Samuel Clemens rather, asking him if he'd like to give a lecture in Carson City. He'd owned a downtown theater at that time, and Clemens had replied almost affectionately.

"Your kind and cordial invitation to lecture before my old friends in Carson has reached me, and I hasten to thank you gratefully for this generous recognition — this generous toleration, I should say — of one who has shamefully deserted the high office of Governor of the Third

House of Nevada and gone into the Missionary business,
thus leaving you to the mercy of scheming politicians."

The whole thing made him smile now, though he wondered then if it Clemens was poking fun at his commitments, his
being a government employee and all.

He looked again. The man was just standing there. A
tall man. Perhaps he thought himself invisible standing by the
sign that way. "You over there!" he shouted. "What are you
up to?" The man took off running like a flat-footed platypus,
not that Helm had ever seen one run, but that's how he imagined one would appear. "Come back here!" he yelled, though
he knew it wasn't a good idea for the man to stop, turn around
and head his direction, which is of course is exactly what the
flat-footed man who had been hiding in the shadows did —
right toward him.

Helm stood in the middle of the street, fumbling with a
wooden match, before giving up all hope that he'd get the lantern
lit in time. He'd simply use it as a cudgel or club, he figured. He
raised the unlit glass lantern high above his head. "Don't you be
running toward me! You get out of here," he shouted, though no
self-respecting Mason or businessman would want to be seen that
way. It looked too timid.

But the man didn't stop. At some point, maybe ten or fifteen feet away, he lowered his head, "like a bull," the Methodist
minister said, though why he was outside watching all of this is
anyone's guess. And plowing into 62-year old Alfred Helm, he
knocked him into a pretty nice pine tree that one day might grow
large enough to be the State Christmas tree, not that the state
needed one, but why not? Caught up in its branches, thinking it
looked a little bit like Jesus Christ hanging there that way, Helm
squeaked out the words, "See what you did! See what you did,"
he repeated, as if the sentiment should have some eternal sense, or

at least business significance, it being a Presbyterian church and all that.

The man smiled! Helm had never seen him before, and hoped to never see him again, his being so tall, flat-footed and all. He was dressed like a Douglas County Mormon, not that he'd ever met one but he'd been told how they dressed, and since everyone was so up in arms over their being upset with things not having gone their way. They shouldn't have left, Helm figured, in 1857 running back to Salt Lake to keep the government off their backs. They should have stayed, like most of the Protestants did, or Catholics or maybe Jews too, who got hold of things when the territory then a state was just beginning. They'd done quite well with that sort of commitment.

"You should have stayed," he shouted, thinking that might be the best thing he could say as he pried himself loose of the bushes and headed back inside. "That's what a Mason would have done," he said, before wondering if the man was a Mason given how he was running — and all, his hands up in front of himself like a bumper on a stagecoach or carriage — it being the universal distress call of Free Masons everywhere.

He pulled the Presbyterian manse door shut, put the back down on the table and gathered up his belongings. There would be a big meeting tomorrow at the church, not a large one but an important one. He could tell the story of the tall, flat-footed man as an allegory of the kind of danger the church was in if it didn't dig deep down. "If we aren't careful," he decided to say, "if we don't take care of the bats in our attic and decide who the bad guys really truly are in this world, we could end up moving in with the Methodists in their building. And wouldn't that be nice?"

Chapter 46

THE MISSION

"You don't think there's anyone out there, right?"

Slavin nodded his head up and down on his way out the back door. It was a practiced nod, like a child might give his parents if the child wanted to appear as if she was listening, which is of course where a much younger Ian Slavin had learned it a dozen or so years back when his mother and father began talking to him about law school. The regular "Yes, ma'am" soon became a set of responses, irrelevant to any specific content or conversation, particularly if his mind had drifted elsewhere, which is in fact where it was when he stumbled against the front door of Emma's house after looking around outside and found it unlocked instead of locked. He drew his gun, and slowly pushing the door open was surprised to see Emma standing in the living room with a Mormon missionary, a man in his early fifties.

"Emma, are you all right?" he asked.

When she nodded and smiled, he dropped his gun back into his holster. "Meet Mister Logan," she said. She gestured to a tall bearded man in a dark suit carrying his scriptures.

"Elder Logan, ma'am."

"Of course, Elder Logan. This is Mister Slavin. He's staying with us at the mission tonight."

"A little late, isn't it, elder?"

"It is, Mister Slavin. Miss Emma here was telling me that you're a Mormon. I don't believe I've seen you in church, sir."

"You have not. I've recently come from Elko and other parts in eastern Nevada. This is my first time in northern Nevada."

"And you are here on business?"

"I'm sorry, elder. I don't generally make it a point to discuss my business with people I don't know. Again, is there something we can help you with?"

"No sir, I was merely stopping back to speak to the directress here about coming by earlier. We didn't mean to spook the young man who was looking out for things in the stable."

"We, Elder Logan?"

"I'm sorry sir, my partner and I. He's gone on and I was about to when I saw Miss Emma here struggling with some packages. I had no idea there was someone staying with her, to help out that is."

"No, I imagine not."

"Well, my apologies again, Miss Emma. I'd like to stop back sometime and share with you the Restored Gospel, ma'am. Have you ever wondered where the Indians came from?"

"Oh, God..."

"I'm sorry, Mister Slavin. Did I say something inappropriate?"

Slavin shook his head "no," but the glare in his eyes made it clear that he didn't want to hear anything more of it. The thought that the American Indian was one of the lost tribes of Israel was "rubbish," his parents told him. And while his conversion to the Latter-day Saints involved a certain warmth and witness to the truth of their scriptures, he'd reserved judgment on those items that seemed strange or out of whack with how he'd been raised. He did not believe Joseph Smith's revelation, for instance, in 1831 that Saints should take multiple wives, in particular Lamanites and Nephites, which is to say native Americans. The revelation, a part of their scriptures suggesting that Indians might become "white, delightsome and just" by marrying into a lighter race. "Even now their females are more virtuous than the Gentiles," the prophecy said. It was simply wrong to assume that an individual might be this or that by virtue of their race, in his experience anyway.

"Elder Logan, I'm thinking it's way past our bedtimes here at the mission. And while Missus Nauman might be interested in the specifics of our religion, there might be a better time for that discussion."

"Ian's right, Mister Logan. When you and your friend come back, I'd like to share with you *our* faith as well." Logan looked confused. He looked first at Slavin, hoping to clarify her meaning, and then back at the mission's director. "I'm only saying that the best teaching, Mister Logan, is when both parties understand where the other party is coming from. Don't you think?"

"Elder Logan, ma'am. And certainly, I meant no disrespect."

"None taken, sir. I'll be happy to tell you the actual history of the peoples we serve here when you return."

"Their history, ma'am?"

"Well yes, Mister Logan."

"Elder Logan, ma'am."

"Of course. I'm sure you'll find it interesting to know that the Washoe people are quite different than the Paiutes and the Shoshone and the others who gather here. And they have so much to say."

"Yes, ma'am. Well, Mister Slavin," he paused, "or is it elder, sir?"

Slavin had never taken the ordinations of the church, nor had he received its temple endowments or blessings. He was a convert, and in his mind not a very good one at that. "It's simply Ian, *Mister* Logan."

Logan turned and headed toward the door, before turning around. "I'm sure we'll see each other again, sir. And Miss Emma, have a generous and holy night."

"Thank you, sir." She closed and locked the door behind him.

"Emma, I thought I had been clear."

"Oh, Ian. I could see that he wasn't armed. And it's cold outside!"

"Ma'am, it's cold inside as well. But that's no reason to invite a strange man to stand in your living room, particularly after you've heard from one of your stable boys that their afternoon visit was so extremely awkward. Am I right?"

Emma nodded. "You are, Ian. Forgive me. Now can I make you a cup of tea? I expect we'll be up much of the night, talking."

Slavin winced. "Ma'am, there's no need for you to stay up all night. I have this. And to be frank, I'd be much more comfortable knowing you were in the bedroom, behind a closed door than sitting out here with me waiting on what might come."

"What might come?" Slavin walked to the front door and locked it.

"Emma. That was an angry man who was standing here a few moments ago. And it was an armed man as well, if you saw the bulge in his pocket, which I imagine you did not. He was not your friend. He is not your spiritual teacher or counselor. But now he knows how many we are, and likely understands a bit more about the house than he did before. Please go to bed, bolt your door. And pretend that everything is okay. I'll make my rounds throughout the night. And I'll let you know if there's any cause for alarm."

"You're right, Ian. Good night."

"Good night, Missus Nauman. I'll wake you when Mister Ronin gets here."

"Oh, I'll be up way before he arrives."

"To be frank, Missus Nauman. I truly hope not."

Chapter 47

MEMORIES, DREAMS AND REFLECTIONS

Ian pulled the covers up over his head. He'd begun sleeping with a blanket covering his head since he was child. He even found the habit helpful as an adult, particularly on cold winter nights in the mining camps outside of the Lamoille Canyon and Elko. Warmer accommodations were fewer and farther between, particularly when he was drinking.

He pushed his left hand up underneath a sofa cushion and bunched the blanket into a tiny ball before pulling it around his shoulders. He'd sleep a half-hour or so then he'd get up and walk around. Every couple of hours he would check on the children and staff. That way he'd get a little bit of sleep.

Staying at the mission with Missus Nauman just didn't feel right. It wasn't that he was sleeping next to her. He had no interest in the woman, nor did she apparently have any in him. Neither cared about how it might appear to others. His discomfort didn't have anything to do with it being a mission of the Protestant Church, either — him being a Mormon in good standing, at least the last time he checked, which had been a while of course because he hadn't been in San Francisco for a couple of years. No, it was because he was living someone else's life — staying there, his rifle by his side, his handgun still on his hip but buried between the cushions of Emma's new leather sofa. "Cool in summer, warm in winter," she said when she handed him a pillow and blanket for the night.

Maybe Ronin was right. It was time for him to be moving on. And how had he agreed anyway to help his new friends with the unruly Saints in Genoa? They weren't his problem.

He rolled onto his back, until his gun and holster popped from beneath the middle cushion, sitting more appropriately at his side. He put his arm across his forehead. He'd be better prepared that way, his sleep lighter because his arm was draped unnaturally, for sleeping anyway. And he could get at his guns quicker, if necessary.

It wasn't as if he owed W. W. Ronin anything. Sure, Ronin had tried to help him with getting a job at the Depot Hotel in Elko, not that it had worked out. And he'd put in a good word for him in Virginia City, not that the Comstock was his kind of town, or towns rather — Gold Hill being the least attractive of the two, Silver City out of the question, a ghost of what could have been but now long past its prime. There was little chance he'd ever be a long-term resident of Nevada's gold and silver towns. And he wouldn't head back to Elko either, even if Jim Clark had a change of mind. The Depot days were over. Maybe these too, in cities piled along the eastern slope. Maybe it was time to head home, back to San Francisco after all.

"Ian, did you hear that?"

Emma's voice woke him. He'd been sleeping. "Hear what, ma'am?"

"The scratching outside my window. You didn't hear that?"

"No ma'am, but I'll be happy to check it out."

Slavin pushed himself up into a sitting position and pulled on his boots. Why anyone would buy a new couch that felt like an old couch — sort of frumpy-looking with cushions too soft to support a grown man's weight — was beyond him. *I'd rather sit on a bench*, he mused as he stood up, *though sleeping on a bench wouldn't be comfortable at all.*

He picked up his '73 Winchester and pulled a couple of cartridges from his belt, sliding the .44-40 cartridges down the rifle's tubular magazine. He checked his revolver — it was fine — and unlocked the front door. If anyone was outside, they'd surely hear the front lock turning and head for the weeds. Pushing the screen door open, he peeked both ways. *Nothing.*There was no point to his being there, when other men, more involved men like Ronin or Dustsucker, could do what he was doing. Maybe he'd head back to school after all.

"A sharpened mind is better than a sharpened sword," his father had said when he headed out the door to make his millions in the gold and silver mines of eastern Nevada.

"I'll be back," he told him. But he was unclear that he'd ever return. Maybe that's why his father said what he did, knowing he was choosing money over memory though he was certain he'd have an adventure or two heading to the American West.

"You just don't understand," he'd responded, though he suspected they did understand, having braved the Sierra Mountains themselves in the years after the initial gold rush when yellow and silver-colored nuggets were literally popping out of quick-running streams and rivers in the Sacramento Valley. Immigrants came from around the world — the Sandwich Islands, China and of course Mexico, Peru and the points in-between. Soon mining towns were everywhere, complete with shops, salons, saloons and other businesses, all hoping to cash in on the new economy. His parents had moved west for the same reason in 1849 — tired merchants seeking a new start, believers in the American dream of capitalizing on the extraordinary rush of people from literally everywhere. Their final destination, San Francisco, was in no small part the product of hundreds of thousands of people having the same dream — the opportunity for prosperity and success through hard work, by people just like him. "All men are created equal, endowed by the Creator with certain inalienable rights..."

The Comstock rush a few years later only complicated San Francisco's efforts to rise above the chaotic growth of America's most significant growth of people west of the Mississippi. "An

American Paris," his father said describing the city, which was probably the phrase that most led to his sleeping on a couch in the front room of the mission director's house.

Heading back to San Francisco — "never backward," Ronin said, "always forward," the bounty hunter insisted as it was impossible, he said, to recapture one's memories and dreams once they'd become a part of one's reflections — didn't seem a satisfactory option at all. *I have no future here,* he mused as he opened the door to enter the house.

He paused to look over his shoulder and thought he saw a movement by the front corral. The horses seemed nervous as well. *Manuel should have put them away for the night.* He walked in the front room and called quietly, "Emma, get up, would you? I'll leave my rifle here by the couch. Stay away from the window. I'll grab a shotgun from the rack in the kitchen. I'm going to check the barn."

"Be careful," she whispered as she opened the door, her robe wrapped loosely around her body, pushing against the plaid, woolen night dress in all the right places. She pulled tightly at the knot and smiled.

He averted his eyes and moved to the kitchen. He lifted a scattergun from the gun rack and breaking it open to see if it was loaded. He took a box of 12-gauge shells from the shelf beneath it and unbarred the kitchen door. "Lock this," he said quietly, stepping out onto the back porch. Crouching behind a pile wood, Slavin surveyed the barn before stepping onto the dirt. A couple of chickens moved noiselessly as he left the boards and looked up.

The barn door was unlatched.

He ran to the left side of the doors and looked north and south along the barn's entrance. The sliding wood door, rusted metal bands holding the barn door erect, left a small gap through which he was able to peek inside. *Nothing.*

It was 3 a.m., Sunday, January 1st, "in the year of our Lord 1882" — not that the Christ could be found so early in the morning at the American Gospel Mission just south of the capital city. Hell, he hadn't seen Jesus in years, even if he did come across in a boat, which of course he didn't. And no thinking Mormon ever said that, though it was just as difficult to believe that the savior of mankind simply appeared in the New World having left the Old World a dying and broken man, with nails in his hands, his legs crossed beneath him, the sagging weight of his body pushing down on his heart and lungs. "No man gets off a tree after being nailed there," his mother said, when he told her he was about to become a faithful man. "Converting?" she asked. "Converting to what?" she said, thinking he was going to become a Baptist or a Methodist, some heart-felt religion that didn't require thinking or brains. It would have been nice to have said that that he was going to join an Episcopal church or a Presbyterian church for that matter, where the intellect was respected and looked at as one of a myriad of ways the Divine presence in the world could be felt and ascertained. But no, he was going to become a Mormon, he said. She just sighed.

He pushed himself through the narrow opening of the doors and moved immediately to the left, where a small room stored the mission's saddles, harnesses and related items. He felt the door's handle, which was locked, and moved on to the first stall.

"That's far enough!" a voice called out. He immediately knelt down, and raising the shotgun, waddled like a duck into a second stall behind a pile of blankets.

"Who's there?" he called out.

"It's not your battle, brother," the voice replied.

Brother? "It is if you intend to harm the children," he said, breathlessly. "Leave now and I won't kill you." It was a bad imitation of his friend, W. W. Ronin, but it was what he would have said.

There was only laughter on the other side, from a couple of men. He pulled a hammer back on the shotgun.

"Brother, this is your last warning," the voice said.

He moved to a third stall and realized that they couldn't see him. Wherever they were, however many there were, they had said nothing. He waited. In the quietness of his own heart — which he found surprising, as he'd never heard the quiet in there before, having long since stopped praying and having never meditated on the scriptures or anything of meaning for that matter — he suddenly felt *fully* formed. The whole of *who* he was supposed to be. Saint or sinner, it didn't really matter. He was *where* he was supposed to be. Or at least he was fully there where he was, which was a good place to be, just inside the compound of the American Gospel Mission, an Indian school at the far end of Stewart Street where the street ran out, past the lumber mills and storage yards, where the weeds and brush began.

He waited, aware that his lack of visibility, having moved from the backlit entrance of the barn to stalls at other end of the barn, was his sharpest weapon. His mind was so much sharper than the 12-gauge shotgun he held at his shoulder, its range sufficient to knock a man down at 30 yards or more and leave him bleeding in the dirt.

A carriage blocked their view. They were apparently there on the bottom floor of the barn, not in the loft. There were two, he figured by the tittering back and forth between them. If there were more, they were disciplined men, and silent. He would kill them both, despite their religion. They were apostate anyway. And even if they were not — who was he to decide? Only the Prophet could call a man such a thing — they were dead men for thinking that the people he had come to love could be pried loose of the land of the living and sent to the place of everlasting judgment and dread.

He kept silent. To speak would give away his intent and location. He waited.

"Pilgrim, we have no issue with you ..."

"No issue at all," another voice said.

Elder Logan's voice.

Then both men stood, apparently secure in their belief that he was not where he was. Unaware that their prey had decided to become the hunter, they stood there and talked!

"Keep your gun up, Elder Logan," the one said to the other. "He's a Utah boy. He understands why we're here."

"Maybe, maybe not," Logan said, before putting a phosphorus match to a bundle of straw he held in his hands. The sudden strike of light allowed Slavin to take careful aim. He fired the scattergun beneath the wagon, skipping dirt and stones into the men standing on the other side. And while they stood there screaming — their holy hands covering their eyes, the flames falling helplessly to their feet — Slavin stood up and took aim again. "Death lays its hands upon those dear to us," he called out. "At times, death leaves us baffled. But truth comes as an angel of mercy!" Logan raised his arm, as if to shoot. Slavin pulled the hammer back on the second barrel and fired at the men just a few feet away, over the buckboard Emma liked to take to town to get the mission groceries. And the two men, likely men of faith but misbehaved and misled, fell dead on their feet, their pants and jackets now burning.

Slavin walked a few steps and extinguished the flames with his boots. It was the first time he'd ever stomped on a man, living or dead. And while it wasn't his pleasure — violence should be met by the rule of law, not by brigands in their own right hoping to make things right or to keep the wrongful doings of even darker men in check — it was his duty. He did it, rejoicing that he had been faithful enough to do what was needed to protect those whom he loved.

"Ian?" Emma called out.

"Yes, Emma."

"Are you safe?" she asked.

"I am, ma'am. We are safe — the children, too."

"Come in then, out of the cold, Ian. Those that you've chased away or killed in service to the Christ will have to wait until morning. Tonight, I want us to give thanks."

"Yes, ma'am."

Chapter 48
THE EPISCOPAL
CHURCH

"I'm on my way to the mission, reverend, but I thought I'd stop by."

The Reverend George R. Davis paused alongside the front doors of the Saint Peter's Episcopal Church with a yellow paint chip in his hand. "What do you think?" he asked.

"I think it looks like the color you already have on the building, reverend. Doing some touch-up work?"

Davis reached for his pants pockets and pulled them inside out. "Not me," he said, wagging his pockets like they were bird wings, "not a brush on me! But W. D. Cotterell is coming by in a couple of minutes to take a look at things. Some of the women think it's time to paint again and I'm not one to stand in their way." He zigged and zagged — a little to the left then a little to the right, and then began laughing.

"No, I imagine not. I never thought it a safe place to be, standing in the way of women, particularly in the church," Ronin said. "What do you call that color, anyway?"

"Man at the store said, 'drab yellow.' Can you believe it?"

"Really?"

"Yup," he nodded, placing it alongside a much darker brown trim.

"Well, it's a nice color, I guess."

"Same color as before, so I imagine it's a safe one." He put the paint chip in his vest pocket and turned. "Ronin, what do you hear about the Mormons in Genoa? Are things settling down?"

The detective smiled. He'd made it a point to get acquainted with the clergy in town, given the inclination of some folks — both good and bad — to confess their sins and to seek absolution. He'd sat inside Davis' sanctuary from time to time, though never on a Sunday and never to listen to a priest. Being there was good enough. And going there every couple of weeks when he had something to think about, or simply needed some quiet, had worked itself into a reasonable friendship between the two men, though they had yet to grab a beer or talk about the women in their lives or share anything truly intimate.

"George, who knows? Fact is, the whole thing might blow over. I mean Orson Hyde's curse has been around for… well, it'd be 20 years this year, I suspect. And not a whole hell of a lot has happened because of it, not from what I can tell." The reverend looked at him sort of peculiar-like, his head cocked to one side. "Did I say something wrong?" he asked tentatively.

"Huh?" The priest looked up and shook his head. "No, no. I was just thinking. It's been a difficult couple of years, William."

"It has."

"I mean with the paying off of the church's debt, and the general depression about these parts. As the mines go, so go the offering plates. You know, it'd be a horrible thing if more suffering is coming everybody's way, wouldn't it be?"

"I'm not a fan."

"Exactly, I mean I get that tough times sometimes make tougher people." He shook his head and then began to smile. "You know what the good book says…"

"Yes," Ronin replied, knowing that the reverend was going to tell him anyway.

"Make every effort to add to your faith goodness; and to goodness, knowledge; and to knowledge, self-control; and to self-control, perseverance; and to perseverance …"

"Reverend?"

Davis sputtered to a stop. "Yes, Mister Ronin?"

"Where are we going with this?"

"I'm sorry, Ronin. I get all excited when I think about what good people can do when times get tough. People get better, don't you think? I was just about to say, this paint doesn't matter a whole hell of a lot..."

"Reverend!" Ronin feigned surprise. No one had a more expressive verbal palate than he did. And it didn't take the Pinkertons or the war to encourage its full expression. The church had done that.

"Well, it doesn't, William. And those men who came by this morning, wondering if I could make a tithe toward their cause ..."

"A tithe, Reverend? The *church* make a tithe?"

"Yes, didn't I tell you? Mormons, from down in Genoa, I think. Or maybe it was Washoe? I don't remember. Anyway, they asked if the *church* might be willing to make a financial contribution toward their "Get Right with God" fund. Well, I thought, that's an odd name. I mean with all the fundraising we've done here at the church recently. I've baptized maybe 60 people over the last couple of years, performed a good number of marriages and maybe twice as many funerals. Of course we paid off that debt. What was that, $3,000? Well, it all goes to the bottom line, of course. And they were just wondering with everything going so well..."

"Reverend!"

"Yes, William?"

"What's your point?"

"Well, I was just saying, with everything going so well, they were wondering if we weren't able to help a few people out."

Ronin's left eye squinted. His cheek began to burn, a facial tick he had come to regard as a sort of internal witness that things didn't sound right. "That's sort of odd, don't you think?" he asked. "Mormons?"

"I sure did, and I told them so. Their campaign theme, for instance — 'Get Right with God?' I told them it sounded kind of Baptist, that I'd never heard a Latter-day Saint use such words."

"And they said?"

"Well, they laughed — an odd couple of cowboys, too, not your normal couple of Saints, no suits or anything like that." The priest raised his chin. "And they weren't carrying their scriptures, either. In fact, they were wearing guns. Don't you think that's odd, William? I know I do. So I told them, I shared with them the same verse from 2nd Peter, chapter 1."

"The one you were just quoting from."

"Make every effort to add to your faith goodness; and to goodness, knowledge..."

"Reverend."

"Sorry. And you know what? Now that I think about it, they laughed. Laughed! They said they were going to add to their faith a good number of things, though goodness might not be a part of it, nor self-control. And that they were doing evangelistic work, they said. Gosh, you know the more I tell you about it, the more concerned I get."

"Well, I don't blame you, George. The whole thing sounds strange. Did they say anything else?"

The Reverend George Davis thought for a few moments and then hesitated. "William, you know they did. I didn't think anything of it when they said it. But now I'm wondering."

"Wondering what?"

"What they meant when they said the 'Get Right with God' evangelistic campaign was going to begin tomorrow night."

Chapter 49

BREAKFAST AT THE MISSION

"William is going to be real impressed with these berries, don't you think?" Emma pulled an apron around her middle and walked over to the shelves above her counter to get a can of berries. "Have you seen one of these?" she asked.

"No ma'am, I haven't," Slavin said, rubbing the morning salt from his eyes. "Guess I've been out in the woods too long, ma'am..."

"...not to speak of the deserts and near-ghost towns you've been frequenting."

"Well, sure Miss Emma. But those are where the tailings are, and it doesn't take much to find a little metal for one's pockets in those places. My dad always said, you've got to work hard for the things of this world. The deeper things come a little easier."

"That's a sweet thing to say. And by deeper, he meant..."

"Well, he wasn't a religious man, as I said last night. But he was a thoughtful man, given to what was most valuable."

"And that is, Mister Slavin?"

"Relationships, of course."

"Yes, of course," she said, setting the can down on the table and turning to show her guest the device she had in her hand. "This claw-shaped piece of metal is a can opener, Mister Slavin. Invented in 1855 by Robert Yeates, an English cutlery maker."

"Well, I guess I have seen something like that, though it had a bull's head on it."

"With the Bully beef cans, right?"

"Exactly."

"Well, I just saying, I bet Mister Ronin hasn't seen a can of blueberries in some time. The syrup is simply divine, Mister Slavin. Would you like to taste some?" She began to whittle her way around the can with the wooden-handled opener until Slavin stopped her. His hand rested briefly on top of hers. She looked up.

"Let me, ma'am. A woman's work doesn't have to be dangerous. And there ain't no rules about a man sharing in it, I always say."

"You do, do you?" Emma blushed, as she pulled her hand away to her side and wiped it dry of blueberry juice.

"I do, Miss Emma. May I call you that?"

"You may, Mister Slavin. May I call you Ian?"

"You may, Miss Emma." He blushed. "I mean, Emma." He pierced the top of the can with the opener's point and levered it so as to tear the can's top. Emma reached forward with a spoon and took a little bit.

"You first, ma'am," he said.

"If you insist." She raised the dark, thick, sugary liquid to her lips and tasted it. "Delightful, Ian." She returned the spoon to the can and then raised it to his lips. He took hold of her hand, to steady it, and was careful not to look in her eyes.

"Delicious is right. Ronin is definitely going to enjoy this."

"He certainly will," she said, putting the spoon down. "I believe that's him at the front door now."

Ronin pulled his coat tight around his neck, and waited with his hands in his pockets. He'd stopped letting himself in when Emma and him had a falling out. And while he figured she might want him to act a little more familiar toward her and the house, he was trying to keep an appropriate distance. He knocked again, then tried the latch and finding it locked, nodded.

"Well, William, you're a little later than I thought you might be. Ian and I have already gotten started. I think you'll be pleased."

"Ian?" he asked. The tone sounded friendlier than he remembered the two of them being.

"Yes, William. You asked him to stay last night."

"Of course." He let himself into the front room and unbuttoned his coat. He kept his gun belt on. A single Colt revolver hung at his right side. He'd left the other one with a gunsmith at the hotel.

"How about some coffee?" Slavin said, walking into the front room from the kitchen.

"I don't mind if I do," Ronin answered, reaching for the cup in Slavin's hand.

"No, that's mine," he said. "Let me get you one. Maybe the two of you can visit while I pour you a cup."

"Visit?"

"Ian found a couple of men out in the barn. One of them, or both of them, I don't know, was here earlier in the day."

"And?"

"And what?"

"And what happened?"

"He killed them, William." She leaned into his arms. He hesitated, but folded them around her and patted her back.

"I'm sorry. I'm glad he was here." He pushed away from Emma and looked over her shoulder where Slavin was standing. "You okay?"

Slavin nodded, smiled and handed him his coffee. "It was damnedest thing, Ronin ..."

Emma looked up.

"Darnedest. I'm sorry, ma'am. Seeing them there, hearing them talking about the mission and the children and torching the barn, set a fire within me. It's like I've changed."

"Few of us remain the same after seeing the elephant, Ian."

"Well sure, but I'm talking about something more. It's as if I know what I want to do, Ronin. There's no more running around, chasing after women and money and ..."

Emma looked over.

"I'm sorry ma'am. I'm just trying to express myself."

"Of course you are, Ian. I didn't mean to look at you that way..."

"Yes, ma'am. William, I think I know what I want to do with my life. I don't want to dig for silver. I don't want to pan for gold. And I don't want to go back to school."

"No?" Emma and Ronin responded simultaneously. Ronin deferred.

"What do you want to do, Ian?"

"I want to remain here, Miss Emma. I mean, if you'll have me." He looked at Emma and then Ronin, who was smiling.

"And you want to do what, son?"

"I want to teach and protect the children, sir. I mean if it's appropriate. I didn't make a whole lot of sense of my life growing up, William. I squandered a good many moments, not listening to my parents and chasing after the wind..."

"Ecclesiastes," Ronin said.

"Yes, sir."

"And you're done doing that."

"Exactly."

"And you think you could be helpful teaching Indian children?" The Mormon experience missionizing the Indians along the Sierra had been disappointing at best, not that they had done much better with settlers, either.

"If you all will have me."

"It's not up to me, Ian..." Ronin began to stutter and looked over at Emma, who had her head down, her hands folded and seemed as if she was blushing. "Emma?"

"It's an answer to prayer, William, so many prayers. Ian, we'll work this out," she said, putting her hand on his shoulder.

There was perhaps an eight-year difference between them, enough that both wondered what the touch actually meant. "Let's settle this Mormon thing first."

"The uprising?" Ian asked.

"No, sir," Ronin responded.

"The bodies in the barn," they said together, Ronin and his Emma, smiling as if they had finally worked things out. Each of them now knew where they stood. They were friends and would likely never be anything more, which was fine, because there was no need for them to be anything more.

There would be a man at the mission again. A good man, not the man Henry Nauman pretended to be, or wanted to be but was never able to be. Nor Ronin, either, who would have been the right man for the job, had he been the right man, his inner commitment to helping people being that much more. Neither one of them was right for the American Gospel Mission, neither Henry nor William, not in any permanent sense. And Emma knew that, more or less, though it was often less but not for want of asking for more.

They'd work it out, Emma figured, whatever needed to be worked out, he and she and all the others that still needed to be dealt with, in Genoa and Carson City and God knows where else, because they hadn't heard from Henry in some time and he still had a say in such matters, still being Emma's husband and all. They'd work it out — all of them, each of them — and it would be fine, more or less, which is the situation of folks everywhere. More or less, life is never right on.

Chapter 50

WAITING ON A TRAIN

Henry Nauman brushed the dirt from his pants and headed toward the train platform. It didn't matter that there wouldn't be another coach to Reno until the next morning. Fact is, he was happy to sit there, as long as sitting there meant having no further contact with the malefactors and miscreants that had plagued him since he'd arrived in Carson City.

It was Henry's intention to visit with some of the women who had brought him pleasure when he lived in northern Nevada. There was Ally, of course, and Emma, though he wasn't at all sure that he would be well received there, and nameless others that lived in some of the homes and hotels along Ormsby Street. "Pick one and move on when finished," he told young Gillom Rogers, when he'd arrived in the city via Missus Rogers' supply wagon. Gillom had been kind, though a little misled, not that he could blame the boy given that he still lived with his mother, whom he'd had the non-pleasure of meeting a couple of years back while calling on area businesses for a contribution to the mission just south of town.

"I can read you like a book," Bond Rogers had said, though the whole pretense of her being smarter than him seemed a little unbelievable.

"Then what am I saying?" he asked her in return. And she'd punched him in the nose, not that he didn't deserve it because in fact he did, if she could read his mind that is.

Gillom might make a man of himself yet, he thought as he ran a handkerchief across the top of his shoes. He should have worn boots. He'd forgotten how dusty the capital city streets were, and hadn't really decided to take a train south to Carson City until he'd started feeling sort of randy. Waiting until Salt Lake wasn't likely to meet his needs. "A bird-in-hand is better than Mormon bush any day," he told the young man who missed most of the double entendre until Nauman's smile sort of gave it away. "Let's go make friends," he told the boy. That simple phrase — meant only to strengthen the boy's resolve to live like a man instead of a mouse dominated by a woman who wouldn't stop being his mother even if it hurt the poor son of a bitch — had turned out to be among the worse decisions he'd ever made in Carson City, short of selling a few Indian children, that is.

They took to the adventure like hungry men after a Basque picnic — steak and beans and fish and lamb and rolls and just about everything else in the Basque family larder — waiting for them right there on Ormsby Street curbside. But some folks had recognized him and taken umbrage to his moving in on their gals — a gift his absence had already made, and now he was trying to take them back. So they had taken to beating him — his head, his belly, his private areas, wherever they could reach — until he and the boy moved to a safer place on Carson Street, where his old friend Jack had put together a new saloon with "a kinder and gentler clientele," Jack had assured them until the first Indian popped him one, right in the kisser. *In the kisser! Jesus Christ, where will it end?*

So he punched him back, the "big old dumb Indian," he said when he hauled off and hit him, something he'd normally not have done had he not been hurting so from all the rejection he and the boy had experienced earlier that evening. "Pick one and move on" had turned into "wish you had one so why not just shoot yourself in the head right now because you're so damned unlucky." But the boy didn't need to hear that, so he had kept on persevering until he'd hit on the damn Indian's wife. And how was he supposed to know? A medicine man, he was later told, who was enjoying a half-dozen women there. Not really, though it seemed like that compared to his entertaining exactly zero women at the time.

If it hadn't been for Jack yelling "Hands," or some similar thing, the tall Indian man in a hat would have taken his head off with that shiny new Remington revolver he had tucked in the front of his pants. He was using it as a hammer, of course, given that it was unloaded, or so he discovered when Gillom was able to get hold of it to ask the Washoe man to take a step toward the doorway to allow his friend to recover. The Indian stood there smiling — would the insults ever end? — saying something about knowing who he was and that there were a couple of men looking for him, which was fine until Mister Hands didn't seem so happy and mentioned the name "Ronin." Right then and there he decided to leave town.

Henry Nauman unfolded a newspaper on a bench outside the train station and was surprised to read that the Mormons in Genoa were upset with something. Emma had been fond of those folks, he mused as he paged ahead to see if there was anything in Placerville that might interest a man of his abilities. And not seeing anything, decided he'd go to Salt Lake City after all, even if the girls were virgins and interested in staying that way until they met a man who could give them their heavenly names, the name their husbands would call them on the day of resurrection when Christ would come back for those who'd stayed righteous in the midst of mounting moral sins and opportunities. Hell, by the time a man turned 40, he had some stories to tell!

He reached for his shoes. There was more cow shit in Nevada's capital city than anyone could explain. He unfolded his handkerchief and watched a train pull slowly out of the station. He'd be a happy guy if all he did was get out of this place, and maybe find some fresh strawberry jam, and a job writing for a newspaper, maybe, or explaining things to young children, or helping someone else's business get back on its feet. He had so much to offer and the world was just waiting for him.

Chapter 51

DOWN TWO

Horace Brown ran breathlessly into the house just as the Elder was getting up from his morning prayers. An open *Book of Mormon* sat before him, where he'd been reviewing the battles of the Lamanites and the Nephites, ancient peoples mentioned in the *Book of Mormon*.

"You know about these people?" Hickman said with unusual enthusiasm, as it was only five o'clock in the morning and he was in the midst of his morning devotions.

"I do not, Elder Hickman..." Brown said, placing a hand on one of the kitchen chairs so as to catch his breath. The old man continued.

"Well, the Lamanites were a wrong-hearted people. For their sins, the Lord turned their skins dark, 'so that they would not be enticing to the Nephites,' according to *2 Nephi 5:21*. The Nephites, on the other hand, were descended from the ancient Israelites, or Jews. They were light skinned and more righteous."

"Why does everyone assume dark-skinned people are bad?" Brown asked, who had been teased many times because his own complexion was darker than many people thought it should be. "I used to be a farmer," Brown liked to say, though he'd never really seen a farm, save to knock on the door of a rural ranch house from time to time and demand money.

"I don't know, Horace. But that's not my point..."

"Please continue," he said, though what he wanted to say was "stop," so that he could speak to him about the night's tragedies — two of their men, dead at the mission.

"Well, the Lamanites were at war with the Nephites, for I don't know, say hundreds of years. They ultimately prevailed, sadly. You know, sometimes evil is stronger than good."

"Yes, sir. I imagine," Brown replied, not really caring about the bad or the good, and being a new convert, not really understanding if the Prophet's words were important. "I do have something to..."

"You probably don't know why I'm reading this chapter, do you?" the old Danite continued, sitting up straight in his seat, a worn and rusty Patterson revolver by his side.

"I do not," he said, though what he was really thinking was that he didn't care about the Lamanites and the Nephites, or the Jaredites or the What-have-you-ites. He wanted to say, "Something awful has happened."

"I'm reading this chapter because in it we find the moral backing for what we're about to do, Mister Brown. Take verse 14 for instance..."

"Sir?" he said, trying to settle himself down. Religious people could be so aggravating. He remembered how his mother used to make him go to a Methodist Sunday School when he was growing up in Iowa, "Because it will do you good," she said, though he usually spent his collection plate money on candy at a small shop he and his brothers had found along the railroad tracks. She was always quoting chapters and verses.

"Well listen," the Elder said. "'Now the Nephites were taught to defend themselves against their enemies, even to the shedding of blood if it were necessary. Yea, and they were also taught never to give an offense, yea and never to raise the sword except it were against an enemy, so as to preserve their lives.' The *Book of Alma*, chapter 48, verse 14."

"That's very interesting, sir. I need to say..."

"So what do you think of that, Mister Brown?" Hickman asked.

The sinner turned Saint, but still very much his own man, had learned to answer, "Well, I think that sounds marvelous!" when he didn't understand what the Elder and Revelator of the church was saying. It would take some time for him to catch up to the others, he figured, given that they'd been studying the Mormon scripture books for years, dozens of years more than he had. Most of his religious training had taken place in a small Iowa German candy shop, near the children's home that had burned to the ground a couple of times. He and his brothers had nothing to do with it, not that he knew anyway.

"In the end Horace, the Nephites don't make it…"

"They don't make it?" he asked. None of the children at the Iowa Soldiers' Children's Home had perished in the fires, not that he could remember.

"They died, like good people everywhere, son. Some of our number will likely die as well."

Horace Brown swallowed hard. There was no questioning that he was a tough guy, what with wearing all black clothes and making sure his hat was generally down over his eyes. And he was fast with a gun, though the conscience thing was sort of new to him. He'd told the Prophet a couple of days before that he was having troubles, given that so much of his old life — carousing and thieving and the sort was now over — but so much of it was still needed, like shooting and beating and murdering and so on. "Yes sir," he replied, pushing his other thoughts aside. "Sir, I need to talk to you."

"I'm just saying Horace, lighter-skinned, lovely and righteous in every way, the Nephites did not prevail. They were descended from the ancient Israelites, you know. They traveled from the Holy Land to the New World by boat, over 1,200 years ago. Isn't that amazing?"

"Elder Hickman…"

"Yes, son?"

"This is all very interesting, sir. And I am most appreciative that you've taken the time to teach me all of this. Except that I need to say a couple of our men — Logan and I don't remember the other man's name, but he was smaller and maybe just as faithful — were killed last night at the American Gospel Mission, just south of town. They were in the barn..."

"I know where it is!" The Prophet's temper flashed. "Goddamn it!"

"Sir?"

"I'm sorry, Horace. Those two were good men. Their wives and children will surely suffer."

"Yes, sir."

"You know Logan was one of the first settlers in these parts. Jesus..."

"I'm sorry, Mister Hickman. I should have protected them. I was nearby, but preoccupied with everything else that was going on..."

"We are surrounded, my friend. Not just by great evils, but by great opportunities. Huge dangers linger ahead for all of us." Hickman paused for a moment, then put his left hand on the Mormon scriptures before taking a deep breath. "Have you claimed their bodies?" he asked. He picked up the gun with his right hand and shoved it beneath his belt.

"I... I don't know how to do that, Elder Hickman. There are others at the mission, now. And we are at war, are we not?"

Hickman frowned. "It's begun, Mister Brown. And we will not lose this battle. God's good people will prevail in this valley. We will not bargain. We will not carp or complain. We will do everything that is necessary for the truly righteous people in this world to finally get what is coming to them — blessings, son. Keeping the commandments, resisting iniquity, the very powers of hell will be shaken!" Hickman closed the *Book of Mormon* and began tapping on its cover with his index finger. "Burn the mission to the ground, son, and bring back those Saints. Talk to Mister Jones when he comes here, and see if he doesn't have a couple of hard men he can send. The Saints will remain here. Until then, gather the others..."

"The others, sir?"

"In the front room, Horace, our Mormon friends and neighbors. There's no reason to wait for everyone to arrive. It's time to go to war. And it's time for us to pray."

Chapter 52

THE HOTEL

Bear Claw hadn't noticed any difference in the *Morning Appeal* after Nellie Mighels hired Samuel Post Davis from the Virginia Chronicle. He'd been a reasonable writer before, and despite his sometimes irreverent leanings, hadn't yet embarrassed himself as the *Appeal's* editor.

What he didn't expect was Nellie's wedding to the man, a year after her husband's death, not that he held any judgment in the matter. The single life was nothing to be aspired toward — it was sometimes lonely and many times difficult. It was just that Davis' assumption of duties at the *Appeal* hadn't included blocking him from any romantic discourse with the woman.

He hadn't even spoken to her, save for a couple of words about her covering the legislature a few years prior. "It's not the right place for a woman to be," he'd said, meaning that if she had been his gal he'd not have had her working so hard, what with the ranch and the newspaper, and then her husband Henry, a former Speaker of the House, getting sick and all. The words hadn't come out right, and now with Davis firmly moved in, there was little chance he'd ever get Nellie's attention. She was from Maine and he was from nowhere, and besides, they were talking about children and she already had a passel of them with her former spouse. It wasn't like he needed all those ankle-biters hanging around.

"Bob?"

"Yes, Mister Goodwin?" Shaking his head, he folded the newspaper neatly before putting it under his arm and standing. He walked slowly over to the Ormsby House's front desk.

"I was simply going to ask if you were going to work today, Bob? Or if you were planning on sitting in the hotel lobby the rest of the day reading one of our newspapers?"

Victor Goodwin could be a real pain in the ass. He'd only been sitting there a couple of minutes. He hadn't even read the headlines yet, and besides, it was January already. The holiday rush was over. There wasn't going to be a whole lot of people checking in. And it wasn't his job anyway, helping folks with their luggage and all. He ran his sleeve over his new silver-colored guard badge, which had replaced the tin Pinkerton badge he had been wearing for lack of any other special designation. It was a gift from his new friends, Marcus T. Slade and William Washington Ronin. He looked up.

"Did I miss something, Mister Goodwin? I thought it was good moment to set myself down and take a load off."

"And it's quite a load, Bob."

Bear Claw winced. He'd hurt people for a lot less.

"But that's not why I'm asking. There's a man looking around out front, who I notice has been there since the wee hours of the morning, and I'm wondering if you would shoo him away?"

"Of course, sir."

For a big man, Robert Bear Claw moved fairly quickly. He pushed the newspaper across the desk and smiled and was out on the street before Goodwin could say thank you or sorry, not that he would have said either. "It's a big shadow," a slack-jawed gentleman had remarked a couple of afternoons prior when there'd been practically no sun on the west side, and no gas lamp inside or out was that well lit yet. So he punched the man, which didn't go over with Goodwin, the hotel's reputation and all. Then there was the issue of the broken table on which the man had finally come to rest.

Bear Claw stepped into the street and came face to face with Charlie Jones.

It barely looked like him, what with the full beard and a good thirty or forty pounds of new weight. And he wasn't at all sure it was him until Charlie opened his mouth and said his name. "Bob," he said, before Charlie's fist came crashing into the side of his head.

Neither of them had been friends previously, but Charlie and him had had a beer or two before his heading off to prison. He knew he recognized him. Bob had signed up for the posse out of Benton Hot Springs in 1871 or '72, he couldn't remember which year it was, when six of the 29 men were hiding up near Convict Lake, though it wasn't called that then. A shop owner named Robert Morrison was killed there. A good man, he was almost married in fact. Now there was a mountain named after him, not that that made up for things. And the Paiute Indian guide Mono Jim was killed up there as well. And he was thinking of all of that when the hairy man's fist hit him in the side of the head, which was probably a fair turn given that he had belted that other guy in the face for doing nothing more than commenting on his weight.

Bear Claw went down on one knee and was feeling pretty poorly about things, the two of them still in the street, when Deputy Marcus T. Slade came running south on Carson Street. "Hey," he was saying when Jones, who didn't know the deputy but recognized the star, began to sprint toward a horse tied up on 3rd Street. By the time Slade arrived to help him up on his feet, Jones was practically out of town, having dodged a couple of children playing outside the St. Charles Hotel a block south.

"Jesus, Bob. You okay? What was that about?" Slade asked, holding his chest to catch his breath.

"That was Charles Jones."

"Seriously? *The* Charles Jones?"

Bear Claw nodded.

"I thought he was long gone from these parts," Slade said, "in California or somewhere." Bear Claw stood up and was rubbing his head when W. W. Ronin came along.

"Bobby."

"Ronin," he replied, blushing.

"Bear Claw took a couple of punches to the head, Ronin," Dustsucker offered.

"Just one, from Charlie Jones, if that don't beat all."

"You sure about that?" He looked over at his friend Dustsucker, who looked at Bear Claw who nodded at Ronin. "You recognized him?"

"I did."

"Hell, Bob. We're going to have to get that Pinkerton badge back if what you're saying is true. Catch him, and we'll both be making a bundle of money."

"Well, I don't know anything about that. But what I do know is that he was standing in front of me a couple of minutes ago. He said my name and then punched me in the head."

"I read in the paper a couple of years ago that he died in a sheep camp near Visalia." Dustsucker said.

"Or Fish Lake Valley," Ronin offered. "Slade, he's a dead man walking. He's been seen just about everywhere."

"Boys, I'm telling you. Charlie Jones was standing in front of me, as sure I am standing in front of you."

The ex-priest smiled. "Well, if that murdering son of a bitch is in Carson City, it's not going to be good for anyone."

Chapter 53

SOUTHBOUND

Jones rode south, along the edge of the Sierra chain. At the lip of Ash Canyon, just north of the timber yards, he stopped and looked back to see if anyone was following. Not seeing anyone, he got off his horse to take a leak.

"That I didn't need," he murmured as he struggled with the buttons on his fly. A long, hot stream sizzled at the base of a small piece of sage next to a solitary pine tree. He stood there a few minutes — his feet wide apart, a Henry rifle leaning up against his side — thinking about the morning's reconnaissance. The V & T roundhouse would be easy, though it would take some wire to make it all come down. And the hotel — hell, that would be easy too. The whole job would be over in a day or two. Then he'd have enough in his saddlebag to head south again or north, or maybe east toward Wells.

Jones had seen a lot of risk in the last few years, after breaking free of the state penitentiary, where they'd eaten a lot of meat and potatoes. Every other day or so they were given stewed peaches, sometimes baked beans. The food had been good, though it wasn't his Ohio momma's cooking. Still, it beat the Union army's chow by a wide berth.

"I'm not headed back, for anything," he said out loud while shaking himself dry. The horse looked at him. He stared back until the horse looked away. He fastened the final button on his fly. They hadn't previously met, the horse and he, not that it mattered. He'd always taken what he needed and ridden what he wanted, including the woman he'd had relations with during the 1871 escape. "It's been a long time," he said to one of the men who had joined him in the violent act, though he had insisted on going first.

Jones had been standing opposite the Ormsby House Hotel for a couple of hours when his old friend Bob Bear Claw ambled outside all curious about what someone was doing just standing there looking at the hotel's front façade and balcony. Not that it was any of Bear Claw's business of course, it still being America and what the hell — when was it against the law to linger against a post anyway?

He'd gained a few pounds over the years, even grown a mustache so that he looked sort of silver-hungry, though no one close enough to look in his eyes would have taken him for a prospector. He was surprised Bear Claw recognized him. He'd never been an *early* drinker, but he *was* thirsty and the original owner of the bottle didn't seem interested in arguing about it when he'd offered the little weasel the back of his hand. Maybe it was the morning bottle of beer that had drawn his friend's attention.

Charles Jones had been a good boy all his life, or rather up until he plunged a long knife into a man's chest during an argument when he worked for a California livery. "Mutual combat," his boss had said, "You needed to defend yourself," he swore he'd testify, though the thought of going to court didn't sit well with either of them, and a judge had also witnessed the act. California hadn't been the answer to everything, but it had given him plenty of work when the war was over, and connections there had helped him escape when the sheriff's posse had driven him up and over the Sierra into the area around Visalia, where he was thinking of seeing the giant sequoia trees that grew south of there. He'd had a subsequent tussle with a man who had caught up to him by the San Joaquin River, and actually had to draw down on the man. He wasn't the quickest with a gun, though he did like his Henry and blew quite a few holes through him that way. The other man died there. Maybe he'd head for California again.

He took a sip from the dusty brown bottle and turned it to look at the label. *Carson Brewing.* It'd be the last time he'd be able to show his face in the capital city, in the daytime anyway, unless he killed the two of them — his former friend and that fat deputy who had come to Bear Claw's aid.

"Let's go," he said, mounting the tiny beast he'd stolen from the post on 4th Street and kicking its flank. The horse stuttered for a moment and then began to trot.

He'd made a reasonable living in Genoa, where he assisted a blacksmith and generally stayed away from folks except for his once-a-week jaunt up to Jack's bar with a few of his buddies. "You've got quite a knack with horses," the Elder had said a few years back, dropping by the forge to repair a bridle or something.

"Joseph," his employer said, "this is Mister Hickman." He turned to face the man. "Hickman's got a ranch near here, and might someday be your employer," he said, though his name wasn't Joseph but it was a reasonable name to offer folks if he feared they might ask, "Charlie who?" or "Charlie what?" Charlie Jones was a well-remembered name in those parts, even by those who didn't know him.

He offered his hand. And while he wasn't generally impressed with religious folk, Mormons even less than Methodists, Hickman seemed to have unusually clear eyes for an old man. "I wouldn't mind that at all," he said, smiling, though he didn't know how he really felt, him being a Mormon and all. *Funny to actually be working for him,* he mused as he started down the road to Jack's Valley. He kept a ways west of the road, which was his habit over the years he'd lived in northern Nevada. He'd kept to himself except when he was with the others, the few men he'd come to trust who were now in Hickman's employ as well.

He pulled a black kerchief up around his mouth, as the morning air was cold and moist. He kicked the horse into a gallop.

- 245 -

He'd report in over breakfast. "I'm hoping there's food left. How 'bout you?" he asked the horse. And he'd meet with Horace Brown, Hickman's man who was ramrodding the campaign, to see who else was on the list before they began blowing things up and killing folks for no good reason. "Any day now, you nag!" he yelled over the wind that was whipping snow up the valley, not a lot but enough to make him nervous. If it got any wetter, they'd have to trim the fuses, and folks would have to be a lot closer to their victims than the Elder said they'd want to be, given that they were religious and all.

"Holy hands," he complained, or something like that before adding, "it won't matter I guess if you can't see their faces," though it *had* mattered, to him anyway, plenty of times, fighting for the Union Army and then later. Hell, he'd even begun to enjoy looking in the faces of the men he was killing.

"Eye to eye, the Good Book says," Jones told Hickman, before he watched Hickman laugh. He said he'd misunderstood the scriptures, though the meaning was pretty much the same, he explained.

"An eye *for* an eye is how it actually reads," Hickman corrected, though it didn't matter any to him. Jones would just as much poke people with a large knife and twist it until blood came out than see their insides blown all over the streets and sidewalks. It was more personal that way.

Chapter 54

BREAKFAST IN GENOA

The group had finished their prayers and begun to fix breakfast when Jones dropped onto the porch, leaping onto the boards leading up to Hickman's crimson-colored front door. An athletic man, Charlie was rarely shy about making such entrances, though he typically didn't show off in town. Some folks remembered him as a much younger man who used to drive freight wagons from Bishop Creek to Carson City. Jones put his foot to the front door and knocked with the bottom of his boot, gently.

"I don't know how you do that."

"Is that eggs and bacon I smell?"

"It surely is, Mister Jones. I'm Horace Brown."

"I sure figured you for a bigger man," Jones said, pulling Brown out the door and disappearing along the large table in Hickman's kitchen. "Charlie Jones at your service," he said, smiling. Hickman dropped the chef's knife he was carving with and rubbed his hands across a clean, white towel spread out on the table, on which sat a fresh loaf of bread, eggs, some fruit and some coffee.

"Welcome to the Lord's work." Hickman gestured toward the food.

"I don't know much about that, sir. But I do know the beginnings of a great spread. And this looks real nice." The Elder smiled. The Lord's work wasn't always easy, but it promised good eating to those who were faithful, at least in his experience. The valley cattle had never failed him. And the crops they'd grown —

distorted and barren elsewhere in the Silver State, particularly as he'd traveled south toward the old Mormon fort in Las Vegas — had never left his table bare.

"Mister Jones, is it?"

"It is, sir," Jones said smiling. "You know we met a long time ago, at the livery in Genoa."

"It wasn't too far back," Hickman replied, picking up the knife again and carving a few extra slices off of a slab of bacon. "You were good with horses, I remember...I understand you're also good with explosives."

Jones nodded as he took a piece of bacon from the fry pan.

"I am..."

Hickman looked at him and waited.

"...oh, and thank you," he said, flapping a piece of pork aloft with his right hand as he reached for a slice of apple. Hickman dropped the flat side of the blade across the back of his hand. Jones withdrew.

"You are what?" Brown said, re-entering the room, wearing a scowl on his face.

"Good at blowing things up, Horace," Hickman said, looking at Jones and then back at Brown, who was brushing sand off of his pants, having fallen off of the porch into a large pile of firewood.

"Ah." Brown shot an angry glance Jones' way. "Then we'll all be happy, won't we? Won't we?" he repeated. Jones stopped chewing.

"Really, Horace, my apologies. But I fully expected you'd be taller given your reputation as a gunfighter. That's what my men said, anyway."

"Quick with a gun doesn't mean you have to be tall, Mister Jones."

"Or smart either, I guess. Say, Elder Hickman ... can I call you that?" Brown clenched his fists but kept them at his side.

"You may."

"When does this back and forth begin?"

"Back and forth?" he asked.

"Between the promised peoples and the Gentiles they've grown not to love?"

"You'll speak to Mister Hickman with a little more respect, Jones. I'll not have…"

"You'll not have what?" Jones said, stepping close enough to Brown to smell the fear, though Brown wasn't admitting to any of it. He'd take a good jailhouse beating before he got his gun up and out. But he'd put a bullet into the son of a bitch. But there was the issue of the Prophet's house.

"I'll tolerate no more rudeness," Brown said, stuttering. It surprised him. "I mean, from a man I hardly know." He looked Hickman's way. The elder nodded.

Charlie Jones smiled. "Well then, I guess we'll have to get to like each other then, won't we?" Jones grabbed a hunk of bread and walked into the living room where a few of his friends were seated, talking to some of the Saints.

"This is a good idea?" Brown whispered.

"It was your idea, Horace," Hickman whispered back. "I told you the Lord's army was enough, but you wanted more. 'A faithful man shall abound with blessings,' Horace. *Proverbs* 28:20."

"You showed me a bunch of farmers with pitch forks and Kentucky long rifles, Elder."

"Not hardly."

"I'm just saying, I thought this Jones character would be someone we could work with. I had no idea he'd come with a bad attitude."

"He did bring his friends, Horace. Work it out. I'm going to finish cooking this bacon. And then we'll get down to work." He looked into the front room. "You know the men are ready to hear what you have to say." Brown nodded. "I mean, we've prayed together. And we've given out what guns and ammunition we have. It's now time to get organized. Why don't you head in?"

Horace Brown's head bobbed up and down, when what he wanted to do was shake it from side to side. If there was anything he hated, it was talk. A fast gun, he was all over that. And killing a man for having a bad attitude — no problem. But standing up in front of a group and telling them what they already likely knew? Well, it brought the whole Civil War thing back to the forefront of his mind. Lying generals, merchants protecting their products, farmers their pigs, sheep and cattle — and the women and children, and broken down old men cringing behind hastily locked doors. Shoot a man down in the street, sure. But blowing up train stations, setting a couple of churches on fire, a hotel and his favorite damn bar? Well, it made his skin crawl. He shuddered.

"Brown, you coming in here? We're all waiting for your little talk," the trouble-maker said. Brown grimaced.

He didn't care if it was the famous Charlie Jones or not. He wasn't going to tolerate any more wise-ass from a jackalope who didn't know enough to stay away from people who might recognize him. Hell, he didn't care who he was. He'd not tolerate a man, however big and tall he was, making fun of him in front of a dozen of Hickman's neighbors and a half-dozen of his own friends. He put his hand on his gun and began to stride into the front room like his speech didn't matter. And it didn't, because what's in the heart of a man, he figured — whether he's good or bad, it's all the same — is as apparent to those gathered around him than any words might show his heart to be. Horace Brown *the Third* was larger than that son of bitch, who should have stayed hidden, or dead, or whatever he was after he'd escaped the damned prison in Carson City. And he'd prove it.

"Horace?"

"Yes, Elder Hickman." He stopped just in front of the arch separating the kitchen from the front room and took hold of the wall with his left hand.

"Wait for me. I've got a couple of words to say as well."

Chapter 55
THE SPEECH

It all went pretty well until Charlie Jones said for the ump-teenth time that he wasn't going to follow any nincompoop into battle against a white man, not that Horace Brown was any less equipped than an average fellow, Brown figured. And he certainly was more intelligent than the average man who was *non compos mentis.* "Look that up, you moron!" Brown yelled, accidentally knocking the Elder away from the makeshift podium he and Brown had fashioned in the front room from old bibles and dic-tionaries.

Hickman fell into a lamp, spilling kerosene onto a trea-sured pine wood table he'd bought in Placerville the year before, about the time he was deciding to do something about the Mor-mon curse and was weighing whether anyone could get killed seeking reparations from the damned Gentiles in the Carson Val-ley. "Horace!" he yelled, but it wasn't like anyone was listening. Because Horace had already grabbed the front of Charlie Jones' shirt and succeeded in lifting the taller man — by about a foot, some said, though they rarely stood close enough to get a good measure — and throwing him into the giant hearth Hickman had made for his beloved wife Winifred, who had left the first winter there before she could enjoy it, but some of the neighbor-hood kids did. The fire ignited the convict's backside and sent him diving out the front door of the house head first into the snow. A trio of friends followed him out the door as two or three others drew their guns and leveled them at Hickman's chosen leader, the almost late Horace Brown who hadn't thought to lift the hammer strap of his gun so that he could grab it if necessary. He stood there, tugging at it.

Hickman yelled again, "Stop!" And the people did, though there was no good reason they should have given that one man's ass was on fire, rolling around in front of the house while another man's friends and neighbors sat wondering what had happened to their church that they were now considering violence toward their otherwise peaceful Gentile neighbors. And all just because an ancient curse from a former Mormon judge hadn't played the requisite amount of divine vengeance. "Put your guns down and go attend to your friend!" he said, and they did. "Mister Jones," he continued, "are you okay?"

Jones nodded, as best he could as everyone's hands were patting snow on his ass outside, hoping the flames wouldn't start up again. He laid there, on his stomach, angry but struck by the luck of it all. "He's okay," someone yelled back.

"Then bring him in here," Hickman said, looking at his captain like he'd made the first giant mistake of his career and there wouldn't be a second one because he'd kill him before he ever made another. "So help me, Horace," he said. And Horace looked down, because he knew he had failed his new friend and spiritual mentor. They dragged Charlie Jones into the house, only because he was kicking and screaming about setting fire to the son of a bitch who had pushed him into the fireplace in the first place.

"I'll not have any of this," Hickman said, looking at Brown Jones' mercenaries. "You all work for the Lord. And if you don't see clearly enough to understand that, if you don't agree that extending God's kingdom in Nevada is important, then try to remember that you all work for me." He pulled the giant Paterson revolver from his waist, and laying it on the table, looked down. Hickman knew his stare was unnerving. He looked up, having given everyone a break. "God has brought us together — Gentile and Saint, believer and not-yet-believer — to rain havoc on these disobedient people and we *shall* do that. And here's how we're going to begin." Jones looked at Brown who looked at Hickman who was staring back at the two of them. "We're going to begin with the bar on Carson Street."

The bar on Carson Street, Jack's Bar, no God, not that bar, Brown thought, with Jones not far behind. But Brown knew the Mormon Prophet had deliberately chosen that place, and he knew why, too. He'd spent the best part of a week's evenings there over the last few months drinking his religion away. His Latter-day Saint friends, who were concerned about his salvation and progression in the things of God, had decided to torch the place rather than count another reprobate among them.

It was much like Joseph Smith had set fire to the newspaper office a block east of the Nauvoo Temple in 1844 after the Prophet had excommunicated a group of believers who had objected to certain new practices in the church. Revelations about the church's early endowment ceremonies hadn't gone well with everyone, plus plural marriage. Then there was the belief that the church's government ought to become the nation's government, or at least the state's government given how serious God was about establishing his kingdom on earth and such. Hickman was doing the same. Eliminating the dangers that would keep his people tethered to the terrestrial world — a gross and sinful world with all of its temptations — when more spiritual thoughts and things in the celestial kingdom competed for their attention. He couldn't blame him. "But not Jack's Bar," he said before thinking.

Hickman looked his way. A holy fire danced in his eyes. "Yes, Horace," he said. "You and your new friend will do this together, demonstrating that God can make a holy mountain out of a hellish mole hill," he continued, "which is the opposite of what you men are doing right now." Brown and Jones hung their heads, not because they were ashamed, but because there really wasn't anything else they could do. Hickman's look was that severe.

"Gentlemen, in doing so you can help us become the mighty people we are meant to be. Am I being clear about what I want?" A three-pound Paterson laying on the table in front of him, and the knife with which he'd been slicing bacon a few moments before still sitting in his right hand. Pounding the flat side of the triangular cook's knife into his meaty palm, it was a message neither man could ignore. "Mister Jones?"

"Yes sir."

"Your answer?"

"Of course, sir."

"Mister Brown?"

"Yes, Elder. I'd be most honored to comply." The words barely squeaked from his lips. He hung his head and shook it from side to side, but infinitesimally as he couldn't afford anyone noticing. It was kill or be killed for sure, even if it meant taking the miscreant offender along with him. "Consider it done, sir."

And the two men — a bad-ass ex-con who hadn't completed his prison term but finished it, in his mind anyway, because he was sick and tired of being treated to peaches when what he really wanted was a decent job and a just-like-mom-makes flaky crust pie — and a slick, black-on-black gunfighter who was smaller in stature than some men but not small enough that his height should be joked about, and after all his heart was unfolding in new and exciting spiritual ways — looked at each other and nodded. They'd do what Elder Hickman wanted them to do, or kill each other trying. Then they'd be back for the others to accomplish a much larger task.

Chapter 56

PLACERVILLE BOUND

When Happy Hands told Ronin who he had run into at the saloon on Carson Street, Ronin didn't know what to do. On the one hand, he felt like grabbing his friend and shaking some sense into him. His Indian friend had let the son of a bitch go. On the other hand, there was no time for that if Henry Nauman had in fact heard Happy Hands say, "I know who you are!" Because Nauman — wanted as he was for questioning in the kidnapping of Emma's mission children and God's knows what else — was likely already somewhere else or sitting on a train or stage platform waiting for just the right coach out of town.

"Jesus, Hands, really?" he said, dropping the two bodies from the mission on the deck outside the courthouse steps. "You left him standing there at Jack's Bar? You and Gillom? The boy didn't do anything either?"

"It was not our business, my friend."

"No, I'm sure it wasn't," he said, wondering what had happened to the wise and compassionate man he'd befriended in the last many months that he'd care more for a couple of women than a mixed-up missionary who had caused everyone a good deal of grief. "Take care of these two, would you? I've got to check the train station."

"What should I tell the sheriff?" Hands said, looking down at two dead Mormons from the American Gospel Mission, wrapped in blankets, who had previously been tied to the back of a mission horse.

"Tell him they stuck their noses where they didn't belong and were hoping to set fire to Emma's barn. Tell him Slavin killed them, and tell him I'm headed to the V & T roundhouse as well. Maybe he should come over and join me."

"Ronin?"

"Yes?"

"I'm sorry. I should have thought about everyone else's needs. I was distracted at the time, and Gillom took my pistol and was aiming it at me and..."

"Gillom had your gun? Your new Remington?"

"Yes. And I am thankful it was unloaded."

Ronin stuttered between quick thoughts of how foolish it was for his friend to carry an unloaded six-gun or concern for Bond Rogers' boy, who clearly was making choices his mother wouldn't approve of, and how the three of them — Happy Hands, Dustsucker and himself — had all tried to steer the young man toward a more appropriate life. "We'll talk when I get back. I'm too flustered right now. I want to catch this man before he leaves town. Find the sheriff!"

W. W. Ronin stuck his left foot in Jackson's stirrup and swung his right leg up over the saddle, before sliding the 1866 Yellow Boy out of its scabbard and laying it across his lap. He slipped a hardened rawhide loop around the saddle horn to hold the rifle in place and kicked Jackson's sides. The horse went to an immediate gallop. He reared up as Ronin pulled him around to the right. *Check the stage office first, then the V & T.*

Henry Nauman woke with a start. Surprised to see the sun up, he went looking for a cup of coffee on the train platform at the corner of Carson and East Washington Streets. An employee was happy to lend him a cup. "Heading out today, Mister Nauman?" the porter asked, a big smile on his face, his hand outstretched hoping for a dime.

"I am," Nauman said, flipping him a silver dollar. The two men immediately bonded. "I sure appreciate you letting me sit here last night. I don't know what I was thinking. I didn't mean to fall asleep."

"That's all right, Mister Nauman. You were tired and all, so I said to my boss, 'Boss,' I said, 'This here man is a missionary of the Lord and needs his sleep if he's sitting here, you know?' And do you know what my boss said back?"

"No, I don't, son."

"Well, I don't rightly remember either, except he was fine with my letting you sleep here. And I was fine, too, you being a minister and all. It's a special piece of God's plan to have men like you caring for men like me…"

"Well, I didn't do much for adults, son. And I'm quite retired now. I'm sorry, I don't even know your name…"

"Sylvester, sir, though my mother always called me Sylvia, because she wanted a girl and all she got was this here boy." The Negro laughed, which was funny, because Nauman had never met a smiling porter before, save for maybe those that worked in the dining cars, but then Emma never really wanted to sit there and eat, having brought sandwiches from home, not that they were as good. And they were always short on money, it seemed.

"Well, Sylvia…" the two men laughed. "I'll be leaving this morning if I can stay awake. What time is the next train to Placerville?"

"Should be in a few minutes," the man said. Nauman took a last swallow and handed the white china cup back to his new friend. It felt good to be alive, starting a new life and all as soon as he got to Hangtown, not that they ever hung anyone there, not many anyways. And they wouldn't be hanging him as he was about to turn over a new leaf.

He smiled. "Thank you." He was looking around for a place to take a leak when he saw a man ride down Telegraph Street toward the roundhouse at a fast gallop. *Ronin! Jesus, God!* "I'm in trouble now," he murmured, though the ex-priest had only met him once. When they were introduced, Ronin had drawn his gun and was about to drill him a new belly button when a fat deputy grabbed at it, shouting, "We need to take him alive!" Alive is what he wouldn't be if he didn't get moving. "Sylvester?"

"Yes, sir?"

"Is there a horse I can borrow? I'm thinking I'd like to grab a quick sandwich before I get on the train. I'll be right back."

"But Mister Nauman, you always like to eat in the dining car. You know that."

"Yes, that's true," he hurried, "but today is different. I want... I want..." he stuttered, "I want to do something in memory of my wife, poor Emma," he said, patting his heart with his right hand while looking down the street. "And the children, I mean without her and all ..."

"Mister Nauman, let me get you one. I'm sorry, I had no idea you lost your wife."

"No, no. You've done so much for me already. A horse — is there a horse nearby that I might grab?"

"Well, you can have my Nellie, I guess. She's not much of a nag, but she'll get you a block or two if you're quick. I can't hold the train, you know."

"No, of course you can't," Nauman said smiling. "And your horse? Where is Nellie?" he asked.

"Right over there by the outhouse," he said, pointing to a small outbuilding at the back of the platform. "We keep meaning to move things indoors..."

"No problem, my friend. I'll just pause for a minute and make myself a little bit lighter, then I'll be on my way."

"On your way, sir?" the porter asked, who hadn't been raised a fool, but still wasn't quite certain what some men meant when they talked about such little things. His mother had said, "Put the big rocks in the bottle first, Sylvester. Sometimes that's all the room there is and you won't have room for anything else."

"Yes, ma'am," he'd always said, learning from the saying that keeping first things first was the most important thing a man could do growing up in the world. Even as a full grown adult, it was important to remember to make the main thing the main thing. That's how he'd been able to afford a horse, praise God.

"You go ahead then, Mister Nauman," he said, ignoring his intuition. There was still a minute or two, and if a man had to go or had to get a sandwich, well what could anyone say about that? "Just leave the horse when you're done, Mister Nauman. Everybody knows Nellie. That way you won't miss your train. He won't wander."

Nauman smiled and stepped into the outhouse. He pulled his pants down around his ankles and sat down. Maybe he didn't need a horse. Maybe he just needed a place to hide. Maybe this whole thing with the mission and the law and this Ronin fellow and the sheriff chasing after him would blow over, and he could move ahead with his life. He'd be Placerville bound in no time. Nauman latched the door. It wasn't more than a second before his not-so-much-a-friend but soon to be his acquaintance, William Washington Ronin, climbed off his horse and onto the train platform looking for him.

Chapter 57

HENRY'S END RUN

It's never a good thing to be seated on the toilet and to have somebody bang on the outside door. It tends to hurry things along, if you're about to do your personal business — which is what Henry Nauman was doing when the former Reverend W. W. Ronin began thumping on the sides of the privy outside the V & T train station in Carson City.

There was really no good reason for Nauman to be sitting there — his first thought having been to borrow a horse and get the hell out of town when he saw the ex-priest turned gunfighter heading his way. But Henry's safety concerns took a back seat to other pressures present in his person, and he found himself unexpectedly in the dubious situation of having an angry man banging first on the front door and then on the sides of a small, yellow-painted-to-match-the-main-building's commode, in a manner that had he been armed he wouldn't have known where the banging was coming from. In fact, it was coming from all around him.

"Henry Nauman, this is William Washington Ronin. I'm a deputy with the Ormsby County Sheriff's Office and I'll need your quick exit of these premises," Ronin said, though he wasn't a deputy and he might have been more patient for the occupant to open the door if it hadn't have been for the following words.

"You'll not take me alive, Mister Ronin! I'll not sit in some county jail waiting for a trial. And I sure as hell won't live out the rest of my years in a state prison," he whined, which is what *you* might have said if W. W. Ronin had been knocking on your outhouse door and you were hiding there hoping the bounty hunter would go away.

Ronin took the words to be a warning of Nauman's intent to hurt himself, with a gun he figured, since he didn't believe the former school master was the kind of man to carry or use a knife. So he did the only thing he thought he could do, which wasn't at all appropriate, Henry Nauman said after being pulled from the messy pile of boards and nails and what-have-you he found himself in. Ronin gave the outdoor privy a heave, hoping the whole building would come up instead of just the top and the sides. And sure enough, there Henry Nauman sat, more or less, because it was only his rear end showing through the hole and it wasn't long before he loosened his grip and fell onto one of the sides. The tall ex-preacher stood there laughing, his gloved hands resting on his hips — it was January out, it wasn't cold, but it wasn't warm by any means — until he remembered that he was most concerned about Nauman using a gun.

"Henry Nauman," he said, "it's time for you to get yourself up and off of there, which is what he did. Which is what accounted for the huge goose egg on the former mission director's forehead, Ronin was quick to point out when the Ormsby County Sheriff, Shubael Swift, came running across Telegraph Street from a small breakfast place just north of the train station and yelled, "Holy crap! What did you do to the shit house?"

The *two* of them now stood there laughing, Ronin with his hands on his hips and Shubael barely able to keep hold of his vest. He had never been the sort of man to wear a coat in the wintertime, but then many men don't, if they're sturdy enough to ignore the weather, which Shubael Swift was, being not only a very popular lawman, but fireman, too. They stood that way sniggering, until Ronin was finally able to blurt out the reason for his somewhat impulsive methods and why Emma's former husband, more or less, was lying on his side, his pants down around his ankles, hearing tweety birds and counting turds and such.

"It sounded to me like Nauman was going to shoot himself, sheriff. So I knocked the outhouse over, hoping not to expose myself to gunfire..."

"You clearly didn't give any thought to exposing your prey," the sheriff said.

"No, I did not," Ronin continued, laughing. "And frankly, when the interior began to sound like a couple of coyotes fighting over a farmhouse chicken, I just figured Henry here was scrambling for his gun..."

"...which I don't see."

"No sir, you do not. And I don't, either..."

"You raised a bit of a welt on the preacher's head here."

Ronin touched his own forehead before realizing that Swift was talking about the former director of the mission, a lay preacher with the Presbyterian Church, though he had apparently laid the religious work down and was now lying practically naked on his side, moaning. "It would appear as if I did," he said.

"I don't think that will go away."

"I don't know that it will," Ronin said, reaching into the outhouse to retrieve his suspect. "Sheriff Swift," he said, "this I believe is Henry Nauman, wanted for conspiracy and kidnapping and all sorts of things, I suppose, if you and Dustsucker wouldn't mind visiting a bit. He's been gone for a good year or so. I think you have some money out on this son of a bitch, which I'd be happy to collect. Where have you been, Mister Nauman?" Ronin ran his gloves up and down the front side of Nauman's body, in part to make sure he hadn't hidden a firearm in his waistband or pocket. Nauman shuddered.

"Keep your hands to yourself, please. I'll tell the two of you nothing I don't need to," he said, straightening his collar and patting his vest pocket to see if his wallet and Bible were still there. "What is the meaning of this?" he said. And that's when the good no-longer-a-reverend snapped.

If there was a sign that W. W. Ronin was about to physically engage his quarry again, it might have been the sudden and unusual cant of his jaw, slightly upturned, his eyes squinting in disbelief that someone who had caused so much pain, who had done so much wrong to his wife and to the children in his care, could stand there posturing like a common thief. A real truth-telling Henry Nauman wouldn't have tolerated such an assumption, he was so much better than that, coming from the Upper Ohio Valley and not the lower, thank you, just a few miles out from the great city of Pittsburgh, though in reality he was closer to Steubenville than anywhere else, not that that was anything to be proud of.

Well, Ronin just couldn't hold it together any longer. Picking up the front of his leg until it floated perpendicular to the front of his shirt, he drove the bottom of his boot into Nauman's chest, his ass landing back into the privy's seat, which hung precariously by a single bolt on the now north side of the water closet, causing Henry Nauman to bite his tongue and begin screaming now that he was sitting in an outhouse pile of poop and paper.

"Now look what you've done," the sheriff said, smiling. "I bet he won't shut up."

"That's a good thing, Shubael, because maybe the truth will come out. Listen, if you don't mind, I want to get back to the mission before anything else happens."

"The two men?"

"How did you know? I just dropped them off."

"Ian Slavin stopped by, about the time you left the bodies at the courthouse doors. Jesus, Ronin," he said, looking at Nauman, who was now touching his fingers to his tongue but was beginning to quiet down. "You've got to stop cluttering up our streets with bad guys."

"Sheriff, I haven't even started yet. But if Slavin is at the courthouse, I need to hurry along to the mission." He took a few steps toward his horse. "Can I stop by later?"

"Absolutely, my friend. We'll get all this straightened out."

Ronin pulled Jackson's reins from around the railroad's porch post, put his foot in the stirrup and then looked back. "Shubael," he said, "I've never said this to anyone before, so I hope you don't misunderstand. If I have to punch, kick or kill another jackass today, I'm going to need a very long vacation."

"You and me both, son... you and me both."

Chapter 58
THE BAR

Charlie Jones and Horace Brown thought they might have lunch first. Jack's offered a free sandwich after a beer or two. They figured that would give them time to empty the bar of their favorite patrons before setting fire to the place.

The Carson Street saloon had been a home away from home for the two of them, though never together. Jones meeting with *his* bunch most Mondays — a fellow escapee who lived in Virginia City as a woman who went by the name of Pat and a couple of other reprobates he'd befriended from the surrounding hills and valleys. And Brown a lonely cast of ne'er-do-wells that rotated most weekday evenings but always included a fellow Mason or two hoping to find their way out of the esoteric fellowship into something that actually might find them a couple of jobs. "You've got to be a part of a local lodge to make those kinds of connections," Brown used to say by way of counseling. But when he came to a more vital experience of faith by joining Hickman's house church, Masonry gave way to Mormonism and the friendships began to show some strain. "There isn't much of a difference," Brown now liked to say, though his Masonic brothers were hearing none of it. "Some of the rituals are like word for word," he argued, until they stopped buying him drinks. So he was now typically silent on the matter though Hickman had counseled him to be bolder and to have more faith.

Which was the only reason Horace Brown was able to even stomach the thought of burning down his favorite meeting place in all the world. He was certain that his prison friend was up to no good, Charlie Jones being a Gentile and all. But the thought of a free sandwich and an opportunity to talk Jack out of the saloon before they set fire to the space seemed like a good thing. One more time at the tap couldn't be a bad thing either, he figured, and Jones said he would buy the sandwich if it wasn't free anyway. He was thinking of having ham and cheese, with a pickle if they had any, when Jones opened his mouth.

"You know this used to be pretty good place to get a drink," Jones said.

"And how do you know that?" Brown said back, given that Jack had moved the bar from its previous Ormsby Street location when folks began to talk about cleaning up the pickpockets and prostitutes and renaming it after Abraham Curry. Curry had been a former lodge brother and city founder, assemblyman and senator, before dying with only a dollar in his pocket, according to his wife, despite being the father of pretty much everything in the city, which was another reason Jack decided to move. He didn't think anyone could be that kind or wholesome or good unless he was a Roman Catholic, which didn't bother Jones but did Brown a little, as he wasn't sure that Catholics got to go to heaven.

"Look the point is after today, there isn't going to be a Jack's Bar," Jones said, "so why don't we live it up a little bit?"

"Suit yourself," Brown said, though having a good time sounded like a good thing, given how badly everything had gone that morning. "Listen," Brown continued, "about this morning…"

"Ah, forget about it," Jones replied. "I shouldn't have said what I said. I get a little red sometimes…"

"…and so do I," Brown said as they pushed open the door to their favorite drinking place in the whole world. "Jack, set us up!" he said, before noticing W. W. Ronin tying up his horse outside. "Holy hell," he said.

"What?"

"Ronin is here."

"I don't know anybody named Ronin," Jones said. "Do I care?"

"You should care. Keep your mouth shut. Let me do the talking."

Charlie Jones didn't get a word out of his mouth before Ronin pushed against the doors and ran straight into Brown. "Mister Ronin," Brown said, his hands in front of him as he backed up against the bar. "Slow down, buddy. Give me a chance to get out of your way. What's your hurry?"

Ronin did a quick double take, registering Brown as the slick little gunfighter Hickman had hired a couple of weeks ago. But who was this other fellow? "W. W. Ronin," he said, "at your service," he smiled, extending his left hand toward Jones, who was trying to make sense of the situation. Brown had sounded alarmed, yet this man — tall, obviously good with a gun and clearly in a hurry given that he'd practically jumped off the saddle — seemed good-natured and friendly.

"Joseph," he stuttered.

"Huh," Ronin said, looking back at Brown, who seemed paused mid-way to grabbing one of his guns. "Joseph who?" he asked, looking back at Jones but keeping his eyes open. Brown looked like he was playing the piano with his left and right hands. The telegraphed movement made Ronin smile.

"Joseph... Smith," he said.

"Like the Mormon Prophet?"

"Um... yeah, like the Prophet."

"Nice to meet you Joseph Smith," he said, shaking hands. Their right hands still free, neither man was bound to keep the gesture friendly. He pointed quickly at Brown with his trigger finger, crossing over his left arm — the speed was staggering, it was like a flinch or spasm, it didn't look anything like a man drawing his gun, not like any man Brown had seen before. "You have the nicest friends," he said before turning back to face Jack, who was standing still, his face as white as a ghost, sweating behind the bar. Ronin passed to Jones' backside, so that the convict was standing between him and Brown. "Jack, I need a quick sandwich for Emma at the mission. The roast beef maybe, with some cheese? I think she likes that."

"I'm all out of roast beef, Mister Ronin," he stuttered. He'd never known Jack to stutter.

"Well then ham and cheese. She'd be happy with anything, I suspect." He turned to face Horace Brown. "I saw your horse out there, Horace, and thought I should stop in. I didn't get to wish you happy New Year. And with all this trouble and all, well you know, I thought it was important that there not be any ill will between us."

"Mister Ronin?" Jack interrupted.

"Yes, Jack," Ronin said, without moving his eyes. Charlie Jones stepped to his right, toward the door, exposing Brown and putting him in double jeopardy.

"I only have enough ham and cheese for two sandwiches. And these boys were about to ask for it, I'm afraid."

"You're afraid, Jack?" he said, his eyes squinting into a sort of 'black-dot focus' — not really looking at anything but seeing everything at the same time. His peripheral vision was quicker, he'd found, in picking up multiple stimuli. If these dirt bags were going to draw on him, he would know it before they did. Their stance would change. There'd be eye movements as they considered targets, tensed muscles, stretched. There'd be a verbal escalation possibly. He was ready. "Boys, did you order a couple of sandwiches already?"

"Nah," Horace said. "We were going to have a couple of beers, and then maybe some sandwiches. Right Charlie?"

"Charlie? I thought you said your name was Joseph?" he started to say when Jones, not to be out-drawn by a man he didn't know, pulled his piece from his coat pocket and blew three slugs Ronin's way, fanning. But quicker than he'd ever seen anyone move before, Ronin's gloved hand slipped over the barrel of Jones' 7½ inch Colt and twisted it in the direction of Jack's new sign. "Jack's Bar," it said in ten-inch red letters. And underneath, in black and gold, the words: "A Saloon Since 1859." Ronin drove his right foot into Horace Brown's chest, propelling him backward into a sixty-year-old square grand piano. Not brand new, but precious nonetheless to Jack, who'd cheated an old woman out of it years ago, when she thought he'd be a possible suitor. "I don't play this old thing," she said before he decided the same thing, keeping the piano but casting the woman aside for someone younger and prettier, someone who could earn him a dime or a dollar, back when he didn't believe in the baby Jesus, his now being Catholic and all.

"Hey, watch the merchandise!" he yelled. Ronin only smiled.

He twisted Jones' gun hand to the side and launched a vicious series of punches to his face, each one capable of knocking a normal man to the floor, but Jones didn't fall, because Ronin was holding his gun. He looked at Brown who was stretched out over the top of the plain, Victorian box, about the size of a fat man's coffin, he'd later remark to his friend Dustsucker, who took no umbrage at the remark, knowing he couldn't fit into a normal man's box no matter how hard he tried, though he wasn't in any hurry. He slipped his long Colt from its cross draw holster and hit Jones across the forehead. He went down. Kicking the gun free from his hand — it spun a good 20 feet across the floor — he leveled it at the gunfighter Horace Brown and smiled. "This isn't your lucky day, is it?"

"It is not," he said.

"Then I'll tell you what, how about you pick the handguns out of your holsters with your thumb and index fingers careful like and place them on the bar?" He looked back at Jones. He was still out. "And Jack, what do you say you run across the street to see if you can't find Sheriff Swift or Deputy Slade?"

"Yes sir."

"And when you come back?"

"Yes sir?"

"I'd still like a couple of sandwiches for the lady at the mission."

"Of course, sir."

"And Jack?"

"Yes?"

"We both like our pickles on the side."

Chapter 59
BY THE FEET

If there was a mistake, it was that Ronin should have waited for help to move Charlie Jones and Horace Brown. Jones was out on the barroom floor when he pushed Brown out the door and onto the boards. And Ronin, generally used to people staying unconscious if he put them that way, wasn't expecting the strapping prison escapee to suddenly stand up and take a swing at him. He'd pummeled the man more than a few times in the face with his gloved right hand, and hit him across the forehead with the heavy barrel of his 7½ inch Colt handgun. Most men, at that point, would have had the courtesy simply to lay there and bleed.

But Jones, a couple of inches shorter than Ronin but beefier — like a man who worked for a living rather than looking for criminals and the like — wasn't your average bad man. Stronger, wiser and sneakier than most, Jones had simply laid down, as a prize-fighter might to get a little extra dough in his envelope. Watching the detective take hold of his friend and ass-kick him out the door, he rolled painfully onto one knee and was about to stand and punch him when Ronin pushed open the café doors and saw his raised fist.

"Whoa, partner!" he said, drawing the shorter of his two Colts from his strong-side holster and pointing it Jones' way. "I thought I might have to carry you out. Looks like you're going to save me the trouble."

Jones wiped blood from his left eye, then grabbed at his partner's hat, a black wide-brimmed "Boss of the Plains" job from Philadelphia, a Stetson of all things. Not that Ronin was surprised to see a Stetson hat — Brown had established himself as a styling sort of guy, and now that he was Mormon even more so. But he'd never seen one of the straight-sided crown with rounded corner masterpieces in black before, they being made more typically in a natural color, like dust or dirt.

"Let me get that," the ex-priest said, putting his boot on it. "Well lookie there!" he exclaimed, kicking the hat to the side. "There's a derringer in Horace's hat. I bet you didn't know that."

Jones screwed up his lips and tried to move his swollen eye. "Nah, I didn't know that," he said dryly, "though it would have been a nice surprise."

"Well, there you have it, the last possible piece of hope you have of not heading back to prison, Charlie. Mister Jones," he said, shoving him toward the door, "I believe Sheriff Swift is waiting for us outside."

The five-term sheriff had hold of Brown by his wrists from behind and was attempting to fix a pair of handcuffs on him when he looked over the bar's outer doors and smiled. Brown seized the opportunity. Spinning around, he grabbed Swift's left wrist with his right hand and, pulling him in, kicked him squarely in the crotch. Ronin watched the sheriff's smile turn to a frown. He moaned. Brown took hold of the sheriff's gun. "Don't move, Ronin. Or one of you is going to get dead! You hear me?" the little man hollered.

Ronin didn't wait to answer. Grabbing Jones by the front of his shirt, he plowed into the doors, knocking the sheriff, Jones and Brown down. The three men spilled into the dirt. He drew his gun and punched it forward, thumbing a shot that split a few boards.

Brown fired next, having fallen onto his back, the sheriff lying on top of him. The bullet broke a window to Ronin's right as Ronin thumbed a second cartridge into battery and this time took more careful aim. "Stop!" he yelled, and the shot hit Brown in the side of his chest, turning him to the left. Brown coughed then pushed the sheriff up and off to his left side.

"You son of a bitch..." Brown shouted.

"Not hardly," Ronin said, catching his balance with his right foot and dropping to one knee. "Drop it, Horace!" he said, hoping to spare the gunman's life. Brown blinked — his heart still unfolding, something within him still connected to everything that is quiet, peaceful and good about life — and then suddenly glared. *Damn.*

Brown raised his six-gun Ronin's way and with the sixth commandment of "The Lord, my God" — a phrase he'd said in prayer that very morning, not anywhere in his mind — he began to pull back on the hammer in order "to kill," as the Bible warned against, "Thou shalt not murder." Ronin fanned three times. A trinity of .45 caliber lead bullets burrowed into the gunman's chest and Brown died, right then and there. His eyes rolled back in his head. His mouth hung open, breathless, unmoving, bleeding — the gentle unfolding of his heart finished before its time. Every dream the man held, gone. Every chance of making things right with Jesus, over. Ronin frowned.

"Well, Mister Jones..." he said, pulling himself together, turning back around.

"He's run, Ronin," the sheriff interrupted. "Got up and left while you were putting the final nails in Mister Brown here's coffin. And let me thank you for that ..."

Ronin's head turned sharply. "He just got up and left?"

"He did."

"You didn't say anything?"

"I was a bit out of it, Ronin, you might remember."

"Which way did he go?"

"South on Carson Street, I think. Give me a hand, we'll go get him. I didn't know how I was going to hold Brown, not that that's a problem anymore. But I've got no issue giving you a hand with this Jones fella."

"Sheriff, I think you've got it wrong. I'm the one helping *you*." Ronin ran toward his horse. "Brown was harboring a prison

escapee, or hindering prosecution, or compounding a felony —
you would have figured it out. But Jones, he's a giant piece of shit,"
he said, his foot in the stirrup. "I'm more than happy to help you
corral that murdering reprobate."

"Well, let's get moving then," the sheriff said. Ronin raised
his foot to kick Jackson's behind.

"Wait, is that Slade coming up the street dragging some
poor son of a bitch by the feet?"

"I believe it is," Ronin said, laughing.

"Well, I'll be damned."

"Not likely sheriff, though these two men probably will.
You're going to lawman heaven, I suspect."

"Mister Ronin, if that there's Charlie Jones bumping his
head down Carson Street, I'm in heaven already."

Chapter 60
THE LATE HORACE BROWN

Horace Brown's dark shirt — purchased from Koppel and Platt's clothing store, a few spaces down from the Ormsby House next to the bookstore at 3rd and Carson Streets, not that Horace had ever been in there — was now darker than he ever imagined it could be. It was soaked with blood, his blood, lying there in the street outside the saloon that had become his spiritual home prior to his briefly finding solace in Hickman's apostate Mormon faith.

Hickman had been like a father to him, accepting him as a son — "just as you are," he liked to say, which felt so very, very kind. "We have this treasure," he explained. It was a big change from the man who had once hollered while heaving a heavy iron at him when he said he was moving west instead of staying east and becoming a part of the family business.

A third generation Horace — the first having left Great Britain for the New World in "seventeen something or other," his dad, Horace *the Second* used to say, "not because he wanted to either, but that's what they did with rogues like your grandfather," his dad explained before showing him the tools that would some-day be his if he took over the shop and became a shoemaker of all things, a goddamned shoemaker.

Horace *the Second* was "a *custom* shoemaker," his dad main-tained, so as to differentiate his efforts from factory-made shoes where uppers and lowers were slapped together like two pieces of bread, with little thought and lots of mayonnaise. Like those of

Jan what's-his-name who was the son of an African homemaker and a Dutch engineer, and was tinkering in Philadelphia with a shoe-lasting machine that would someday revolutionize the shoe industry.

Horace was proud he'd finally made something of himself, having found his way back to the family's religion, though Mormonism wasn't it. Still, it complemented the "inadequate revelation," as Hickman said talking about his father's Paterson, New Jersey church. Was it Presbyterian or Congregationalist? He couldn't remember. "It doesn't matter," Hickman said. "One is the same as the other."

But now he was laying in the street, breathless, an artery cut by a bullet or maybe two, he didn't know, not that he could do anything about it. Hell, he couldn't even move. The sheriff didn't care, or the ex-preacher son of a bitch who had shot him when all he really wanted to do was get away from it all and keep on living, whether it was in Genoa or not, it didn't matter. The Mormon thing was simply a job at first, though he'd begun to believe in what Hickman was saying, though his new found faith wasn't helping him right now.

Laying there in the middle of the street, next to Shubael Swift the fireman/sheriff — indeed there *were* sillier things to be than a gunman serving the Latter-day Saints, or a shoemaker, serving just about everyone who wanted a nice pair of shoes, left or right didn't matter as much as "the fit," his father used to say, "and their finances, of course. A man's got to pay his way in the world," he said. Now he was exiting the world, as he knew it anyway. Maybe there was something afterward. Maybe he'd go on to meet his grandfather after all, who was likely a better man than many and not nearly as nasty as what everyone after him had made him out to be.

Horace Brown coughed as Shubael Swift put his big fat palm on his chest so as to get himself up from the ground. But no breath came out or in. And it was getting more difficult to see, the darkness becoming his new home he guessed, though he was still hoping there'd be something more, something different even for a man such as he, who had combed through too many canyons of good people and their jewelry to be considered a good person, a saint of any sort except that the Saints in Genoa didn't seem to care. They'd become his best friends, even after his saying that he'd come from a very disreputable stock, at least three generations of it in fact, coming to America when the states were simply colonies in some English lady's crown. They loved him just the way he was... just the way he was, he thought as the lights began to go out and a subtle inner glow began to form in Horace Brown's mind.

He'd "handle their dirty work," he'd said, though now he wouldn't be handling anything he guessed unless something wonderful happened, something miraculous, something crazy — and it didn't look like it would with the sheriff saying "It doesn't matter now" and Ronin standing over him saying they would have gotten him for something — hiding a prison escapee, or hindering prosecution, or fucking up their felony. *Goddamn it, is this all there is?*

He turned over onto his right side, though he was pretty sure it was only in his mind, but it felt better that way to pass into the light, or the dark, he didn't know but he'd sure figure it out, he laughed, though he was pretty sure he didn't really laugh, either.

He liked Nevada best of all of the places he'd ever been.

Texas had been too hot. California too dry. Arizona had too many Mexicans in it. Then there was Mexico, of course.

He wanted so much to be better a better man than his father or grandfather, he thought as he expired there in the street, just out front of Jack's Bar. "A saloon since 1859," though he knew it really hadn't been...

Chapter 61

HOME MEANS NEVADA

Despite the disconnect Hickman felt with the Church in Utah, the old man liked to think he'd taken the best of the Mormon Prophets to heart.

He felt Joseph Smith's resolve — to do what was right no matter what the price, even if it meant his life, which in the end of course it did. And he possessed Brigham Young's careful consideration of the truth. Hickman had once read that the second of the Mormon Church's presidents had received no real or immediate witness to the truth of *The Book of Mormon.* Instead, he'd considered it for a couple of years, wanting to make sure that the faith had made a difference in the lives of those who believed in the good news and the golden plates. He even suffered seeing the baptism of several members of his family into the faith before he himself acted on what he came to regard as the Restored Gospel of Truth.

Hickman wasn't sure about John Taylor, however, though he had seen Taylor's palladium of homes in Salt Lake City last summer, sheltering six of the Prophet's wives and families. The six attached houses reminded him of how he was using his own home in the Carson Valley to nurture and protect. He didn't consider multiple wives a real part of any reasonable person's revelation. How could any thinking man want so many women? Still, Taylor was a pastor's pastor — so maybe he had taken *that* to heart, despite all of the new groups and scriptures.

So when the news of the gunfight in Carson City reached his ears — a good man, his son in the faith, sent to a sinner's heaven — and a lesser man, more so a very wanted man about to enter a sinner's hell at the Ormsby County Jail, he wondered. What would become of the movement? Even more, what would become of the people he had gathered in God's name?

The initial dream, of course, had seemed so real. Settling down in a valley once owned only by Indians practically promised that a small amount of effort would turn everyone involved an extraordinary reward. Thirty-some years ago, the valley had only three or four homes in it. And any one of their occupants — his friends and neighbors — would have traded multiple acres of rich Carson Valley farmland for a sandy and unproductive plot in Salt Lake City.

His wife used to talk about how their first visitors to the corn crib that acted as their home were snakes, toads and scorpions. She'd left him of course, gone all the way back to Salt Lake City and married another man, had children, too — which might have tainted him on the Utah Church, he didn't know.

It seemed like the devils reigned at first, but in time everything got better. More people settled alongside. Five years after the pioneer John Reese began selling produce and meat to people heading west over the mountains, Mormon Station was an oasis of cool water, clover, grass and cottonwood trees. But in September of that year, it all came crashing down.

"There's an army of 2,500 to 3,500 men en route to this territory," a letter from the Salt Lake headquarters of the church said, "besides 1,200 teamsters and 700 wagons, loaded with supplies. Four-hundred mules and horse teams packed with personal effects and 7,000 head of beef cattle." The missive meant the Carson Valley mission was over, and the personal dreams the men and women of the valley had along with it. "We have concluded," the local LDS president read, "that you should dispose of your property as well as you can. Make no noise about your business, but let all things be down quietly and in order."

As if they could. As if he could! And he wouldn't, he said to no one in particular because pretty much everyone else was packing up to go. Twelve-thousand dollars in gold was sent to San Francisco to buy Mormon guns and ammunition. And before long more than 200 wagons with practically every living Latter-day Saint riding in them was headed to Salt Lake. Good men, like Chester Loveland — the ward president — William Smith and John Lytle took charge, leaving their farms and businesses, and many their Gentile friends to defend "the State of Deseret" — Brigham Young's dream, but what about *his* dream? And what now, since his two best soldiers were gone?

"Excuse me, Elder Hickman," Hyrum Smith said." The Negro who worked on the short line railroad at Lake Tahoe was standing in the door, adamant as ever. *He is a proud and annoying man.* "The men and I are wondering if you know what we're going to do yet, with Mister Smith and Mister Jones gone. They were our two best guns. And the others have left, you know..."

"The others?"

"Well, yes, Mister Jones' friends. When they heard he was arrested they picked up their guns and walked out the front door. I am surprised you didn't see them."

"I've been in prayer."

"Yes sir. We all have."

"Well, that's why I didn't see them leave."

"Yes sir. I didn't mean nothin' by what I said."

"Then what did you mean, Hyrum? You've been hinting since you've been a part of our church that we ought to live a little more like Jesus and a little less like Jehovah. That's what you said, right?"

"It is sir, a while back. But you corrected me. I'm happy to be corrected, Elder Hickman. I suppose I was wrong. I simply meant..."

"You meant that we shouldn't be waging war is what you meant. Is that right?"

"Well, yes sir. Latter-day Saints, well, we're a religion of peace, right? 'Glory to God in the highest, and on earth peace, good will toward men.' *Luke* 2:14, sir."

"Oh Hyrum, come off it. You know better than that. These are tough times, and when faced with tough times God's people get moving. Do you believe that?"

"I do, I suppose. I mean, if that's the word of the Lord ..."

"It is."

"...then I guess we'll all get moving, sir. Just tell us what to do."

Orrin Hickman, the old Danite, stood up. There was a pain in his shoulder. He looked around for his cane, and not seeing it, turned around to enter the living room where everyone was gathered. But then he realized he didn't know what to do. And he didn't know what to say. But if he was going to be anything like the American Saints who had gone before him — Joseph Smith, who lived and died from 1805-1844; and Brigham Young, who was born in 1801 and died in 1877; and John Taylor who was the first Prophet of the Church not to be raised in America, but was British-born in 1808 and was still living — he'd have to give the matter some real consideration, because that's what good church leaders do. They consider.

"Hyrum," he said, the right side of his face drooping slightly, "I apologize. I don't mean to treat you like the irritant you sometimes are. But this whole thing has caught me a little stumble-footed. I don't know what we should do. I really don't." And he just stood there, looking at him. And Hyrum Smith — who despite sometimes pretending that he was related to Joseph Smith's family, but how could he be? He was black and Joseph the Prophet was white — smiled. Because he knew for sure that he had found himself a home. Hyrum — who was an educated man despite being a former slave, who had recently taught himself to read using an Woodrough & McParlin Ohio Saw Works cata-logue from Cincinnati, Ohio, and who imagined someday buying a place along a gentle stream where he could retire from his job at the lake because it was too expensive to buy a home there and if he remained he'd only end up working — grinned. Because Hickman's hesitation meant that *his* Prophet, Elder, Prophet and Revelator Orrin Hickman was human. Everything would be okay. Because being human meant that they'd figure it out together — he and him, and everyone else in the front room who now mat-tered most to him, his neighbors and friends who were just like family.

Chapter 62

THE SUPPER CLUB

William Washington Ronin unwrapped a couple of ham and cheese sandwiches and slid them across the table at the Ormsby House Supper Club toward his friends, Emma and Ian. Emma had a smile on her face as the mission's new English Literature teacher looked on. "So you're going to be talking about books?" Ronin asked as he set the two pieces of wax paper on top of each other and began to fold them. He'd clean them later and maybe use them again.

"You know Edison invented that, right?"

"What?" Ronin asked.

"The paper."

"Ian, I think a guy named Gustave Le Gray invented this stuff."

"I don't think so..."

"Jack said it was made for photographic applications. He'd been using it for a couple of weeks now to wrap food. What do you think?" Ronin asked, taking it back out of his pocket and unfolding it to show the two of them.

"I suspect it's a lot older than that," Emma said, "paraffin paper has been around for a long time," she nodded.

"Whatever," the ex-priest replied, before looking toward the door of the Supper Club. Sheriff Swift and his deputy were just coming in. "Dusty!" he exclaimed, standing up. "How did it go?"

"With Charlie Jones?" Dustsucker asked.

"Exactly." Ronin pulled a couple of chairs away from the table and sat down.

"Well, he's got more than a couple of bruises between what you did to his face and what we did to his head and backside. I imagine some of the bumps will take some time to heal. But then that's okay…"

"It sure is," Sheriff Swift replied, scooting up to the table. "You're going to make yourself some money, Ronin, between the good for nothing missionary you caught and the prison escapee. If you don't mind hanging around for a couple of days, I'll be glad to get it together." He put his hand on the ex-priest's arm and smiled.

"You caught Henry?" Emma looked up from folded hands, where she'd been praying Ronin guessed, while they were talking about Charlie Jones. He would have shot him in the back had he seen him trying to escape. Emma had little tolerance for violence, despite the overwhelming evidence in the scriptures that her God was all for it. She'd not yet connected the dots between the shootings at the mission, the Mormon bunch in Genoa and the genuinely wanted ex-convict Charlie Jones from the 1871 prison break. She looked with surprise at the sheriff and then at her friends.

"We didn't have time to tell you," Dustsucker and Ronin said together. "It all happened pretty fast," Dustsucker continued. Ronin put the wax paper away in the pocket of his duster, adjusted the black scarf around his neck — cut from one of his late mother's dresses — and sat back in his chair. "Henry was over at the train station looking to get back to Placerville, apparently," Dustsucker said.

"Happy Hands told me," Ronin said.

"Happy Hands?" Emma asked.

"Your husband…" He looked at Slavin and then began again. "Your ex-husband ran into him at Jack's." He pointed to the sandwiches. "That's where I got the ham and cheese, and pickles. Seems like there was a little bit of a fuss between the two of them. Gillom Rogers was somehow involved. And Hands told him that he knew who he was. Well, that scared your husband, I mean, your ex-husband, and the rest is history, I guess." He nodded back. She smiled.

"What will become of him?" she asked.

"Well, ma'am," the sheriff said slowly, "he'll be questioned first. And then if there's any evidence connecting him to the kidnapping of those Indian children, he'll be tried. Right now, I'm holding him in custody as a material witness. I've got nothing else on him until the district attorney takes an interest in him."

"I see," she said. "And the Mormons? How is that going? Mister Slavin and I aren't sleeping very well I'm afraid, knowing that there are some real religious lunatics out there."

Slade raised one eyebrow.

"Mister Slavin has been staying at the mission, Dusty. He shot those two boys the other night, and decided to stay on until things straightened out."

"I'll be staying a little longer than that, Ronin," he said.

"I'm sorry. Dusty, meet the new literature professor at the American Gospel Mission."

"Really?" He extended his hand. Slavin took it and shook it.

"Yup, if they'll have me."

"I didn't know you *read* books," Ronin said.

"They don't make lawyers out of people who don't read books, Mister Ronin."

"No, I guess they don't, Ian. Well you've got quite a start then."

"The Mormons? What's happening with them?" Emma asked, impatiently.

"That's an interesting thing, Emma. With Charlie Jones in custody and Horace Brown now dead, folks tell me the movement has pretty much fizzled out."

"I just came from there, actually," Swift said. "It looks like Orrin has had a stroke — drooping lips, a bizarre gate and weakness in one of his hands. And the guns he'd hired? Brown, Jones and others, they've all disappeared. That's left a pretty big hole in things. In fact, I met a man who says he knows you. He tells me that it's all over."

"Who's that?"

"A black man named Hyrum Smith."

"Sure. Dusty and I met him in Glenbrook last fall. The man put me on the V-flume, told me to sit down actually. I was standing at the time. I guess he was happy to hear that I'm still alive."

"He didn't say," Swift replied. "But he did say that you'd remember him. And that you'd likely trust his word that things were over for the Danites, as they were apparently calling themselves."

"Danites?" Ronin laughed. "What's with bad guys having names? Hell, the Danites haven't been around since 1838 or so."

"If they were ever real at all," Slavin said.

"Whatever, Ian. Yeah Shubael, I trust him. He's a good man, and I wish him well. So is the Mormon war over?"

"With Hickman in the hospital and his gunmen gone, I'm afraid so, Missus Nauman. You'll not be having anymore night-time visitors," Shubael said, his thumbs pulling at his suspenders. Emma blushed. "But you will have this, ma'am — a well-deserved peace and quiet. All of us will. It will finally feel like home."

"Yup," Dustsucker said. "Ronin, how about you?" The deputy scratched at a couple of table crumbs.

"What's next, you mean? I think I'm up for a rest, Dusty. Might take in a hot springs or two. Sit there, read a book. Say..." he said, looking over at his friend. "Why don't you go along?"

"Oh, I don't know." Dusty brushed the front of his vest. It was supper time and no one had ordered yet. He'd been thinking of a steak, but cash was short. "Miss Emma, are you going to eat that sandwich?"

She put her hand on top of it. It was maybe the last gift W. W. Ronin was ever going to give to her, given that their relationship was changing. She'd not share it with anyone. Slavin was already biting into his.

"Slade, why don't you go with Ronin?" the sheriff offered. "We've got the county troubles pretty well wrapped for now. There's plenty of time before the trials start. Hell, the district attorney isn't even back from Christmas break. You'd enjoy it."

Ronin and Dustsucker looked at each other and began to smile. A couple of good friends, riding off toward the hot springs in Reno or Markleeville. Maybe they'd start in Carson City at Shaw's. It sounded too good to be true. Time with each other, that was the real blessing, and a place to stay, Nevada.

"Beers?" Dusty asked.

Ronin laughed. "Beers it is, my friend."

Chapter 63

WINTERTIME

The snow began falling later that night, blowing down from the Sierra Mountains immediately west of the city. By morning a few miles south, the American Gospel Mission sat beneath a robe of sparkling diamonds and white flakes a couple of inches deep.

There was no finer place to be in Nevada, in northern Nevada anyway. A soft alpenglow — its purple and blue and pinkish hues putting the valley to rest at night — and the stark poetry of winter crispness glimmered in the morning light. *If there is a heaven it will be just like this*, Emma thought. No reflection or change would do as the final resting place of Nevada's heaven-bound Saints, Mormon and otherwise. Emma knew that.

And Henry knew that, too — the damaged and dented man of God she'd traveled to the Silver State with more than a dozen years ago. He'd become so much less over the years of his living there, though Nevada hadn't changed. Not really. The setting sun, the wind blowing wild and free, the hills, the sage, the pine — the whole experience of Nevada bouncing between moon beams or trembling in the morning's sun and light. *Home means Nevada*, she mused as she puttered around the living room, knowing that the state had changed, her relationships too in the last couple of years. But in some very real way, the beauty of her experience there had remained the same.

The marriage she'd had with her husband, corpulent seeds that God had planted in his fullness within the two of them — an uncertain greenness in the early years flowering toward heaven's hiding place. But watering and weeding, too. It hadn't all been easy. It was as God planned it, she figured, though the mystery and pain of those years were at times too difficult and demanding to sit with or to understand.

Then there was her knight in shinier armor. Ronin, or William as he'd finally allowed — his given name, after a father or grandfather she thought, not that he had ever said. Sometimes sullen, other times so focused that the sun itself couldn't be brighter. And yet, never truly happy nor present in the way she had hoped for, even prayed for when it became clear that her husband was lost or dead but certainly never coming back and that she was staring God's gift in the face, an unexpected flower in the weedy patch that had become her life.

The two men were so similar at times, and yet so different. Then when her husband reappeared, the truth of her relationships — with Henry and William, and maybe others before and after — stared her in the face. No man really knew her, not yet anyway.

She stood at the large window in her front room, looking out toward the Sierra. The snow on Job's Peak made her wonder if the weather would prevent Ronin and Dustsucker from leaving town for their holiday among the warm, steamy waters of nearby hot springs. She'd been to Shaw's of course, when the spring was owned by Thomas Swift, who had built a number of bathhouses there, even a clubhouse and hotel — though she thought $14 a week was rather steep. James Shaw was talking about a "plunge," he called it, a much larger pool where men and women could recreate together. It seemed inappropriate, though the idea of an outside bath was appealing in the January snow and sun.

Her house guest, Ian Slavin was up and about, having stayed on the tufted leather front room couch the last few nights. Her new protector, though no more protecting was needed — the threat of angry Mormons, apostate Mormons now past. The Prophet Joseph had intended a peaceful religion, she thought as she looked toward the peak named after Mormon Moses Job, who settled the Carson Valley in 1854 and operated a store, not the

Biblical Patriarch whose name was synonymous with pain and heartache, having lost all of his family in a bizarre biblical test of faith.

Life was as it should be, she thought as she gathered the sweater around her shoulders and listened to a younger man, her guest and now employee, push additional logs into the front of the iron stove that heated the room. The fire crackled.

"Ian, it is beautiful, isn't it?" she said, as she looked out on the fields and mountains that had become her home. "I don't think I could live in a more beautiful place."

"I've been to a good many places, Miss Emma, and I'll give you that. It's nicer than any place I've ever lived."

"Me, too," she said as she dried the tiniest of tears that had slipped from her eyes onto her morning cheeks. She'd not washed her face yet, remembering there was a man about the house. Not her William, but that was okay. She had her work. And she had whatever possibilities God had raised up for her, each day a new day, each person a new friend or member of the family.

"Should we have coffee this morning?" she asked.

"Already made it, ma'am. I hope I wasn't being presumptuous."

She turned and smiled, then covered her face, more or less, with her hands as she walked into the kitchen to draw some water. She lit the stove, placed a half-full kettle on it and waited. "Mister Slavin?"

"Yes?" Ian answered from the other room.

"I've appreciated you staying here these last few nights. You've helped me. I couldn't have gotten through this time without you."

"Missus Nauman, you would have been alright. You're a strong woman."

"That may be. I just want to say thank you. I know it's important that we get you proper quarters. We can attend to that today, if you like."

"I'm willing to accept God's timing in the manner," he said, thinking he'd said too much, that God's timing certainly was sooner than later, as he couldn't imagine the Savior being pleased with his staying in the house alone with a woman who was not his wife. And there was the matter of differences. He was a Saint, and anxious to practice his religion again. And she was a Gentile, he reminded himself, no matter how spiritual a woman she seemed. They were not the same faith. "Ma'am?"

"Yes, Ian," she answered, putting down a kitchen cloth.

"Is it possible that we've developed a friendship, Miss Emma? I don't want to be disrespectful."

"I think we have," she replied from the doorway between the front room and kitchen. He turned to face her, a good and proper distance still between them. "Why do you ask?"

"I'd like that to continue, ma'am. I really would."

Emma Nauman smiled. She'd moved to Nevada because God had wanted her to. God had told her exactly the right spot to stop, despite her husband's protestations and later misbehaviors. And she'd built a school, homes and boarding houses she could be proud of for the Paiute and Washoe and Shoshone children, and the families their mission served. She'd done exactly what she'd set out to do, what God had asked her to do. And then her husband left, but she'd found another man, though nothing had come of it save perhaps an intimacy she'd never known before, and the challenge of a truly human relationship. It had not been easy. Sometimes, he wasn't easy. But it felt right. And this did too, though it raised as many questions as it did answers.

"Ian," she said. "Is it your hope to stay here?"

"It is," he answered, his hands on top of each other, splayed across his heart, sitting there naturally, not to emphasize a feeling or to communicate a point.

"I hope you'll stay. And maybe..."

"Maybe ma'am?"

"Maybe this friendship will be exactly what it is meant to be, Ian, if we're true to ourselves and our faiths as well."

"Exactly what it's meant to be, ma'am. Despite our differences, you mean?"

"Your being a Latter-day Saint?"

"And being so much younger."

"Not too many years younger, dear one."

And the two of them smiled at each other, as the kettle on the stove began to hiss and shake, feeling good about the differences, and sensing that if others had made it work — the Washoe and the Paiute, the area's natives and those who had come after them — they might make it work, too.

The snow began to slow, the morning's crispness growing into a warm and sunny winter day. As her friends — the former Reverend W. W. Ronin, a detective and bounty hunter, and *his* friend Marcus T. Slade, whose middle name she'd never learned, perhaps no one had ever learned — walked to Benton's Livery across the street from the Ormsby House to saddle their horses and to rent a mule, Emma knew it would be a wonderful day, or week or month, or even longer for the two of them, and for each and for all of them. And why not?

THE END

AUTHOR'S NOTE

While this isn't the end of the W. W. Ronin series of Westerns, it does mark the end of the initial serial.

Some of my earlier readers thought we were writing a trilogy at first. The first book, *East Jesus, Nevada,* was set in northern Nevada, where we had the privilege of raising our children in the mid-eighties to early nineties, when I was pastor at the First Presbyterian Church in Carson City. The second, *Lady of the Lake* was set at Lake Tahoe, one of the most beautiful places on earth. The third, *The Pinkerton Years,* leant a back story of sorts while pushing forward the series' aim of speaking about "real people and real places."

If you've already read the fourth book, *True Believer,* you know why that followed the other three. (I won't ruin things for you, if you have not.) The fifth in the series, *Home Means Nevada,* signals the end of some of the initial tensions in the first four books, and sets us free — in the relationship you and I have as writer and readers — to explore other locales, stories and emotional edges.

I recently counseled a fellow writer to be clear, in his own mind at least, who his audience was. While readers of this series of books, I hope, are many, first among them are my own children — my late son Jared, who encouraged me to move ahead when I was spending too much time thinking about the particulars; my daughter Rachel who still perseveres as a preacher in Presbyterian circles despite her father going a different way; and my youngest, Josh, who works for a wonderful nonprofit, Habitat for Humanity, doing good work all across the globe.

Writing these books tells my kids something about the area where they grew up and the family they grew up in. However, if they read W. W. Ronin to be a simple reflection of their father — an ex-pastor wanting to experience more of the world than his church work sometimes permitted, a sometimes black and white thinker who believes that some folks "ought to die sooner than others" — they'll catch a dim reflection of the real truth.

Ronin stands alone. As do I.

While living in Carson City, we owned a white Chevrolet station wagon. It was a boat. One day, after pulling into a local filling station to buy fuel, an African-American man happened by. One of the children blurted out, "Mommy, what's wrong with that man's face?" I don't remember which of the kids it was, but I recall the hope and shame I felt when I realized how homogenous my children's experience was in Nevada's capital. The Indians lived in "colonies," the chairman of the search committee told us when we first toured the city. The rich multi-cultural fabric I grew up with — raised initially in a Philadelphia neighborhood though later experiencing a suburban but similar quilt of Italians, Polish, Jews and what have you — was not my children's experience.

In some small way, the five books offer a contrast by pointing to the rich differences of the people that populated the Silver State more than 150 years ago, and truth be told, very much before that, too.

Home Means Nevada tells the story of a pretend early settler, Orrin Hickman, a name conflated from those of two early well-known Danites, one of the more militant groups of Mormon settlers that populated the American West. Hickman's desire to see the Mormon dream of a sacred corridor from Utah to the Pacific Ocean reconstituted propels him to violence.

It might be said that the story of the American West is the history of the Church of Jesus Christ of Latter-day Saints. And while too short a treatment would be reductionist and dishonoring, speaking about Nevada history without saying something about its first white settlers, which is to say Mormon settlers, is impossible.

In addition to more recent texts, I am particularly indebted to the work of the late but much respected LDS Church historian Leonard Arrington, the founder of the Mormon History Association, whose books and co-authors have greatly informed my understanding. Specifically, *Great Basin Kingdom: An Economic History of the Latter-day Saints 1830-1900* (Lincoln, NE: University of Nebraska Press, 1958); Davis Bitton's *The Mormon Experience: A History of the Latter-day Saints* (New York: Vintage Press, 1980); and also Jon Haupt's "Intolerable Zion: The Image of Mormonism in Nineteenth Century American Literature," reprinted from *The Western Humanities Review,* Summer, 1968. If you can only read one thing, see the series of twelve articles published by the *Las Vegas Sun* in 1979, bound together in a small and still available volume entitled *The Mormons in Nevada.*

One of my beta-readers tells me that she didn't much understand "the spiritual stuff" in this book. So let me say, I've tried *not* to write a religious book. *Home Means Nevada* is fiction after all. But the silent murmurings of most men and women being what they are, and the real history of the Nevada being what it is, saying something about the religious quest of these early Mormon folks is only fair. The reader will notice that I've cast much of the discussion in more concrete ways, economics for example — Hickman stays behind to capitalize on what others have left behind — or moral decision making, as in the hesitant, double-mindedness of members in Hickman's house church, but also Emma Nauman, who continues in her role of director at the American Gospel Mission. Its location, "just south of town," is a hint to the reader that I've modeled the mission and its ideals on the early Stewart Indian School in Carson City.

The reader should know that my primary interest, aside from what I've already stated, has been to accurately reflect Nevada history in the 1880s. But my second focus is just as dear. I confess a long term fascination with the mystery and complexity of what makes people live, relate, grow and get along.

In that sense, I hope the book has a much larger appeal — to the person who is just beginning to understand the history of the Silver State, but also the reader of Westerns in general. It is my unstated goal to write the best and most accurate Nevada Westerns ever written. If I get close to doing that — sell a few or sell many, it really doesn't matter — I'll be satisfied.

A few final notes are appropriate.

Some of the people mentioned in this book are real, though the details of their lives may not be. Interested readers will know the difference. The "Mormon curse" uttered by the Latter Day Saint pioneer Orson Hyde is real. A great deal is written about Apostle Orson Hyde, I won't elaborate except to say that he figures prominently in early Mormon history and was a very interesting man.

The 1871 prison break is real also, as are some of the characters and details I share. In that respect, I want to express my gratitude to Richard Delaney, who's brief and entertaining book, *Gunplay at Conflict Lake* (Prather, CA: Talahi Publishing, 2008) answered my initial questions, but led to my reading his lengthier volume, *Quest for Freedom: A Saga of the Men and Women Impacted by the Murderous 1871 Nevada State Prison Escape* (Prather, CA: Talahi Publishing, 2009). Delaney does a nice job in telling the story. His books include pictures from the period as well.

True also is the history of the first Christmas tree, the invention of the can opener, factory made shoes, aspects of life in Carson City's early churches, businesses and so on. I love including these pieces of historical memorabilia in my books and I hope you do, too.

The continued inclusion of certain fictional elements beyond my regular characters, such as Gillom Rogers and his mother Bond, should signal the careful reader my favorite Carson City film, "The Shootist," featuring John Wayne (his last), Lauren Bacall, Ron Howard, Harry Morgan, Richard Boone, Hugh O'Brian,

Jimmy Stewart and so on. These and other small details are testimonies to the films I grew up with.

Allow me a few additional thank yous. To the late Willa Oldham, who was a bright and decent human being and an encouragement to my writing when she worshiped at the First Presbyterian Church in Carson City, my belated thanks. Her book, *Carson City: Nevada's Capital City (Genoa, NV: Desk Top Publishers, Inc., 1991)* is still an important work. Journey well, my friend. Richard Moreno's more recent and interesting volume, *A Short History of Carson City*, (Reno: University of Nevada Press, 2011) was and continues to be helpful in my writing. My thanks also to David Thompson, who compiled *The Tennessee Letters: From Carson Valley, 1857-1870* (Reno, NV: The Grace Dangberg Foundation, 1883), whose compilation of early unsigned letters to California newspapers from a Carson Valley was truly wonderful. Their value is perhaps best illustrated by this note published in 1857: "The return of the Mormons to the Great Salt Lake has removed one serious drawback to the settlement of these fertile valleys. The country is now filling up with substantial immigrants from the Atlantic States and California. From 5,000 to 6,000 head of immigrant and California cattle will winter this season on the east side of the Sierra Nevada. The crowd of immigration causes Carson Valley to present a scene of unparalleled life and animation. Wagons, horses, mules and cattle are to be seen in every direction. Every shelter is filled with women and children."

Home meant Nevada to every one of those early Mormons who returned to Salt Lake, at the behest of their Prophet Brigham Young, as it did even more to those that remained, as it still does to my children and to me.

This book is dedicated to my brother Scott, who has made a new home for himself on the East Coast, after losing his previous one in the wake of Hurricane Sandy. And to my father-in-law Derwood "Del" Lashbrook, who has made a home for himself on the West Coast. They are good but very different men. I love them both, dearly.

ABOUT THE
AUTHOR

Gregg Edwards Townsley is a reflective, free-thinking ex-pastor, martial artist, writer and western fast draw enthusiast living in St. Helens, Oregon. No stranger to the places his Western characters inhabit — Reno, Carson City, Virginia City and Lake Tahoe — he raised his children in northern Nevada, from 1984  through 1993, as pastor and head of staff of the First Presbyterian Church in Carson City.

Gregg enjoys hearing from his readers, posting updates and background to his work on his website where he writes two blogs: Silver State History (Nevada), where many of his Westerns are set, and The Writers Edge. Additional information on the W. W. Ronin series of Westerns or his new series, Tommy Valentine, PI, can be found on the publisher's website, www.twobearsbooks. com. Join the official mailing list on either site, and you'll get a free preview of other books and stories yet to be published.

You can write to Gregg at Gregg@greggtownsley.com, or friend him on Facebook: www.facebook.com/GreggEdwardsTownsley, or subscribe to his Twitter updates at http://twittter. com/greggtownsley. He encourages your review of his books, short stories and other publications at www.amazon.com and www.goodreads.com.